MW01132371

By His Hand

Stefanie Bridges-Mikota

Edited by: Grace Augustine
Cover Art by: Tell ~ Tale Book Covers
Author Photo by: Heidi Marshall Photography

Stefanie Bridges-Mikota

Published in the United States by Stefanie Bridges-Mikota

This book is a work of fiction. While the events leading up to and regarding the fire are true, most of the characters are a work of the author's imagination. A few mentions of notable true people are used when appropriately necessary to keep the historical information as accurate as possible. All effort was made to convey the true events factual as much as possible. The author accepts all faults for any errors that may be found.

ISBN: 10: 1986516296
ISBN-13: 978-1986516297

Stefanie Bridges-Mikota

DEDICATION

TO DAN, MY OTHER HALF

ACKNOWLEDGMENTS

Thank you to Jan Sass for being my first editor and helping build confidence to pursue publishing. To my beta readers for not only reading but providing encouragement along the way. Grace and Linda for all the encouragement and support, and to my fellow Indie authors who have all assisted me to get this far. A big thank you goes to Dan, my loving husband, for being patient while I was busy typing away instead of running the house (my regular job), keeping me focused and driven throughout, providing ideas to guide me, and loving me in all the ups and downs during this process.

**Available now In His Time, Book 2
Carried Through Chaos series
by Stefanie Bridges-Mikota**

CHAPTER 1

Allie's hazel eyes fluttered open. Her head was pounding and she had that metallic taste in her mouth again. She spat blood out on her cold, hard bedroom floor. *Where was he now?* She was panicky but kept still to listen. No sounds, nothing but silence.

She took a deep breath. *He's gone...for now. But he'll be back.* Allie tested her strength, pulled herself up, and stepped to the wash basin. She kept her eyes down to avoid the dreadful mirror that no longer reflected the independent girl she was finding harder to remember. She didn't want to see the wreck of a women she'd become. She splashed water in her face then cupped water into her hands to rinse out her mouth. The once clear water was now tainted, much like her life that was so full of promise.

She was resolved! It was time. She had been planning, hoping to save more, but she needed out...now. She carefully put weight on her tender ankle. It still smarted from last night. Slowly she reached her dresser and the canister tucked in the back of her drawer.

She took in mending from the local bachelors. Eddie set it all up. They would come to him. He would bring her the clothing. When she finished the mending, he would deliver it back and collect the money. She never saw a red cent...or so he thought. Some of the men knew what was happening and slipped her money. Sometimes it was hidden in the mending they would send. Other times, Mabel, her closest neighbor, delivered it when she saw Eddie leaving.

Allie was grateful, yet terrified, that Eddie would discover their donations. Those few people kept her hopes up. *Some people still cared.* She held on to those thoughts when Eddie allowed her to head into town. Many folks turned their heads, some even looked down at her with arrogance oozing.

Like you are better than me. Please! We all have our secrets, some are just more visible than others. That brought a chuckle! She knew a few of those secrets. Mable didn't just bring the money to her, she was also a great gossipmonger. *Probably how some had learned her full story! I better not let Mabel see me leave or Eddie might get tipped off too early.* She opened her canister and forty-two cents jingled out onto the bed. *Not much, but it will have to do.* She placed the money in her coin purse and threw a few necessities into her bag. With one last look around the room, she took a deep breath and opened the door into the darkness...and a new beginning.

March was warming up early. Allie still needed her wrap, but it was nothing like the bitter cold and snow that had blanketed this whole area and seemed to never want to leave. *Maybe this would be a good sign? Spring's coming early this year in more ways than one, I hope.* She marched on toward Falcon. *Either Eddie is having himself a good time, or he found a place to sleep that good time off.* Her stomach churned.

Usually at the height of the evening one could faintly hear the patrons of Grand Forks, even from this far away. Falcon and Grand Forks were about half a mile apart on opposite sides of the St. Joe River. The name of the river brought a bubble of laughter to her throat. There was nothing saintly about this area. The populations were small, but that didn't stop them from making a loud ruckus in the many fine establishments that formed the midtown square.

The whistle was like clockwork. No one needed a clock if they knew the train schedule.

It must be closer to morning than I thought. At least I won't have to wait too long for a train.

Allie was thankful that the depot was not in Eddie's direction. Her plan would never work if she had to appear in the same town he spent most of their money in. She just needed to slip in unseen—then beg them to let her ride. Even with fare, they might laugh her out of town.

The train was used to transport the local rail

workers to various areas to lay track and blast tunnels. They ran at regular intervals to get the men to work on time. She knew some non-workers were allowed to ride under special circumstances, but many men wouldn't see her situation as a problem.

With most of the notable town folk spending their time and money in the next town up and the remaining few good souls sound asleep in their beds, her first step should be easy. As she neared town, Allie pulled her wrap up to cover her head and pointed her eyes down in hopes she wouldn't be recognized.

The depot serviced the Milwaukee line and lay at the edge of town. Service was pretty dependable except for the occasional delay from a tree on the tracks or a slide. With the depot door in front of her, Allie quickly opened it and slipped inside. Not many were waiting for the morning train. She gazed to the wall and found the large round clock—4:43 A.M. Good, just a few hours and she could pull out on the first train. She found her way to a bench and sat. Her eyelids were drooping, and her ankle was downright throbbing. *Two hours of sleep won't be enough...but maybe I can sleep on the train.*

CHAPTER 2

Allie woke with a fright. She was vaguely aware of footsteps and a voice from behind her. Her heart was pounding, and blood was rushing in her ears too loudly to hear clearly.

"Miss? Miss? Can I help you? "I am Walter Templeton, Ma'am. I work for the railroad. Can I be of assistance?" He walked around to face her.

"Oh! Yes…ah…dear…pardon me, please," she began, sitting upright to rub the kink in her neck. She took in the freshly pressed uniform standing before her. "I am Mrs. Alice Coghill and I'm hoping I'll be permitted to ride. I'm on my way to meet my family in Montana, sir," she added, folding her hands in her lap to hide their shaking.

Mr. Templeton paused, assessing the multiple colors that donned her face and replied with a barely disguised edge to his voice.

"Mrs. Coghill! This rail line is for workers only, ma'am. Is there any way your family could come and meet you or maybe your husband could deliver you to your destination?"

Her hands stilled, and her throat held a lump that refused to dislodge itself. She coughed, then choked. One hand flew to her mouth to cover her coughing while the other hand formed a fist as she patted her chest.

"Oh dear, ma'am! Let me get you some water." Walter grabbed a tin cup and ran out back to pump some water. He returned quickly, the water still sloshing back and forth as he held it out to her. "Here you are, ma'am. Please, take this."

Allie grabbed for the cup and emptied it in one gulp, with hopes she would dislodge the fear in her throat. She regained control over her breathing and voice, took a deep breath, and pleaded with the man in front of her.

"Sir, I am in desperate need. My husband...well...he...he can't find me. Please!" She was whispering, with her head bent and eyes on the hands that were trembling in her lap.

Placing his hands behind his back as he filled his lungs, Walter delivered his reply in a tone that did not allow for further conversation.

"Ma'am, I am sorry! Policy will not allow me to let you ride the train. Your circumstances are not a necessity. Please, will you head on home?" The words were formed in a question, but the way he spoke them let her know she had no choice.

Tears threatened to fall, but she refused to let him see them. Allie pulled herself up, turned, took a breath, and walked out into the morning sun.

Once out of Mr. Templeton's view, the tears flowed freely. *What now? I can't go back. Eddie will already know I wasn't there last night. What will he do if he catches me? Can I walk?* While she was deep in these thoughts, someone tapped her on the shoulder and she jumped.

Twirling his hat on his hand, a man Allie had never seen before broke through her thoughts.

"Ma'am! I...uh...well, I overheard you in there talking with that railroad man. I have an idea to help you, if you think you can trust me."

Allie was stunned speechless for a moment. "What? I'm sorry. You...you want to help me? Why?"

He chewed his lip. "'Tisn't right, Ma'am...what happened in there. You clearly need assistance. And...well...he plumb refused you. Here, take my handkerchief."

Allie hesitantly reached for the handkerchief and then dabbed her eyes and wiped the end of her nose. "Thank you, sir. But, what plan? He won't let me ride and now...well...he knows me."

The man's mouth formed a smirk and his eyes held

a sparkle. "That's why we need to change your looks, ma'am. Would you be comfortable enough in men's clothes?"

"What? I'm not sure I'm following you, mister."

She looked to her left and right to make sure no one was close enough to hear their conversation. The town was waking up, but it wasn't as busy as it would be in about an hour when the first train was due. The sign at the mercantile was just flipping from closed to open. Someone at the restaurant across the street was sweeping the boardwalk in preparation for the breakfast rush.

"Name's Fred, ma'am. I have a change of clothes here in my pack. I usually change after work. My missus likes me in clean clothes for dinner. And I prefer to eat right when I get home. Works out better for both of us that way." Fred rubbed his belly to accentuate how much he loved his wife's cooking. "Would you like them? You could put 'em on and I'll buy a couple of tickets for me and my...uh...work buddy." He put his hat on his head and smugly placed one hand in his pocket while holding the bundle of clothes out for her to take.

Allie's head began to swim. *Can I pull it off?* "Well, Mr. Fred," she said, smiling, "I do believe I have nothing else to lose." With resolve she grabbed the bundle from him, thanked him, and headed to the outhouse. "Please wait for me, sir. I'll try to hurry."

Fred turned his back to attempt to be respectful,

even though she would change in private. *What is proper in this situation?* He chuckled to himself.

Allie fumbled in the tight quarters. She slipped her dress off and then her skirt. She would keep the rest on to make changing back a quicker process. *With the extra underclothes, it may make me look a little rounder than normal.* She pursed her lips in thought as she pulled on the once-white shirt. It hung down too far...even though parts of the shirttail had been ripped off. She knew what that was from and didn't want to think of what this man used his shirt for out in the middle of nowhere with no proper toiletries. She shuddered and pulled the pants up. They were baggy, but not so big they would fall off. And, unlike the shirt, they were intact. She shivered as she gathered up all of her garments and placed them in her bag before she headed out. The pants felt odd on her, but she would take odd over pain any day of the week.

Fred stood across the street and, by the look on his face, she must look a fright. His mouth was open and eyes where bugging.

She stepped up onto the boardwalk. "Well, Mr. Fred! How do I look?"

He quickly clamped his mouth shut and began to stutter, "Uh...uh...here, take this." Fred practically threw his hat at her and she then realized what others might think when they saw her. She was only half disguised.

With quick hands she pulled the hat down over her

brown hair and then pushed the hair that bunched out up and onto the top of her head. "There. Is this better?"

Fred gave a quick nod. "Yes, but we better be quick about this. Anyone sees you up close and they're gonna know." He pulled his lips under his teeth to keep from laughing and marched into the depot with her following slightly behind.

Fred stood at the counter, slapped some coin down and asked for two tickets for today's 7:00 A.M. work train. Walter grabbed the coin and passed Fred two tickets and change; apparently not noticing the figure standing in the corner closest to the door.

Allie was motionless. *Am I even remembering to blink?* She tried to calm herself and act casual. Fred took the tickets and walked passed Allie. He never looked directly at her, but she caught his eyes pointing to her and then the door. She waited a few seconds and followed. Her eyes needed to adjust once outside. The sun was climbing higher in the sky and more people were bustling about. She did not, however, see Fred. *Which way did he go?* She could hear a pounding sound to her left. When she approached the corner of the building someone grabbed her arm and pulled her into the shade. Immediately her arms flew to her head. "Please don't hurt me," she gasped as the tears began to fall.

"There you go with that again!" Fred reached into his pocket and retrieved the handkerchief once more.

Allie took it and tried to calm down. "I'm sorry, I don't know what came over me."

"That's okay, I should have been more considerate. Stay here until the train stops. Here is your ticket. Don't let anyone see you before you board that train." Fred turned to leave, then stopped. "Oh...and...uh...keep the handkerchief."

Allie looked down at the tattered red and white cloth then back up at the spot where Fred had stood just a moment ago. "Wait, Fred! Thank you." She peeked out from the shadow, but he was already gone. Allie tucked herself back into the shadows that Fred thought safe for her and waited to hear the glorious sound of the whistle.

Minutes dragged out, but it wasn't long before the whistle could be heard in the distance. The mighty green hills in these parts were tall and steep. Sound tended to ricochet off them. The whistle sound was usually a startling, loud repetition, but now it was sweet to her ears. She waited until the train pulled in and the big steam puff cleared before she made her way out. She needed to move fast. If anyone she knew saw her, or someone noticed she was not really a man, the whole scheme would be lost. She tugged Fred's hat down, pulled her ticket out, and headed for the line that was beginning to form.

There were three men in front of her, so she just stood and waited with her head down and her heart pounding in her ears.

"Ticket, Sir." The ticket taker towered over her and he looked down his nose to find her eyes.

Allie jumped. "Oh!" Then she cleared her throat and willed it to sound deeper. "Here!" She shoved the ticket in the man's face in an attempt to take his eyes from her. It worked. He took the ticket and stepped aside so she could board. One step, two steps, three, and turn. She was in. *Can't mess this up now.* She made her way to a bench and settled herself with her head down, so she could pretend to sleep.

Her long, dark eyelashes gave her an advantage. She could see through the small slit, but it looked like her eyes were completely shut. This was a trick she had used on more than one occasion with Eddie. More men were making their way into her car and finding benches. *How could anyone sleep on these trains?* She shifted on the hard, backless bench. She knew they could and often Eddie did. *I just might fall off this bench if I fall asleep.*

Several of the men who filled in the seats around her appeared to have had a rough night. They all looked tired and old, and a few still seemed drunk. Some huddled up and took the same posture she had taken. Others chose to stand in the isle and hold onto the grab bars. It would be a while in this position for her. She must remain a man until they reached Missoula. That is where she could change back and ride on a proper passenger train the rest of the way. The train whistle blew a short toot to signify that it was time for all to board.

I can't believe this is working. Allie thought about the last several hours. *Once this train moves, Eddie will be at least two hours behind me.* That's when the next train departs from Falcon. The train came to life and slowly began to move. A lone tear fell down her cheek.

CHAPTER 3

Eddie was walking home just before the sun came up. He worked the afternoon shift so there was still plenty of time for sleep before he needed to head to Falcon to catch the work train.

I am going to have to work an extra shift to pay back Tom. Why can't I be better at my cards? Even with my extra one, I still lost too many times. At least they didn't find it on me last night. I better be more careful, or I'll be a dead man in no time.

He opened his front door and stepped inside. It was cold in the two-room shanty. The fire had died and nothing was cooked for breakfast.

"Allie," he growled out. "Why did you let the fire burn out? You better have a good reason. Man doesn't deserve to come home to have to start his own fire and cook his own meal." Silence echoed back. "Allie!" He shouted and punched the air.

"Come out, please, I'm sorry 'bout last night, sweetheart," he said as sweetly as he could with his teeth glued together. He tried to unclench his fists as he moved toward their bedroom door. He opened the door more forcibly than he intended, but it didn't hit the wall this time.

"Allie?"

He looked around the room. Bed was made, room looked tidy. *Maybe she's in the outhouse.* As he made his way out to the outhouse, he noticed the door slightly ajar. He decided to turn back and grab his shotgun. Last time the door was left open, they had a nasty critter hanging in there.

Just add it to the list I can be upset about today. Curse that woman. She doesn't do a damn thing right.

With the shotgun secured in the crook of his arm, he headed back out and quietly approached the building. He got into position with gun pointing straight ahead and reached out to open the door quickly. *Surprise attack is the best way to deal with the coons 'round here,* he thought. The door flew open, but nothing looked back at him this time. He breathed a sigh of relief.

At least he didn't have to battle any pesky animals, but where was Allie? He fired one shot up in the air as he yelled her name. The only response came from the crows that cawed and flew away. Silence returned. The thought struck him to check with Mabel. She was another woman not worth her salt, but at least she knew the goings on in these parts. Maybe Allie had gone to visit her. If not, at least Mabel would know where to look. He decided to leave the shotgun behind. He certainly didn't want to frighten her, but more than that, he didn't want that high and mighty husband of hers on his case again.

He placed his shotgun back above the bed and headed out to find Mabel. She was right where she was supposed to be, in the kitchen making bread. She didn't know where Allie was though.

Now what? He rubbed the back of his neck. *Guess I'll have to check in town. She knows not to go there. What is she up to anyway?* Eddie shoved his hands in his pockets and marched to Grand Forks.

He had yet to make it to the main portion of town before a velvet voice washed over his tense muscles.

"What are you doing back here, honey?" Pearl gave his shoulder a gentle rub.

Eddie warmed and leaned into her hand, then cleared his throat as if to refocus. "Ah love, I can't right now. Have you seen Allie? She wasn't home this morning'." Pearl pursed her lips. "'Tis no way to treat a gentleman! Come with me, darling', and I'll show you how she should treat ya."

Eddie was tempted, but his anger was more powerful right now. He brushed a curl from her forehead and gave her cheek a peck. "Sorry, Pearl. I got to find Allie. I need to give her…eh…something. Next time though."

Eddie pushed his hands into his pockets and strolled over to the mercantile. He pushed the door open, jingling the bell above, and made his way straight to the counter. "Morning, Joe. Have you seen Allie?"

Joe was rubbing down the counter top. "Nope, can't say that I have."

Eddie tried to hide the growl. "If you see her, can you send word?"

Joe nodded and bent down below the counter pulling up some pants. "Sure thing. Hey, Eddie! Got a hole in my pants yesterday. Can you have her mend 'em for me?"

Eddie reached out and took the pants. "Sure. Just as soon as I find her." He gave Joe a nod and turned as more frustration built. Eddie stepped back out in the sun just as he heard the faint sound of the Falcon train whistle. His eyebrows wrinkled. *She wouldn't, would she? No, they wouldn't let her on. Especially without any money. Better head back home, maybe she's there now.*

When Eddie got home he opened the door to find nothing had changed.

"Damn it, Allie! Where are you?" He threw the pants down on the table and heard a clink. *What was that?* He grabbed the pants back up and started to search them. As he methodically felt every inch of the pants, he felt something round and hard inside the cuff of one leg. He knew some ladies sewed weights into their skirts, but had no idea why Joe would do that? *Better see what this is.* He pulled out his pocket knife and cut a slit in them. A shiny silver nickel clinked down on the table. Eddie stood stock still and stared down at his table. His heart suddenly dropped.

She had the means. How long had this been going on? Let's see…maybe four months or so he'd been bringing her mending. How much could she have now? And how many men were helping her? He snatched up the coin and pocketed it. *I'll deal with Joe later! I need to get to Falcon. Now!*

CHAPTER 4

Allie sat as still as possible and continued to keep her eyes closed. She was tired, but her mind wouldn't allow her to sleep. The train was chugging slowly...but moving...east towards Saltese, Montana. *Five stops total to get to Missoula—and I've already passed one!* Then she could change and ride properly the rest of the way home.

Fred bought her two stops. He did not board back in Falcon. *Did he need his ticket for the day or was that just for show?* She needed to change positions but feared someone would think she was awake. There were about twenty or so men on the train with her. Some looked friendly enough when they boarded, but others she didn't want to cross.

The train reeked of alcohol. The scent was so strong it seemed the liquor was running off the walls. Fortunately, she had adjusted to that putrid smell or she wouldn't have been able to keep what contents were in her stomach down.

These mountains were rugged and tough, and she needed to match that to make it. The train crept along the tracks, winding its way up the steep terrain and through some glorious valleys. It was pretty. She knew this landscape was like none other but wouldn't allow herself a glimpse. The whistle blew. That meant she'd soon be headed to her second stop. Saltese is where she must purchase more fare. She would wait until the last second to open her eyes and disembark with the crowd.

As the train came to a stop and the last whistle blew, Allie stood and quickly swept her eyes over the men. She had one shot to do this right. Those getting off were making their way to the aisle. She put her head down and worked her way into the middle of the line.

Eddie comes home drunk many nights and sometimes he's still hung over by dinner. If I keep my head down and stumble a bit, maybe they will think that of me? Can't hurt to try, I guess.

As the line moved forward, she shuffled her feet like she was groggy. She was careful, however, to not bump into anyone. No sense drawing undue attention. The sun was high in the sky as she came down the steps. She kept her hands in her pockets even though she could have used one to shield her eyes. Her stomach was growling, but she couldn't risk being out in the open any longer than necessary.

Keeping her head down prevented her from seeing much of the town. It sounded like a busy place. She could hear wagons, horses, and people. There was even a dog barking off in the distance, but she refused to look up. She entered the depot and headed straight for the line. Her plan was to get the exact change out early so there was less time for the man to see her hands. *From a distance I might look enough like a man, but there are too many feminine things about me up close.* She palmed her change and waited her turn. Three men were ahead of her in line. Her heart raced, and she needed this to be quick.

It seemed to take a very long time for her to get up to the counter, but it really was only minutes. She slapped the money on the counter, quickly removed her hand, and hid it in her pocket. "Need fare to Missoula." She grunted as deeply as possible. A second man approached from behind the first holding a telegram. Allie was starting to perspire under her shirt and pants.

"Says here we need to watch for a woman traveling alone. Have you seen her?" The second man laid the telegram on the counter for the first to see it.

The first man gathered the coins and placed the ticket on the counter. "No, can't say I have. I'll be watching though. Says the lady stole some money and left her husband back in Grand Forks."

Allie was shaking and hoped it felt worse than it looked. She grabbed the ticket and walked toward the door as casually, and quickly, as possible. Once outside, she ran to the side of the building. Breathing hard, she braced and willed herself not to cry from fear.

He can't find me. Not yet. She tried to calm her breathing as she pondered what was meant by "stole money." *Did he know about the hidden money? Did he know before or just now? No. Must have been now. That knowledge would have brought pain...and a lot of it.* Allie put a hand on her stomach to ease the nausea she was now feeling. *At least now I don't feel hungry.* She hunkered down in the shadows and waited for that first short toot.

Luckily those toots weren't long in coming. The trains liked to keep moving so the workers could keep working. She did as before and boarded with no problems. A similar mix of men came aboard this time and some of them even looked familiar. *The plan worked the last time so why change things up.* She plopped down on the hard, cold bench, folded her arms to tuck her hands in, and closed her eyes.

The train jostled her back and forth and she was beginning to see how some could sleep. She was exhausted. Even if she wasn't tired, sitting in the same position for hours on end was boring, and the rocking added to the allure of sleep.

The farther away from Grand Forks she went, the calmer she became. She needed to keep that in check. *Just because I'm a few hours away doesn't mean Eddie can't catch up. He will know where I'm headed.* She pulled her shoulders back to stretch her back. She knew the landscape was moving by her, but still didn't dare to open her eyes wide enough to get a look.

The train kept chugging east, stopping at Regis, Quartz, and Lathrop. She had to disembark at all stops but didn't need to purchase more fare. She was starving and knew she could safely purchase something to eat at the next stop. There, she could also change back into her true self.

Knowing that was encouragement enough to keep her going. Her legs were starting to chafe with Fred's pants rubbing on them. How she wished she could change now. She never wanted to wear pants again and was thankful that she had her skirts with her. She would use the facilities at the next stop, too. Not eating or drinking anything allowed her to control her need with ease. Her time with Eddie had taught her to control it. Why he wanted her on a schedule for going outside to use the privy was beyond her.

He is so controlling. How did I not see it before? She sighed and continued to pretend to be asleep.

The whistle blew to signal the arrival in Missoula, Montana. Allie jumped, she must have fallen asleep. Quickly trying to compose herself, she looked around briefly and noticed a male figure looking at her. He was perched a few benches behind her and angled so that he would have the best view of her.

Her heart started racing, but she kept her calm appearance on the outside. Immediately she began planning. *As soon as we stop, I'll head off the train and find a suitable location for changing my clothes—maybe in the facilities in a restaurant. Then I might get a meal, too, if I can lose this man. Who is he anyway? Does he look familiar?* She spent the next couple of minutes thinking back, trying to determine who the man might be and wondering how long he had been watching her. Before she could place him, the train stopped...and she was in flight mode.

This time she didn't care if she was noticed. She bumped and pushed her way to the front of the crowd. The men grumbled and yelled in response, but she never looked back. It is now or never, she thought.

She stepped off the train and made a beeline for the first establishment she saw. This was a glorious building with a sign that read *Savoy Hotel*. It was new since she had last been through this booming town. As she moved quickly toward it, she caught the man following her out of the corner of her eye. He was sweeping back and forth trying to decide which way to go. Once inside the hotel, Allie realized there were no windows. Light came in from above. She approached a man, and as deep a voice as she could, asked for the facilities. He paused a moment and nodded with a that-a-way glance. She did her best to act as though nothing was amiss and ducked into the small wash room.

After she locked the door, Allie collapsed to the floor. Exhaustion seeping out of her, she let the tears come. As they fell, she felt her hunger return. She continued to sit on the floor as she quickly removed the disguise and allowed herself a moment to compose herself. The floor was cold and hard—much like she had made her heart to keep from falling apart these last few months.

She needed to remember she was still in survival mode. She was not protected here and needed to keep moving east. She dressed in her now wrinkled dress. *At least I'm back in my own clothes. I don't need to pretend as much from here on out.* She brushed her palms over the flow of the mud-colored brown skirt. *Always practical.* The color showed less dirt, so she didn't need to do her own wash as often...allowing more time to deal with Eddie's commands. He kept her busy all day. What she wouldn't give to be able to read or sit by Pa's creek and dream again.

Allie stood in front of the sink. The train left her skin dusty and grimy. She would clean up as much as she could. Many places only had outhouses in these parts. Here, she could wash up and feel like she was a lady again.

As she splashed water onto her face, she noticed muffled voices coming from somewhere beyond the other side of the door. She heard a male voice asking something about someone entering. Her hands stilled, and she quickly bolted for the door, leaving the male clothes in a pile on the floor. Opening it slowly, she could see the man speaking with the same gentlemen who had given her directions. She slipped through the door and headed away from the entrance, making her way to a door on the far wall. The door led her to the back of the hotel. *This must be the workers entrance.* She needed to go around the building and head across the street to the train depot. Fare to Drummond and beyond to Deer Lodge needed to be purchased before she could buy something to eat.

Moving quickly, but carefully, she made her way to the edge of the building and peeked around the corner to see if she saw the man. *I wish I could place who he is and why he is following me. Does he know who I am, or does he have other intentions?*

Allie picked up her skirt and flew across the road. She needed to run, to save herself from being run over. This was a busy growing town. It was so much bigger in only a year since she was last here. Once on the other side, she made her way into line at the station. *No pretending—no hiding!* She sighed. *If I can stay away from that man I should be good.* She approached the counter and asked for the tickets.

The man at the counter was a short, robust, middle-aged man. He had a fancy gold watch on a chain that he pulled out of his pocket to check the time. "Train for Drummond leaves in half hour, ma'am. You have good timing."

She passed the coins across the counter and took the ticket. "Thank you, sir." With a slight nod of her head she turned to leave.

He gave a small grunt. "Ma'am, you okay? You're...uh...well...your face, ma'am. Don't mean to be rude..."

She froze and didn't turn back to him. "I'm fine. Thank you. Good day, sir."

She walked out the door and around the corner. *No one noticed or commented when I was a man. I guess that disguise helped in more ways than I knew.* She placed her hand on her stomach and willed herself to feel full. She wouldn't be out in public again without necessity with her bruises, no matter how hungry.

Allie stayed on the side of the building—hidden once again in the shadows—waiting for the whistle. She was thankful the wait would be a short one. She'd planned this part of her trip hours earlier while pretending to sleep. The sound of the whistle could be heard in the distance as Allie rubbed her eyes to prevent them from permanently closing. Once on board, maybe she could truly sleep.

She peeked around the corner again before stepping back into the light. He—whoever he is—was not there. She made her way to the line slowly, so she wouldn't draw undue attention. Fortunately, there were many people to blend in with this late in the day. This was much different from when her journey began. She reached the front of the line and handed her ticket to the man. As she boarded the train, she regretted her flight prevented her from enjoying the sites of this magnificent countryside.

CHAPTER 5

Frank Hubbard was sore from riding the rails. He had only been traveling for a few days, but his body felt like it had been a full month of nonstop jarring. His mind and hands sat idle since leaving Portland. The views were beautiful, but it just wasn't enough to keep him entertained.

Medicine was his life now, and he was growing restless just sitting. He had gone home to Deer Lodge after graduating, but quickly returned to take on the internship in Sandy. Logging was picking up steam, and with it came the accidents. Doctors were needed everywhere. His leg started to cramp, and he decided to take a walk. Trains certainly didn't offer many choices when it came to needing to stretch. He stood and reached up his arms and arched his back briefly before stepping out into the only exercise area aboard a train, the center aisle.

The train was almost full and only a few seats remained open. As he walked to the front of the train, he took in who was on board with him. Some were sleeping, others reading. He noticed a few entertaining young children. On the way back, he was able to see their faces. He secretly enjoyed watching people, and seeing their faces gave him a glimpse of understanding those riding with him.

Frank slowed his pace to allow a longer view of the faces. One face caught his attention. It wasn't what she was doing, since she was only sleeping. It was the coloring. Different shades of black, blue, purple...and even pale brown with a lip that was swollen on one side. This halted his pace altogether. The face was vaguely familiar, but he was having a hard time placing it. *Maybe because it was banged up. I know that person, though. How?* He walked up to the row and took the open seat next to her. He decided to sit and watch for a while hoping to place her.

As he sat thinking of the possibilities, Allie began to stir. She opened her eyes with a feeling that someone was watching her. She jolted awake and braced herself. Her heart was once again racing and making her deaf to the sounds aboard the roaring train. Her hands went to fists and flew to her head.

Her reaction startled him, and Frank reached out a hand to her. "I'm sorry, ma'am, I know you from somewhere—but can't remember from where."

Allie's breath came rushing back into her lungs. She slowly lowered her hands and forced them to unclench. *When will I wake up without panic controlling me?* She attempted to calm her heart. The man was talking, but she was struggling to hear him.

"Ma'am, I'm sorry for startling you. What's your name? I know I've met you." Frank thought better of touching her arm and placed his hands in his lap.

Allie turned her head and blinked. She could not believe who she was seeing. Only one man she knew had the deepest chocolate brown eyes paired with light brown hair. Here on the train with her was a childhood friend. Well, to him a friend, but to her…he could have been so much more. *Of all the places and timing.* She lowered her head. "You know me. We went to school together. How are you, Frank?"

The puzzle quickly came together. She vaguely looked like Allie, but those bruises made it hard to see the girl who was once his playmate. Last he knew, his parents said she had married and moved to Idaho. *What is she doing here—alone—and looking like she got hit by this train instead of just riding?* "I'm good! Surprising my parents for an impromptu visit. Winter was awful this year and as soon as the snow melted enough to make the trains run smoothly, I decided it was time to head back home. Allie, are you okay?"

Inside she sank. *What was I thinking going home looking this way? What will people think of me?* "I am much better now, thank you." She brushed some falling hair behind her ear.

"Allie, your lip looks like it might need some attention. I have my bag with me. Let me go grab it and

I'll see if I can do something for you." He stood to leave but didn't take his eyes off her.

Tears threatened to fall. "No, thank you, Frank. I'm sure it's fine. Doesn't hurt real bad." She was falling apart inside but refused to let him see. *He could have been my future—not this. If he only knew. He needed to leave, though. He had to chase his dreams...and leave me behind.* "Please, Frank, I don't mean to be rude, but I am awfully tired." She needed him to leave.

"Of course, you sleep. We can talk later." He refused to leave her. He would sit and wait for her to rest. He folded his arms and pretended to sleep, waiting for her to close her eyes so he could watch her again.

Frank's mind began spinning, thinking of the last time he was home. *Allie's father would be furious with me if he knew I left her like this. Clearly something is wrong. I need to know what happened. Last time I was home, I was hoping to find her, but found out she had moved away. I can't let her go again. I won't!*

Allie closed her eyes and struggled to fall asleep. *Why won't he go back to his seat?* Most people knew Frank as just nosy, but Allie knew the real reason behind his nosy behavior. He cared for people...deeply. She opened her eyes and turned her head to face him.

"Frank, I'm not ready to talk about it."

"Okay, then we'll just sit here. But, I want you to know I'm' ready to listen whenever you need me." Frank sighed and then crossed his legs to prove he was

31

not leaving anytime soon.

She closed her eyes again. *Might as well sleep. He won't leave me. And this way I can avoid him longer.*

Frank watched Allie sleep for a while. There were three stops before they reached Drummond where they would need to change trains. Allie was in such a deep sleep she didn't budge when the train whistle blew to signal the next town. Passengers continuing through did not need to disembark, so he let her sleep.

She has obviously been through something. Might as well let her sleep. I better stay with her, though. Something's not right. Frank stood to stretch his legs but didn't move from the row. His bag was back at his seat. *I'm staying with Allie whether she wants me to or not. I will see her all the way to her pa's place.*

When the train slowed to a stop, Frank waited for those getting off the train to clear the aisle. Then he walked back to his seat, grabbed his bag, and was back by Allie's side before any new passengers boarded.

As Frank watched her sleeping, he felt a sense of sadness for what could have been. He had liked Allie, but had to get out of that town. He didn't want to follow his pa and run the family business. Banking bored him. He wanted to help people. His parents accepted it easier than he thought they would, but he knew Allie was devastated. She had never actually told him how she felt, but he knew...and he felt it, too. With those thoughts, he started drifting off to sleep.

Frank woke suddenly to find Allie flailing and crying.

"Allie! Allie! Wake up! You're dreaming." Frank gently shook her.

"Stop, Eddie! I'm sorry. I won't do it again. Eddie, please!" Allie's eyes flew open and she jumped at Frank's touch. "Don't tou...touch me. Please!" She was shaking now. *Where am I?* Her head was fuzzy. She rubbed her eyes as everything started coming back to her. "Oh, Frank! I am so sorry. I didn't mean..."

Frank shushed her. *Something was really wrong, and who was Eddie?* "Allie, I need to know. Are you in trouble?" Did someone do this to you?" He gently touched her check and she winced at the pain.

"Frank, I am so sorry!" The back of her hand touched her lips to try to control a sob. It was useless though. She couldn't hide what was blatantly on her face. She had to talk to him. Maybe if she got it all out, it would be easier to talk about with the next familiar face. "Might as well start from the beginning. That's the easier part to talk about, anyway."

Frank wanted to gather her in his arms, but knew she needed space to talk about this. Allie always liked to keep things to herself, but when she was ready she came to him. He was always ready to listen to her on her time.

They had been friends for years through school. Everyone thought they would eventually marry, but they didn't know Frank's dreams to be a doctor. No one knew he was planning to leave, not even Allie. He was regretting that decision now. He turned his body and kept his hands in his lap, preparing to hear something that was bound to shake him.

"You remember Andrew's accident, I'm sure? He had such promise. My parents needed his help. That stupid, stubborn horse. The head injury made it impossible for him to work, and I was forced to take a job to help out. The job I got was at the restaurant, but it wasn't enough. Ma and Pa were struggling. I could see that. They tried to hide it, but Ma was getting thinner. She was eating less and less to save food for us. Pa's tools kept disappearing, and I knew he had sold some. Ma couldn't work since Andrew needed a caregiver. He had seizures. I never saw anything like it before.

"Well...one day, a guy showed up at the restaurant. I thought he was nice looking and, apparently, he thought the same of me. He asked me to dinner the next night—and I went. Eddie was passing through town on his way to Idaho to work on the railroad. He stayed in town for a week and we saw each other every day. When he asked me to marry him, I saw a way to help my parents. I would not bring in any money, but I was one less mouth to feed.

"We eloped and then told my parents. They were not pleased. I thought they would be thrilled, but I was wrong. I was wrong on everything. But, here we were married, nothing else to do but go with my new husband. He took me to Idaho with him. At first it was fine. We fell into a routine quickly. He liked me to stay home. Didn't want me meeting the town folk. He claimed they were a rough sort that I didn't need to know. That was true. Grand Forks people are not our kind of people. They are rough, crude, foul mouthed... He partied with them and would come home smelling of alcohol most nights. After a while, he began to get upset if dinner wasn't just right or my dress was dirty. Little things began bothering him. Before I knew it, he started hitting me. Just slaps at first, but it didn't take long for them to become punches. Then I began missing chunks of time. One minute he was hitting me, and I would wake up hours later. I didn't know what to do. I hid some money and waited for an opportunity. And here I am."

Frank sat frozen. *Allie is such a sweet girl, how could anyone...*

"Allie, I am so sorry."

He was torn between stopping the train and finding this Eddie guy right now or grabbing Allie and never letting go. He knew neither of those options would help. *Why did I leave her? I thought I could return with my degree and we could start a life. When I was told she started her life with someone else, I assumed she was happy. How stupid could I be? I should have found her then. Then what? Steal her? What could I have done?* Frank decided to gently touch her hand. Allie flinched, then let him lay his hand on hers. If felt good. Almost protective.

35

"Frank, I'm going to try to sleep again. I haven't slept well in a long while. And, knowing you're here, I think I could sleep for a week." She didn't wait for him to answer, but instead laid back her head and closed her eyes.

Frank scooted closer to her and gently nudged her head on his shoulder. It wasn't exactly appropriate, but he dared anyone to call him out on it. They stayed that way through the next few stops. He dozed a bit, too. It felt right having her here, leaning on him. He was not going to let her slip out of his life like he did the first time.

CHAPTER 6

Frank woke Allie for the train change in Drummond. There was a little gap of time before the next train, so they had time to grab some proper food. The train usually had some food on hand, but at this hour there was no meal. She was hungry. He could tell. She had tried to eat slowly, but eventually the hunger won and she finished her meal before him. Now they were back on the train making their way to Deer Lodge. Only two towns to go until they were back home, and he could safely deliver Allie to her Pa.

Allie felt better with sleep and a good meal, but a sense of unease washed over her. The closer they got to Deer Lodge, the sooner she would need to retell her story. This time she felt people wouldn't be so quick to let her stop talking. What would they do when she suggested divorce?

Before she could continue her thoughts, Frank picked up his bag and set it on his lap.

"Allie, could I please look at your wounds?"

She exhaled and gave a gentle nod. "Is it really bad?"

He opened his bag and pulled out thread and a needle. "It is. But once I clean up your eye and that gash on your cheek, it will look much better. Can't do anything about the bruising and that swollen lip, though."

He set the thread and needle down on his seat, placed his bag on the floor, and stood to flag down the conductor. He requested a glass of water and a towel. Once those items were brought to him, he sat back down and dunked the towel into the glass.

"This is going to hurt a little. I'm sorry."

She closed her eyes and gave a slight nod. "Can't be any worse than it is already."

He began dabbing her eye and wiping away the blood streaking down her face. Once that was clean, he moved to her check.

"Just as I thought. This needs a couple of stitches. What was it? What did he hit you with?"

Her shoulders drooped.

"A leather strap," she replied.

Allie couldn't tell him about the metal grommets. She felt like crying, but no tears would come. She had choked them back all day. Now, it was pitch black outside. No one could see her. The dim train lanterns weren't even bright enough to read, but she couldn't cry.

Frank managed to get his needle threaded, but it took longer than usual, and not just because of the dim light. He needed to steady his hands, but he was so angry it was a struggle.

"Allie are you ready for this? I don't have anything to numb it. But I'll work quickly."

She gave a nod, unable to speak, not from crying. She still wasn't able to shed a tear, but her body felt tingly and numb all over. She felt detached...like she was floating above looking down and watching this happen. She was in her protective mode. The mode she sought when Eddie was in true form. But now...here it was. Over the last few hours—in bits and pieces and chunks...here and there—she'd told Frank her story. He's the only one she'd told. It felt awful...shameful.

What is wrong with me? I can't do anything right. Now what? I'm going to go cry to Ma and Pa? They can't take me in. They couldn't afford me before. Nothing has changed. And then the tears began.

"I'm almost finished...and...there!" He tied off the stitch and cut the end of the thread. "All done! I'm sorry I hurt you. Here! Use this towel."

"Thank you!" She grabbed the towel and used it to wipe the tears from her face. "I'm getting tired again. I think I'll try to sleep a little more."

Frank placed his items back into his bag and offered his shoulder. This time she opted for the window.

CHAPTER 7

Eddie paced the floor of his house trying to figure out his next move. That was hard to do considering he only suspected where she might have headed. Going home was the only option he would have considered before he found the money. Since then, he realized there was more to her than he once thought.

Allie was a sweet, pure girl. Being able to hide money and lie about it for who knows how long showed she had a side to her he had yet to learn. He wasn't sure if she had the gumption to leave everything behind and go someplace where she knew no one. He did know, though, she left quickly. He found most of her things still in their place. It didn't look like she took much of anything with her. A knock sounded on the door.

"I lost her, Eddie!" John shifted on his feet. "I was headed to work early...trying to get in a few more hours before my shift started, and I saw him...well...her."

"Come in, come in John" They both made their way to the small table and sat. "What do you mean him...her? That makes no sense at all, John?" Eddie was clenching his teeth.

"She was dressed like a him. Her hair tucked up under a hat. She rode the train and I followed her all the way to Missoula, but I lost her on the street. She walked into the hotel and must have run out the back. Missed my whole day of work for you. Boss man will be angry. Hope I still have a job." He put his hands in his pockets.

A small smirk formed on Eddie's unshaven face. "Thanks, John! At least now I know for sure where she's headed. Figured she'd go back home. But this is big country and I wasn't sure who was helping her. Can't trust anybody these days. People should stay out of our business. She's my wife! My business...no concern for the rest of the town. I'll handle her how she needs to be handled. Darn girl didn't know her place. Just trying to teach her how to be a good wife." He slammed his hand down on the table a bit harder than necessary "Thanks, John. At least I know I have someone I can trust."

John gave a nod and walked out the door. Hollering back, "Gonna go talk to the boss...see if I still got a job."

Eddie closed the door without acknowledging John's concern and started to work on a plan. Let her go home. Get comfortable for a while. Let her feel safe. Then I'll go bring her back where she belongs. Satisfied, he poured himself a cup of coffee. Knowing where she was took care of half the problem. He could get her back with the law on his side. A husband has rights! No one could legally stand in his way. Traipsing all over the country side trying to find her didn't sound very appealing, but knowing she wasn't too far away...and would stay put...settled him.

Keeping her home was the other half of this current issue. He sat drinking his coffee with a bubbling anticipation brewing in him. His little house was getting messier by the minute...awaiting her return so she could tidy it all up again. But inside the chaos her leaving brought him, his plan to bring her back and keep her here was beginning to form.

CHAPTER 8

Allie woke to the sound of the whistle and the rays of the bright morning sun penetrating her eyelids. She was home. That thought gave her the strength to open her eyes and look through the window. The town was coming into view and it looked glorious. It wasn't a fancy town, but it held good people. The hills were tall, green, and snowcapped. And the water was crystal clear. Everything about this area seemed to be more vibrant. The colors were brighter and clearer. The people were cheerful. And most of all—not everyone was a drunk! Sure, the town had their share of drinking establishments, but nothing compared to where she had been.

"Good morning!" Frank was still sitting next to her. He had stayed by her side through the night. "How are you?"

"Mmm...good." She looked over and gave him a small smile. She was sore and stiff from riding for so long, but nothing was going to get her down now.

The train whistle blew a few more times as the train came to a stop at the depot. Allie and Frank picked up their belongings...which didn't take Allie very long. Frank had a trunk that would be waiting for him outside in addition to his doctor's bag that he kept with him. They made their way to the front of the train and walked into the cool morning breeze. There were a few people waiting outside, but no one was waiting for either of them. No one knew they were coming. She wrapped her shawl back over her head, needing to get home before anyone recognized her.

"Let me arrange for my trunk to be delivered home and then I will walk you home." He placed his hand on her arm to direct her over to where they were removing the luggage.

"No, thank you. I would like to walk by myself." She turned just as Gladys approached. She was another school friend who knew them both.

"Frank? Frank...is that you?" Gladys waved a white cloth in his direction while almost running to him. "What are you doing here? I just saw your mom the other day and she said nothing of your return."

"Mom doesn't know. But Gladys, I am in a hurry, if you don't mind." He moved passed her and walked toward his trunk, realizing that Allie was not following. Turning back, he couldn't find her anywhere. That Gladys was a pain back in school and nothing had changed.

He ground his teeth in frustration. Leaving his bag with his trunk, he made his way back past a confused Gladys. He ran to the edge of the walk and looked in a circle. Allie was gone. He knew where she was going. She had walked that path for many years and he knew she would be fine, but he wanted to see her home. He needed to make sure she would be all right. He also knew that she was independent, and he needed to give her some space for a while. So, he turned back...only to see Gladys standing next to his luggage. *Great!* He thought. *This is already shaping up to be a very fine day.*

Frank walked back and picked up his bag, and thanked Gladys for guarding it. Why she needed to do that here he didn't know, but he needed to remain polite. *The Lord knows I don't need her mother on my case...again.* "Gladys, I hope you have the most splendid of days," he said with the sincerest fake smile he could manage as he turned to leave.

"Oh...well...you, too, Frank. You, too." She fiddled with her hands and tried to decide what to do now. Knowing she was flustered put a genuine smile on his face.

He decided to head home and surprise his parents. He would find Allie later.

Allie watched the whole scene unfold. She tried to not laugh out loud and give herself away. The side of the old restaurant made for an excellent hiding spot. She would come here when she needed to get away for a while when she had worked at the restaurant. She could see much of the town, but they couldn't see her. Gladys was one of those people who had a good heart deep down, but with her mother's encouragement, she got into everyone's business. And she had a broken heart over Frank. She was devastated when he up and left. That made two of them.

Allie turned around and decided to head out of town in the wrong direction for a while and then she would turn the right way. She wanted to avoid the depot as there were a few people that would probably recognize her even with her shawl on. It was still early, and she was going to make this walk last. She needed time to think and reflect on her life. Now that she was home, she felt she could breathe and think...finally!

Her ankle still smarted, but she'd had worse. Once she was home, she could put it up for a while. The walk was beautiful. It contrasted starkly with her life. Everything was bold. Her life so dark and the light so bright. The sun poured warmth on her face and warmed her clear through. It was only March, but it sure was warmer than normal. She hoped that meant the crops would be better than other years. She removed the shawl from her head and folded it over her arm. Seeing the towel draped over her arm brought a memory from her work at the restaurant about a year ago.

Allie was waiting tables. A man walked in, surveyed the room, and took the table to her right. He was sweet looking and appeared out of place. She approached him with the coffee pot and offered him some. He gladly accepted, but she missed the cup as she began to pour and dumped the steamy liquid all over the table and onto the floor. Pulling her towel out from her apron she began to clean up the mess. He grabbed her hand and removed the towel telling her that it was his mess and he would take care of it.

That was the first time she met Eddie. He was so different then. Was he faking it...or did he change? Did she make him change? She shook her head to erase the thoughts. Once she started them, they were hard to stop. So many questions—never enough answers.

She decided she had traveled far enough out of the way that she could turn north and head home. If she went any further east, she would head straight into some of her neighbors. Going home first was best. She wanted to see her parents first...hoping to hide out until her face cleared up a bit. That might keep the gossip down for a while anyway.

CHAPTER 9

Arriving home wasn't as dreadful as Allie thought it would be. The house looked like it was shining with the sun hitting it just right. The fields lay beyond the two-story house. There was a garden and laundry line on the far side that couldn't be seen from this angle. The barn was just west of the front yard. Everything seemed in order except for the chipping paint here and there.

Some things couldn't be done since the money was tight. Things seemed quiet. *Pa must be out in the field with Andrew and Ma is probably inside somewhere.* She slipped into the back of the house unseen.

The room right off the kitchen was a mud room that housed not only coats, but dry goods. The house was quiet. She made her way through the kitchen and was making her way to the front room when she heard the door bang closed. Ma must have been outside. Taking a deep breath. She knew she couldn't wait. She had to step into the front room and get it behind her. Gently nudging the door open between the two rooms,

Allie stood with her hands folded in front of her. Ma was a slender woman and had her back turned to her. She had a basket of laundry she was folding. Allie cleared her throat and softly whispered, "Ma." The towel Ma was folding dropped to the floor as she whipped around. Her eyes were normally large, but now they seemed to take up half of her face.

Ma's hand flew to her chest. "Oh, Allie! You scared me half to death. What are you doing here? Is Eddie here, too? Well, don't just stand there, come here and give me a hug." Allie approached hesitantly. She knew Ma would quickly discover the bruising on her face. "Oh, dear child! What happened?" Ma's hand shook in front of her mouth for a moment. Then she quickly wrapped her arms around her daughter. Allie let herself fall into her mother's safe embrace.

The sobs started slowly, but before too long her eyes were a faucet that drenched the front of Ma's navy-blue dress. When she started to calm down, she found herself sitting on Ma's bed in her protective embrace, wrapped around her like a warm wool blanket.

It was comforting at first, but then became suffocating. She didn't want to talk about it, but knew her mother wouldn't let her stay silent for long. With Ma, it was better to get it all out and over with because she wouldn't drop the subject until it was.

As she wiped her eyes with Ma's hankie, she scanned the room and began to tell the story. Ma sat silently, not wanting to interrupt or cut her off. Releasing the words to her was like releasing her soul. It was humiliating and exhausting. Telling Frank was difficult—but paled in comparison to telling her Ma. She knew she wouldn't have any energy left and Ma would need to speak to Pa for her. She couldn't bare that after this. Ma was a stern lady who expected perfection from her children, but Pa was at least twice that. Fortunately, they both had a soft spot for their children. She focused on Ma's bright yellow curtains covering the one window in the room, hoping to draw from their cheeriness. It wasn't working, but she continued with her story.

When Allie finished, Ma remained silent. She stood and walked to her dresser and pulled out one of her nightgowns. Then motioned for Allie to follow her up the stairs and into her old bedroom. Gently laying the nightgown on the bed she took Allie's hands in hers and closed her eyes. Then released her and left the room. Allie changed into the nightgown and crawled into bed. She was overwhelmingly exhausted and quickly fell into a deep sleep with her head laying on her old feather pillow.

Her eyes were heavy, and she struggled to open them. She heard voices, but couldn't make out who was talking. Gently pulling herself up to a sitting position she felt sore and dizzy. The strain of the traveling—and her wounds—would take a while to heal. The door opened, but only the glow of candlelight could be seen. She had slept until dark.

"Allie, Dr. Leman is here. We want him to look at

you. When you are all finished, I have supper ready for you." She ushered the doctor in and closed the door behind him.

Dr. Leman walked in. He was a tall, lanky man. He carried his doctor's bag in one hand and a candle in the other as he made his way to the side of the bed.

"Hello, Allie. I just want to take a look at you, see if there's anything I can do to help. Tell me...where do you hurt?"

Allie sighed. "Where don't I. If I don't have a visible wound somewhere now, I've had one there in the past. Right now, my ankle is really sore."

"All right, that's a good place to start. I want to look you over and I will start down at your feet. I'll try to be gentle. You just let me know if you hurt anywhere when I touch you." Dr. Leman began examining her feet. He wiggled her toes before beginning to move her ankles back and forth. "Yes, I can see that one hurts. It's only strained, though. I will wrap it up and give you something for the pain." Working his way up, he poked and prodded her legs and finally rested his hand on her abdomen. "Allie when was your last cycle?"

Allie closed her eyes trying to think. "A month or more ago, Eddie came home and was upset that I hadn't given him a son. He started calling me names and punching my stomach. I bled for a few weeks after that. I still spot and cramp up sometimes now."

Dr. Leman grunted. "I need you to come to my

office soon, Allie. I need to do a more complete exam on you. We can keep it quiet, if you want. Just come in sometime this week and I will look you over more closely."

Allie nodded and placed her hand on her stomach. "Is everything going to heal?"

With a nod, he reassured her that she should be back to normal soon. "The ankle will take a few weeks, but the bruising and swelling should heal much sooner. Let me look at those stitches. Who did these?"

Allie touched her eye and a small but definite smile formed on her face, "I met Frank on the train on my way here. He tended me while in motion."

"Frank's back in town? Good, good! I will have to catch up with him. He did a fine job. Should be minimal scaring there." Dr. Leman felt Allie's mood had improved...if only slightly. "I'll make sure and thank him and congratulate him on his work. His parent's sure brag about his work he's doing over in Oregon. Such a fine young doctor!"

"He owes a lot to you, Dr. Leman. You took him under your wing and fostered his love of medicine." Allie grabbed his hand and thanked him for looking at her. She promised to come and visit with him later in the week for a more thorough exam.

They said their goodbyes and he left. Allie stood and pulled the sheets up on the bed. Then she wrapped the blanket around her to cover the nightgown.

Confronting Pa has to be done! Might as well get it over with. She stepped out of the room and walked into Pa's arms.

Pa was not an overly big man, but he had an authoritative air that seemed to surround him. His eyes were deep set and dark with hard-work lines covering his face. The three most important people to her were waiting outside.

Dr. Leman had already filled them in about her initial examination and let them know she needed to come in for a follow-up. Ma was dishing up a plate and placed it on the table. Andrew was using the firewood he brought in to stoke the fire. Pa just held her and stroked her hair. Allie made the first move to break free, hobbling over to the table. She lowered herself down to the chair and was the first to speak, "This looks wonderful. It is a treat to have your good cooking again, Ma."

Pa and Ma both stole a glance at each other before joining her at the table. "So, the doctor says you'll heal up nicely," Ma said nervously from the end of the table. Pa grunted in agreement.

"Yes, should be quickly, too," Allie said between bites. Her appetite had returned. Pa was very quiet—not like him. "Pa, could you slide the other chair over here, so I can put my leg up on it?"

"Of course!" He stood and slid the forth chair that was Andrew's to her side. Allie shifted to lift her leg and still be able to eat, "Thanks, Pa."

"Well, got to head to the barn...check on the horses." He grabbed his hat and flew out the door.

Ma released a breath. "He's a bit shaken up. He'll settle back down after a bit and be the same old hard man you remember. Not everyday someone harms his baby." Ma placed her hand on Allie's briefly and then got up to do the dishes.

Andrew remained invisible until everyone else left the room. That was impressive given his size. Everyone always said he took after Ma's family. He was close to six feet tall and had a broad chest. Pa depended on Drew's muscles. Drew sat in Pa's chair and stared at Allie. Attempting to make small talk, she said, "Hello, Drew. How are you?"

"Good. Allie's hurt." He said with an even tone not giving any emotion away.

"Yes, Drew. I am hurt, but you heard Doc Leman. I will be good as new in just a little while." She hoped this would settle him. He was usually cheerful.

Drew stood up, walked to Allie's chair, and knelt down next to her. "No. Allie hurts in here." He placed his hand on her heart.

"Oh, Drew! I could never hide anything from you. Yes, but I will be okay. Come here and give your big sister a hug."

They embraced, and she could feel him softly sobbing on her shoulder. That accident damaged his mind, but he was still in there. Not everyone could see her sweet Drew, but he wasn't hidden from her and for that she was thankful. Such a shame. He would have made a wonderful husband and father, someday. He had such a sweet heart. Ma and Pa had a choice after the accident. Many people thought Drew should be sent to Warm Springs, the hospital for the mentally ill. Drew was harmless though. She was grateful that her parents stood their ground and let him remain at home.

Allie heard the door creak behind them. "Andrew, could you come here and help your old ma dry the dishes please?"

Drew quickly wiped his eyes and started laughing. "Ma, you are not old! Don't tease like that." And Allie was left alone.

CHAPTER 10

Frank's family was surprised to see him when he strolled into the house, just as he did when he was a kid. His ma made a big feast that night for dinner to welcome him home. Her roast beef was the best, although, compared to the cooking at the logging camp he'd recently had, anything would have tasted great. He still didn't understand how people could survive like that.

He certainly needed a change, but for now, his focus would be on Allie. He'd let her have a few days to herself, to adjust to being home and recovering a bit. He hurt that he couldn't go to her, knowing she needed someone, him, to be with her. She was more important to him than his stomach or anything back in Oregon. He couldn't hold off any longer. Today, he would see Allie.

Frank's father had him busy working in the bank, and his mother decided she needed all his off time to tell her stories about his life and do odd jobs that his father hadn't done. So, he hadn't had time to check in with his mentor, Dr. Lehman, yet.

He decided to take a quick detour and stopped by Dr. Leman's office. As he opened the door and heard the familiar jingle of the visitor bell, his heart sped. This was his passion, no matter how many times his father tried to convince him otherwise. He felt awful for not carrying on the family banking tradition, but numbers, numbers, numbers made his mind numb. He needed the excitement and energy that being a doctor offered him.

Nothing compared to the all-consuming investigation and discovery of an ailment and being able, most of the time, to help someone improve their life. Of course, there were always those he couldn't help. The suffering was maddening at times, and sometimes made him question his abilities. But, the pure joy seeing the recovery, and knowing he was part of it, outweighed the stressful times.

Dr. Leman hollered from the back. "Take a seat, I'm with a patient and will be with you shortly."

Frank did as he was told, admiring the room while he waited. It was small with two waiting chairs, a table and coat rack over by the front door, and a bookcase against the opposite wall. The bookcase held so many medical books, it was a wonder the nails were still holding it together. This was where he started his dream. Doc Leman taught him so much with those books. And, some of the town folk had let him observe

Doc's examinations from time-to-time. He owed so much to this town and Doc himself. One day, maybe, he could do something to thank them all.

Growing voices could be heard and Frank knew that meant Doc had finished his examination and would be escorting the patient out soon. He stood, waiting for the swinging door to open.

"Why, Frank! How are you?" Mr. Jonson came out and hobbled over to shake his hand.

"Great, great! But looks like I should be asking you that question." Frank looked down at Mr. Jonson's left leg but couldn't discern the problem through his shoes and pants. He was a fit man in his late thirties. That information alone must mean an injury, not an illness.

Mr. Jonson looked down at his leg and gave a brief nod. "Darn bull came down on my foot awhile back. Doc says it's not broken, but sure is taking its sweet time to heal up."

Frank quirked a smile and nodded in reply. Logging and farming could sure mess a man up in no time flat. Both were dangerous lines of work and he'd seen many examples from each.

"Well, I'll be. Heard you were in town. Wondered how long it would take you to show up here." Doc came in wiping his hands on a towel.

Frank stepped over to him and pumped his hand.

"Jon, you be sure to go home and get that foot propped up for a spell. Needs to rest if you ever want it to heal. Ya hear?" Doc raised one brow to show he meant business.

"Yes, sir! On my way now." Mr. Jonson hobbled out the door.

Doc couldn't contain himself. He started chuckling. "Why his momma saw fit to name that man the same name is beyond me. Jon Jonson! Huh! Course she never had a creative bone in her body. Always cut and dried...to the point, that one. You never knew the late Mrs. Jonson did ya son?"

"No, sir. She died when I was just a babe," Frank replied.

"Fine people, the Jonson's. Jon's pa was a Gandy Dancer. Now, those are hard workers and probably where Jon learned his work ethic. By the time his pa was worn out, they retired here and started up a farm. Jon's been running it ever since. I sure wish his foot would heal. Either I'm missing something, or he isn't resting it like he says. Which, knowing him, is probably the case. That man doesn't slow down." Doc walked across the room and checked for his next appointment in the book sitting on the table.

"I could look at it if you want me to, just to make sure?" *Why am I nervous about offering that? Of course, Doc wouldn't mind, he never did. It does feel odd coming back in here, though. Like I'm encroaching on another man's territory.*

"I would love it, Frank. There are a few people here that you could look at with me later this week. Oh...and I wanted to thank you for helping Allie out. Her face is going to heal up fine with your nice stitchery. Shouldn't leave too big of a scar. If I didn't know better, I would think your momma used to have you doing some sewing." Doc raised both eyebrows and tried to hide his grin. That usually meant he thought he was on to something and found that notion quite funny.

Frank blushed a bit. "You're right, there. My mother thought it was important for me to know how to stitch up a few things along with a few other household chores. I guess knowing I was college bound and wouldn't settle down for a while, she decided I needed some basic skills to get me by before I took a wife. Living in a logging camp, I sure have put those skills to use. You wouldn't believe how many times I have had to stitch up my own socks. I put more holes in those now than I ever did when I was a boy."

Doc patted him on the back. "You're a good man, Frank! Good man! So, what brings you by today?"

"I just wanted to say hello and see if you needed me for anything. Pa has me working the books and my head is going to explode if I can't get away from them," Frank confessed, running his hand through his hair. He sighed to exaggerate the point.

"Sure thing. Like I said, there are a few patients you

could come give a second opinion on later this week if you want. First one's due in Thursday around eleven. That one, I only need you to agree with me. Mrs. Wimble is a stubborn one. Hoping you and I can gang up on her." Doc tugged on his beard.

"Sounds good, I'll be back by then...if not sooner. Headed out to go check on Allie." With that Frank put his hat on his head and reached out to shake Doc's hand.

Doc returned the hand shake. "Good! That will save me a trip. Remind her, though, I want her to come into town soon, so I can check on her again."

"Will do, Doc. Thanks!" Frank walked out into the sunshine and headed straight for Allie's home.

CHAPTER 11

Allie found the cool water of the creek that ran out back of her home to be heaven sent. Not only was it stuffy in the house for March, but her family was a bit stifling as well. She knew they cared for her, but she needed time to think. She couldn't do it when someone was hovering over her everywhere she turned...like she was fragile and about to break.

The mighty pine that stood next to the creek was sometimes her only friend. It would hold her up when she leaned against it and fell apart. This was her spot. She would come here often during her childhood. Anytime she wanted to get away for a while. The side corner of the house could still be seen up the hill...but barely. That meant no one could see her. She used to climb up the tree and sit among the needles, like a bird. A few daring times, she undressed and took a dip. It was still too cold for that. Here she could think and look for answers in the gushing flow of the water, rustling of the needles, and whispers of the gentle breeze like the one blowing today.

Allie made it home. That was her plan. Now what? She hadn't thought this far. It seemed like such a feat to just get away, that her mind couldn't even fathom the idea of the plan actually working and being here now. She had a few options, but none of them sounded great: go back and make do, kill him and become a widow, or divorce. The first wouldn't work of course. Once she went back, he would see fit that she never saw another day herself. And, that would make him a free man to snare another victim.

She supposed she couldn't kill him, either. That one did sound promising, but she would just trade one form of chains for another. Divorce was the only half-decent choice. That word was not spoken aloud much around here, and when it was it came from the husband, never the wife. The law allowed for wives to divorce their husbands and there were some that went through with it, but she only heard about it through hushed whispers. She was wrestling with the idea of it when she heard steps approaching.

Frank knew right where she would be when Ma couldn't find her. The creek was a common place for Allie and he had found her here many times in the past. He could watch her all day, but knew, for her sake, he needed to approach and let her know he was there.

"Hi, Allie," he said as he walked over and sat next to her.

"Hi, back," she said only turning her head slightly in his direction.

Frank reached into his pocket and pulled out a shiny penny. "Penny for your thoughts?"

She took the penny so she could have something to fiddle with while they talked. It was a game he used to play with her. He would give her the penny to pay for her thoughts and when she was done she would give it back to buy his response. How she wished she could go back to those times where her problems were much simpler. "Just sitting here thinking about my options."

"And what options would those be? Which way to inflict revenge on Gladys for stealing me from you when we got off the train?" His voice sounded like he was playing, but his face was serious.

Allie held the penny and her fingers to her mouth stifling a laugh. "No, but that was quite rude. I wonder if she has figured out who you were looking for yet. I bet my story has spread through town like wild fire by now."

"I didn't hear anything, but I also don't get out much. My parents have kept me busy until today—when I forced my way out. Went to see Doc. He says to remind you that he wants you to come and see him. You okay?" He leaned into her and nudged her shoulder with his own.

Her heart gave a hiccup. "Yes, yes! I'm fine. Just wants to double-check me is all, I guess."

"Well then, let me have a gander at your face? I want to see how it's healing up. He tugged on her chin and encouraged her to turn her head. He held her eyes in his own for a moment. Tried to peer into the depths of her thoughts, but she was always a deep thinker. He never could quite pin-point where her thoughts took her.

"Your bruising is looking good. It's turning lighter in color and there aren't too many broken veins showing. That stitching looks pretty good, too, but I might be bragging about that!" He gave her a wink. "How are you feeling?"

Frank was a fine-looking man. If he only knew about her childhood crush! Maybe...maybe her life would have gone differently. She tried to shake the thought from her head without him knowing her mind was elsewhere right now.

"I'm okay. My face doesn't hurt anymore, and I can look in the mirror a little easier." She ducked her head. Why she said that, she had no clue. Quickly changing the subject away from her face, she added, "My ankle is still sore, but I can tell it is improving."

"You know...putting it in the creek a bit might help." He motioned for her to take off her shoe and stick her foot in the cool stream of water.

Once she settled her foot in the water, he asked, "Are you worried he'll show up here?"

"Who? Eddie? No! He's more of a coward than anything. He knows I have many people here to fuss over me and wouldn't come waltzing back in trying to take me back by force. He'll sit back and wait for me. He knows I have few choices." She relaxed back a bit more letting the cool water soothe the ache.

Frank hesitated and cleared his throat. "You know he *can* take you by force. Right? A lawman can do that for him...or supervise him doing it. Law's on his side, not yours, in this situation. Sure, enough people here would fight for you. But in the end, you can't fight the law."

A sob bubbled up out of her and Frank wrapped her in his arms. They stayed that way for a while until she calmed down some. Through her tears she agreed. "I know. I've always known. That's what kept me from leaving for so long. I wanted to leave the first day he hit me, but knew it was pointless. I just...I just had to try, you know?"

"You are strong, Allie. Probably one of the stronger women...people...I know. Even back before Eddie, the way you stepped up to care for your family was heroic. There has got to be a way and I will help you find it." He tucked some loose strands of hair behind her ear. "What were you thinking about when I came?"

"My options: go back willingly, kill him, or divorce him. They would all amount to killing myself." She pulled her head against her bent knee. "I don't love him...never did. I thought in the beginning maybe I could. He was good looking and a smooth talker, but the hitting came on very fast. It didn't allow me a chance to truly fall in love with him."

Allie wanted to continue, telling him he was the one she loved, but why would he love her back? Sure, they were friends...had been for a long time. But, she was a married woman who would either remain married and untouchable, widowed and in prison, or divorced—ruining her chance for any kind of decent future. She would be branded the rest of her life.

Frank sat quietly for a long while tossing her choices around in his head. The first was not an option, if he had any say about it. The second she couldn't do but wouldn't mean he couldn't. And the third, well, that one seemed the best for now. "You should talk to Sheriff Griffin. Let him share some insight into your "options."

"I probably should...just to be on the watch in case I am wrong in what I think he might do." Her brows pinched together making worry lines on her forehead.

"Come on. Your foot has been in the water long enough. Time to take it out and dry it off." He assisted her while she placed her shoe back on her foot and stood.

"Thanks, you didn't solve my problem this time. Does that mean I get to keep your penny?" She smirked in a teasing way.

"Keep it, I gave it to you in the first place remember?" He took her hands in his. "Time for me to be going now. My mother will be pacing before too long if I don't get back. Can't share me for nothing, can they?" He gave a wink and walked back up the hill.

She fell back down and stifled her tears in her skirt.

CHAPTER 12

Time passed and Allie decided she should check in with Doc. She didn't want to. But knowing him, if she let any more time pass he would show up out here and she would not have the privacy she desired. Her ankle had improved immensely in the few days she had been back. Rest and cooling it in the creek was helping.

Walking into town wouldn't be too painful now. With the bruises subsiding, she could show her face and not be too embarrassed by what others might see. Powder would have helped more, but she did not want to be associated with those who chose to wear that. She had heard rumors of some women back east beginning to wear powders and blushes, but that hadn't trickled out to the far reaches of Montana yet.

Only those in certain industries wore it out here. Why anyone would want to cover up their natural appearance daily was beyond her—until recently. Some women had reason to hide. This she understood all too well now. Maybe those women who worked questionable jobs and allowed their bodies to be used also had reasons to hide. Life was not what she thought it was when she was just a girl. She had received quite the education over the past several months.

The walk was not long, but it was beautiful. Many of the birds had returned from their winter travels and could be heard in every direction. She loved this time of year. Spring was a new beginning. Everything was coming back to life. For Allie, the colors seemed more vibrant than normal. They were almost calling to her...letting her know she could take hold of her life and it could be more colorful than it had been in recent months. Of course, that could be attributed to the fact that spring had come early this year. Everything had grown more by now than in years past. She would need summer clothes before too long, if the weather kept this pace up.

Allie needed to do a little shopping for Ma while in town. Ma had sent her with a list and some coins...and told her to go to the restaurant and buy herself a sandwich while in town. She knew she was just trying to get her out and back with her friends. Allie had put a protective shell on and Ma was going to try to bring her out of it any way she could. Since money was so tight and Ma was suggesting this, she knew she would go to any means to achieve her goal. Allie was in for it. When Ma set her mind to something, she always got what she wanted. What Allie wanted was more time to think about her future. She wanted time alone, but she couldn't fault Ma. Allie knew Ma just wanted what was best for her.

Town was at the peak of the midday bustle. First, she would go to Doc's and see if he was free. Then she would run her other errands. And Doc's office was closer than the grocer. Maybe she wouldn't be seen just yet. Keeping her head down, she made her way as quickly as possible to his office and let herself into the waiting room. No one was in the waiting room, but she could hear voices coming from the exam room. She sat and waited quietly for whoever was in there to finish.

It didn't take long before Allie heard a voice she would rather not hear...Mrs. Wimble. "Oh, good morning dear! I heard a rumor you were back in town. Just visiting your parents for a while?"

Allie could tell she was trying to sound sincere, but she knew all Mrs. Wimble wanted was gossip and she refused to give her more than what she could outright see across her face. "Yes, I am back as you can see. That rumor is true. I am at my parents' house, but I don't know for sure how long I'll be staying." This wasn't a lie. She knew she could be hauled back to Idaho by her bully of a husband at any time.

Frank pushed through the doors as he spoke to Doc over his shoulder. "I will just make the notes in the book out front for her next appointment. Ah! Allie! What a pleasant surprise."

Frank drew the attention of both women. The grin on his face calmed Allie's nerves a bit and she certainly didn't mind that he was here right now. "Hello, Frank!" Allie kept her eyes on Frank and she could feel

Mrs. Wimble staring a hole in the side of her head.

"Well, then! I must be going now," said Mrs. Wimble with a defeated sigh. "Allie, I do hope we can catch up another time. Tell your mother hello for me."

With her eyes still on Frank, Allie replied, "I will, Mrs. Wimble...a pleasure as always." She and Frank both stifled a giggle.

"Allie, are you here for your check up?" Frank looked at the schedule and finished entering Mrs. Wimble's name for two weeks out.

"If Doc has time for me. Are you staying awhile?" Her heart started beating louder in her ears. She could not go through with this exam if Frank was anywhere near this building.

Frank's brows drew together. "I was just going to head over to my house and grab a bite for lunch, but I would enjoy your company more. Would you care to go to lunch with me after you see Doc?" He could clearly see her nervousness.

Allie tried to steady her hands by intertwining her fingers. "That would be lovely. After I finish here, I was going to grab a bite and then head to fill Ma's list before returning home."

"Good, good! I will scoot over to let my mother know I won't be there. I'll come back here and pick you up in a little while and we can visit over lunch." He reached for his hat and placed it on his head with a slight nod in her direction.

With a deep sigh that Frank was gone, Allie slumped in the chair to wait for Doc, which didn't take long.

"Hello, Allie. I am glad you came. I was going to come find you if you hadn't shown up by tomorrow. Just finished straightening the exam room. Come on back?" He said it with a question, but Allie could hear an underlining order in his tone. It was clear he was worried about something.

They made their way back and Doc closed the door behind them. There was no window in this room, so Doc had two lamps burning. "Allie. I'm going to need to do an extensive exam on you. Could you please remove your shoes and outer layers?"

She was nervous. His tone was not settling and increased her fear that something was indeed wrong. "Of course, Doc, I'll only be a moment."

"Thank you. You can step behind the screen, if you wish, and I will wait for you right here." He turned his back providing more privacy for her.

Undressing quickly, she returned to lay on the table. "I am ready, Doctor."

Doc turned and walked next to Allie. Starting at her head, he examined the stitches and bruising. Then he bypassed her midsection and moved down to her ankle moving it in small circles.

"Things are progressing nicely, I would say. Your ankle seems much better. The swelling is completely gone, and the little movements don't seem to bother you so much. Your bruising is also greatly improved and won't be visible before too long. As for the stitches, those will need to be removed in a few days. That gash is healing nicely. I think Frank should do the honors of removing them since he had the privilege of placing them. What do you think?" He took one step back and clasped his hands behind his back.

"That would be fine Doc, are we finished?" Allie asked, but knew the answer already.

"No dear, not yet." I must do an abdominal exam first. When did you say your last monthlies were?" He placed his hands on her lower abdomen and gently palpated it.

"A few weeks ago. I had bleeding that lasted for over a week and was quite heavy and painful. Now, I just spot sometimes, nothing I thought to worry about." Allie closed her eyes wondering what was coming next.

"Your uterus seems larger than it should be. Allie, I need to examine you internally." Doc urged her knees up and apart while she stiffened her muscles and fought him. "Allie, I must do this. I'll be gentle, but I think you may have had a miscarriage that didn't completely take."

Shocked, Allie pulled herself up on her elbows.

"What can you do?"

"If my suspicions are correct, I will need to put you out and perform a simple procedure to remove any remaining tissue. Right now, I need you to lie back and take deep calming breaths. This part will be uncomfortable but shouldn't hurt." He began by inserting his fingers to investigate internally. "Just as I suspected. I want you to remain where you are. I am going to find Frank, so he can assist with the next step."

"No!" She quickly pulled away from him, sat up, and hugged her knees. "I don't want him to know."

"Very well, I can do this myself. Just thought he could learn and help to make this go faster." He walked over to his medical chest and pulled out some tools and ether. "I am going to have you lie back down and breathe for me. That is all. I will do the rest and when finished you will wake up and not remember anything."

Allie lay back down and closed her eyes. She felt a tear slip out the corner of her eye at the same moment a cloth was placed over her nose.

She could hear a murmur and felt a tickle on her hand. Slowly, she blinked open her eyes and saw Doc staring down at her. "Good girl!" She could hear him, but she felt like he was speaking to someone else. Her head and body felt separate. She felt a woozy feeling just before she leaned over and retched on the floor. She moaned and wiped her mouth with the back of her arm.

"That is normal and common. It will go away soon. In the meantime, just stay still and let the ether wear off. You'll feel better in no time and I will let you go home soon." Doc began cleaning up the mess and brought over a bowl in case there was more.

After a few minutes passed, she felt well enough to sit and listen to what Doc had to say.

"Everything went really well. However, there was damage to your uterus. The injury that brought on the miscarriage was significant. Allie there is no easy way to tell you this, but you may have difficulty carrying a child in the future." They heard a rustle in the entry just then and Frank called out to Doc. "Hang on a minute, Frank. I'll be right out. Allie, take your time getting up. I'll get Frank out of here for you."

Allie's heart was pounding. She needed to get up and dress quickly. She wrapped the sheet over her and spun off the bed collapsing in a heap on the floor. Her legs were still weak, and she was groggy, but she pulled herself up and made her way back to the changing corner. She dressed quickly and used her fingers to comb through her hair. When she made her way out she saw Doc and Frank quietly discussing something.

Frank smiled. His eyes held concern for her. "Sorry I took so long. I didn't expect you to still be here. Are you ready for lunch?"

At the sound of lunch her stomach flipped. She

placed her hand on her abdomen willing it to calm. "I...I forgot. I must go home." Flying passed them she moved as quickly as possible out the door and down the stairs.

Frank ran out after her but stopped short when he noticed a slip of paper laying on the ground. It was a grocery list. He turned and went back to Doc.

"What happened?" He felt his face flush with anger, but he didn't know why.

"Frank, listen. Allie is my patient and she asked me not to say anything. She will be all right. She needs to get home and rest for a while, though. I'll go out in the morning and check on her. You should stay away for a while." Doc knew he was talking to deaf ears, but felt he needed to say that for her sake anyway.

"She is very upset. Is she hurt, too?" Frank's anger was turning to confusion.

"Allie should be just fine, but I can't talk to you about this. She needs to be the one to talk to you." Doc turned and went to straighten up the exam room.

Frank looked at the paper he held. Worry was settling on him like a thick wool blanket in the hottest months of the summer. He needed air and he needed to think. He also needed to talk with Allie. Deciding it would give him a better reason, he headed off to get the items on the list, so he could drop them off at Allie's house.

Allie had just entered the house when she fell to

her knees in pain. Ma came rushing over. "Allie, what's the matter?" she said as she knelt on the floor next to her daughter.

Allie lay grabbing her midsection with her knees pulled up. Her face was wet, and tears were dampening the floor boards.

"Pa, Pa! Come quick," Ma started shouting.

Allie quickly wiped her eyes and shakily pulled herself up. "No, Ma! Don't. I...I'm fine. I will be fine." She used the side table to help pull herself up and smoothed out her skirt. "See! All better." She hoped that she could convince Ma that she was and would be fine. She did not want to relive this day ever. "I am sleepy, though. I think I will put myself to bed and rest awhile."

Ma was not buying this, but for the time being she would play along. She knew her daughter, and if she wanted her to tell her anything she would have to wait on Allie's time. If she pushed her, Allie would just clam up. She just hoped that her face had relaxed enough to make Allie believe that she would back down for now. "All right. Would you like some help? Or...maybe I can get you something?"

"Water would be lovely. It is so hot right now. Do you think we will be getting rain anytime soon?" Allie was desperately trying to change the subject, but knew she needed to lay down quickly. The pain was intense.

Ma walked over to the kitchen sink and pumped

water into a tin cup. "It is very hot. At least our well is deep, so the water stays cool."

She didn't share the troubles she knew they could face this summer if the weather didn't change. Pa was already carrying buckets to keep the seeds watered in the garden. They had the creek, too. Some were not as fortunate to have a direct water source on their lands and had to rely on their wells alone. Wells were known to dry up, though. If your drinking water was also your garden and farm water, you could end up in big trouble...very quickly. She heard Allie climbing the stairs and followed behind with the cup of water. They both entered the bedroom and Allie sat on her bed and bit her lip as she attempted to remove her boots.

"Here hold the water and let me help you." Ma passed her the cup and began untying the laces. She slipped the boots off and Allie wiggled her toes...a small, but palpable, relief. Allie took a few sips of water and handed the cup back to Ma to put on the night table. Ma lifted her feet and helped her slide under the covers before tucking Allie in. "Let me know if you need anything more. I'll be downstairs or just outside."

"Thanks, Ma. I'll be fine after I rest. I'm sure." Allie rolled to her side and tried to breathe through the pains that came in waves. Ma left the room with a click of the door and could be heard making her way down the wooden stairs. It took a while, but somehow, she found a way to sleep through the pain.

CHAPTER 13

Allie woke to a knock on the door. She quickly checked her bed covers before responding, hoping that it was just Ma, but she knew Ma wouldn't have knocked. The door creaked open slowly.

"Allie, can I come in?"

She heard the familiar male voice. She closed her eyes and mentally tried to prepare for what would happen next.

Frank entered slowly with his hands at his sides and his head hanging a bit.

"I told your mother that Doc sent me to come and check on you. That was the only way she'd allow me to enter your bedroom. Wouldn't be proper otherwise, she said. She gave me strict orders! Said she'd be up to shoo me out if I didn't make it quick." He shifted side-to-side—unsure of what to do or say next.

Allie busied her hands...straightening the covers again...as she tried to hide her uneasiness at his presence. Ma would be even more curious now and she would be forced to say the words out loud. The words that she didn't...couldn't even think yet.

Frank's gaze landed on the spot on the blanket that her hand was stroking. "Allie! Is that blood?" He walked closer to the bed to take a closer look.

"What?" she glanced down and then closed her eyes. "Yes...I forgot. I should have taken precautions, but I was trying to just get to sleep so I wouldn't feel anymore." She shut her mouth afraid to say more. She needed more sleep...and to clean up. Frank needed to leave so she could handle all of this, because handling it while he was here...and telling him...was not an option.

Frank rushed and knelt beside the bed grabbing Allie's hand. "What is going on? Please...talk to me?" His eyes were drawn together in concern.

She closed her eyes and took a deep breath. "Frank, you are not my doctor. Doc said I would be fine and I will be. I just didn't think of doing womanly preparations before sleeping." Irritated by the lack of privacy and hoping that this would satisfy him at least for now. She lay back down briefly catching Frank's blank stare as she closed her eyes.

"I will find out what's going on one way or another. I *am* a doctor. If you won't come right out and tell me what is going on, I will eventually put all the pieces of the puzzle together. If he hurt you...well...anymore then he already has...I swear he will beg me to end his life before I am through with him!"

Frank stood, crossed his arms, and stared at Allie. She remained still...pretending to be asleep. He wasn't fooled. He knew when Allie didn't want to do something, no one could convince her. With a sigh, he turned and left the room—closing the door behind him more harshly than he intended.

Allie continued to lie there for a while, hoping that Frank would not return. She could hear faint voices from below. She couldn't make out what they were saying...although she could guess. Once Ma heard the word blood, she would race up here and demand answers. Answers that Allie didn't know if she could give as the moments ticked by following Frank's departure.

He had never barged into her business before. He was always patient and waited for her to come to him. There were times when she never did talk to him and he just let those issues die. Why couldn't he do that now? She didn't understand. *Couldn't he just keep to himself and let me deal with the damage?*

The more she confided in people, the more she couldn't pretend it was only a dream. And pretend was what she longed to do. When she was finally brave enough to open her eyes, her room was empty, and she could hear footsteps on the stairs. She knew the sound of those footsteps. Ma was marching her way up—the same as she always did when she was upset about something.

Ma burst through the door.

"What is this about blood stains? Frank said he saw blood. He was rather persistent that I tell him what was going on, but I had to tell him I didn't know. You will tell me right now or I will march to Doc's office myself and hear from him." She stood across the room with her eyes focused on the bed coverings.

Allie lost all control then. "Oh, Mamma! There was a baby!" Tears began racing down her cheeks soaking the front of her nightgown.

Realization dawned across Ma's face. She went to the closet and pulled out more bed coverings and sheets. Then to the dresser and took out another nightgown. Finally, she approached the sobbing Allie. "Get up. Let's get you cleaned up and then you can tell me all about it."

It didn't take long. Allie was out of bed with clothes changed and ready to reenter bed just before the bedding had been changed. Rushing downstairs, Ma grabbed some extra towels to place under Allie— knowing they would be ruined and never used to dry dishes again. More would need to be purchased soon and money was precious, but that couldn't be helped. Ma finished up and helped Allie back into bed. Then she waded up all the soiled linens and placed them by the door to take down to wash when she left. She made her way back to the bed and sat next to Allie, silently waiting for her to begin the story.

By His Hand

Allie twisted the sheet between her fingers. She knew she needed to talk to Ma, but it was so hard. She didn't know if she could put words to her thoughts or if it would be too unbearable.

"Eddie was a passionate man. He was stubborn and set in his ways." she began, pausing and taking a few breaths. "If things didn't turn out as he thought they should, he became violent. A few weeks ago, he came home and decided that it was my fault that I hadn't given him a son. He figured, since we had been married for several months, things should have worked by then. And he accused me of doing something to prevent it. I didn't, Mamma! I wouldn't have. You know I would have loved any child that God saw fit to give us...me."

Ma put her arm around her daughter. She pulled her to her and began stroking her hair as Allie continued.

"He decided to take out his frustration on my stomach. I hurt for days. And when the bleeding started, I assumed it was just my normal cycle. It was when the bleeding continued and then...oh...I don't know. It was just different. It hurt and lasted a long time, but it wasn't steady. It would go away only to return and repeated the process a few times. I thought something was different. I thought he damaged me. It wasn't until Doc saw me that I suspected a pregnancy. When I went to town this morning he examined me to confirm and then did something to help clean everything up. He told me to go and rest, and in a few days I should be good."

Talking seemed to solidify everything. It felt good, like a stone had been removed from her gut, but her heart began to feel large and heavy. The beats of her heart slowed as her brain finally allowed her to acknowledge what happened. She sunk to her pillow and sobbed silently into it. Ma just kept stroking her hair and letting her mourn the child she would never know.

She lay that way for a while before Ma spoke.

"Many women have lost their children. The fortunate ones lose them before they ever get to know them. You are not different or special. Yes, it hurts, but you will move on with your life. There will be times you will wonder what it would be like if this child was here. You will estimate when you would have given birth. You will pause and reflect every year around the time the child would have been born...always wondering and thinking, what if? You *will* not...you hear me...*will* not give that unborn child a name. The pain becomes too much to bear when you name them."

Ma rose, grabbed the soiled linens, and flew down the stairs leaving Allie feeling dumbstruck. She had never heard Ma talk that way before. It was as if she had secrets and a past she had never shared. Her parents had two children—Allie and Andrew. Were there more that Allie didn't know about or was Ma speaking about someone else she knew? Ma always had a soft soul with a rough exterior. At least, Allie always knew her that way. Was she always that way or did something happen to make her that way? Her mother suddenly became mysterious to her. That gave Allie something else to ponder while she remained in bed the rest of the day.

CHAPTER 14

Allie recovered quickly and was out of bed the next day. Doc came to check on her and was happy with her progress. He still wanted her to come back to his office in two weeks to have a final exam...just to be sure. And, of course, if anything came up, she was told to send for him right away.

Frank hadn't made another appearance, and for that she was grateful. Allie didn't think she could handle him yet. He had changed since he left for Oregon only a few years ago. She wasn't sure if the change was for the better or not.

Ma had been somewhat distant, making Allie wonder more about the mystery in Ma's past. Ma was a hard egg to crack sometimes. Allie didn't know if she should put thoughts about Ma's past out of her mind or if, in time, Ma would open up to her. Time would tell, and Allie had more than she could handle on her plate right now without adding someone else's business to it.

Over the next few days, Allie was able to do more and more. She was out in the sun finishing up the last of the wash, and it felt good. Rain was needed, but clouds could be seen in the distance. She hoped that meant a good soak was in their near future. However, that also meant she'd need to pack the water-logged laundry back into the house and hang them to dry from the strings in front of the fireplace.

Normally, this time of year, there would still be a fire burning part of the day, but this year it was too hot for that. The laundry would take longer to dry, but at least it wouldn't get rained on and need rewashing.

April was just a few days away and that was usually a wet month. Hopefully, the next month would turn the drought around and all would be well again. Flowers were dying off that bloomed closer to May. The warm weather brought plants out of hibernation early, but also left them to wilt from lack of moisture.

As she lugged the basket inside to hang the laundry, Allie spotted Andrew following her movements from across the field. He had been silent for the past few days. That wasn't like him. She was unsure if he had overheard and knew what had happened or if he was just wondering. She knew he was thinking something, though. He stared at her whenever they were together, and she even caught him on the floor in the hallway outside her bedroom door the other night.

His injured brain gave her another mystery that she didn't have time to unravel for the moment. When she reached the door to the house, she heard Pa calling to Andrew for something. Pa was another story. He acted like nothing was amiss. She couldn't decide if he was completely oblivious or extremely uncomfortable with her situation.

Doing the same chores she had done when she was little was peaceful. Allie's body instinctively knew what to do and that allowed her brain to wander. She wished she could quiet her mind. It was tiresome trying to figure out how her life had ended up this way, not to mention what she should do next. Rest was fleeting. If only she could close her eyes and open them a year from now.

Wishing away all the struggles sounded refreshing, but not possible. A decision needed to be made. Should she go back and endure life with Eddie, stay married and continue to live with her parents and hope that he wouldn't come back to retrieve her, or file for a divorce.

Maybe she could run away from her troubles and change her name. Start a new life for herself. She shook her head hoping to dislodge the solution. So long as she was still married to Eddie, that life would eventually catch up with her. She needed finality. That really left only one choice, divorce.

Could she live with the backlash of it? The sideways looks and whispers when people thought she couldn't hear them? Hanging the last skirt, she took a deep breath. Decision made. She would tell her parents first. Then she could travel to town and speak with the sheriff.

A knock at the door startled her out of her thoughts. She grabbed the towel on the table to wipe the moisture from her hands left by the damp clothes and checked her appearance in the wall mirror. As she opened the door, she smoothed one side of her hair with her palm.

"Blinne?" Allie flung her arms around her lifelong friend, pulling her inside as she closed the door.

"Oh, Allie! It's so good to see you. I'm sorry I couldn't come to visit earlier, but I'm here now." Blinne pulled out a chair and sat a bit awkwardly.

"Well, look at you! My! Do you want some water?" Allie could tell she did and walked to the kitchen before Blinne could even respond.

Blinne fanned herself. "Thank you. I'm afraid I am turning into a watermelon! And the weather has been so warm lately. The walk over was exhausting." She drank half the water, wiped her mouth with the back of her hand, and giggled. "I didn't come to talk about me though, I want to know how you are?" She grabbed Allie's hand and pulled her over to the table.

"I want to let Ma know you're here first. Then we'll head to my room to talk...just like we used to."

She left Blinne sitting at the table with a concerned look on her face. Blinne knew talking in Allie's room meant she didn't want others to hear them.

Allie and Ma returned a few moments later.

"Hello dear, how are you?" Ma asked, bending to give Blinne a hug.

"I'm as good as can be expected. Just trying to survive the last little bit in this heat," Blinne said as she placed her hand on her belly and sighed.

"I feel for you honey. It will all be over soon enough, though, and you will be wishing you could shove 'em back in there from time-to-time…just for some peace and quiet." They all laughed at that. "I'm sure you have some catching up to do. I have chores that won't do themselves, so I'll leave you two to talk." She gave Allie a knowing look and headed back out of the main room.

Allie grabbed Blinne's hand and helped her climb the stairs to her room. After closing the door, Allie made sure Blinne was sitting comfortably on her bed before she pulled the desk chair closer for herself. It was a comfort just to see Blinne again. How she missed her. Blinne was her oldest and dearest friend. They told each other everything and knew their bond was sacred. It is not very often two people connect like that.

"I want to know how you are. It looks like there are some big changes coming." Allie looked at her *watermelon*, as she called it, and smirked.

Blinne sank into the pillows. The bed was a blessed relief after her walk. She could close her eyes and drift off, if she wasn't careful.

"Life is good. George and I married shortly after

you left. He fixed up his grandparents' old place after his grandma passed. It needed some work, since she was up in years and his grandpa had died three years before. George was determined, though. It is such a beautiful little piece of heaven and not too far from his parents' place. Of course, my parents are still on the other side of town. That is too far for me to walk right now, but I was making the trek every couple of weeks."

Allie gently smiled and closed her eyes. "It all sounds so wonderful. I am so happy for you."

"I didn't come here to talk about me—I came to hear about you. Unfortunately, some gossip is going around town and I needed to see you to see if I can help."

Allie stood and walked to the window. "I knew people would talk. They are going to be doing a lot more of that shortly. How much do you want to know? It isn't very pleasant news and I don't really want to upset you." She turned back around and faced Blinne.

Blinne took a deep breath to prepare herself. "All of it. You know I care about you and I want to help you, if I can."

Allie paced across the room, gathering her thoughts. Blinne's eyes followed her as she paced.

"Eddie was different when we left. He seemed sweet and caring here. But once we reached Idaho, he became controlling...at first...and...after a while...abusive. I couldn't do anything right. The last couple of times I blacked out. I'm not sure if it was self-protection or if he just hit me that hard. I still have gaps in my memory."

Blinne gasped, but Allie was lost in her thoughts and didn't notice. Her eyes were glassed over, almost as though she was outside of her body, retelling what she'd gone through.

"I had a baby. Well...was going to have one. He thought I was purposely doing something so I wouldn't give him a child. But he didn't know...I didn't know...I was already carrying one. He beat me and caused me to miscarry. At least that is what Doc said. He performed a procedure to finish what Eddie started. Apparently, my body wanted to hold on to that and it didn't take care of the job. Imagine a body wanting something so badly that it will hold on to remnants of a life that once was," she paused.

"Anyway, I ran away from him and came home. Frank and I ended up on the same train. Imagine meeting him when I was broken and bruised... the last person I would want to see me like that, and there he was. He wouldn't leave me be, either. He was so sweet and gentle, but kind of suffocating. I don't want another man close to me right now. He hasn't come around lately. Maybe he took the hint last time. I don't want to hurt him, but I can't. Just being around a man has me nervous and uptight. I worry that what I say will irritate him. Just because I knew him growing up, doesn't mean I know him now. I need space and time right now. I'm not sure if I will ever be able to trust another man."

Allie blinked a few times and saw Blinne's tear-streaked face. She was holding her stomach with one hand and her other was covering her mouth.

"Oh, I'm sorry. I shouldn't have said all that."

Allie grabbed a hankie from her top drawer and passed it to Blinne. They held each other and sobbed. They stayed like that for a long time before Blinne pulled back.

"What will you do now?" she asked.

Wiping her own eyes, Allie blew out the breath she was holding. "Divorce!" she said, as she stood and walked back to the window. They were silent again as that word sunk deep into both women.

This was the first time Allie had said it out loud since she made her decision. It sounded so definite...so final...but she knew it was just the beginning. Even if she was heard in court and her request was granted, the town would be abuzz for a long time. She would not be welcome in certain circles. Could she even walk down the street with her head held high or would she be watching her feet? People will stare and talk behind their hands to their neighbor. Would she be able to find work? She needed to help her parents out, but not just anyone would hire a divorced woman.

Allie felt arms wrap around her and Blinne's stomach pressed into her back.

"I will be here for you. I'll talk to George, too. He'll

understand when he hears what Eddie did to you. Our home will be a refuge for you."

They stood like that for a while. Allie felt courage surge within her as if Blinne was sharing some of hers. "I hate to leave, but I better head back before George sends a search party for me. He is very protective, especially now that I am so close."

They walked out of the room and Allie helped Blinne down the stairs.

"Why don't I walk you home? I could use the fresh air."

Allie found Ma and told her where she was going, then they headed out. Allie's story wasn't mentioned again that day. Instead, the talk was of happier times, times when they were inseparable. They remembered the adventures they had when they were younger.

Blinne caught Allie up on the lives of the other girls from their school. Once they arrived at Blinne's home, she was given the tour of the little farm. It was beautiful and had the look of hope. Did she dare to dream of a life like that? For now, she would be happy for Blinne and not think about her future. She had enough worries for today without thinking about tomorrow.

After leaving Blinne safely in her home, she used the time by herself to think. Knowing her next move gave her a little bit of calm for some things...but added new concerns. Knowing she had at least one friend on her side was enough for her though. She could do this.

She had to do this.

CHAPTER 15

Eddie led John to the table. He grabbed two cups and poured some coffee before taking his chair. "So, what do you know?" Eddie had promised to pay John for a couple of weeks of missed work so he could spy on Allie.

John sipped his coffee and looked around the room before he set it back down. "She seems good and settled. Has a nice little routine going for her. Other than her family, the house has been quiet. Only one guy coming and going a few times but haven't seen him lately. She keeps busy with chores and stays away from town."

John's eyes kept moving, taking in the space around him. Everything was in disarray. Eddie apparently needed Allie here to run the place. There was a mess in every corner. Clothes were piled, and the remains of many meals were left on the counter and much of the table. He wondered if the coffee cup he was drinking from was clean.

"Good, good!" Eddie rubbed his chin and was

absorbing the information. "Seems like it's just about time for phase two of my plan."

"What might that be?" John couldn't help but be curious. After following Allie around for two weeks he was getting bored with the situation. A change was just what he needed to keep him interested.

Eddie took a drink and stood. "Time for me to go visit. Shake her up a bit. Unsettle her routine. Make her feel a bit unstable again so she doesn't know what to do. I can't have her comfortable for too long or she might start making some bad decisions. She will come back to me, I just need to play it right. Get her to forgive me. Play to her heart."

John slowly shook his head in agreement. The plan coming together in his own mind. "You need me to go back?"

Eddie turned and faced John, "Not for now. I will go myself. I don't want her seeing you with me. That way if I need you to keep an eye on her again she won't connect us."

"All right. I suppose I can go back to work here. Need some payment though—to keep me wanting to help you." He stood with an expectant look on his face.

"Sure, sure. I'll go to the bank first thing in the morning and withdraw the money. I'll meet up with you tomorrow afternoon." He raised his hand and waved it dismissively.

John was not completely pleased with that answer but knew not to question Eddie. He said he would pay him and he needed to trust that. He gulped down the last of his coffee, grabbed his hat, and took his leave.

Eddie started pacing. He had to finalize his next step and needed to think it through so there were no mistakes. He would pack and pick up a train ticket for the next train. He should pick up some new clothes, too. He knew he stunk, but washing was woman's work and he refused to do anymore of that than necessary. He needed her. She had a responsibility as his wife and she was not keeping up her end of their legal contract. He could do this. He just needed to keep himself in check, at all times. It wouldn't hurt to watch her a day or two first to be safe. Just to make sure John wasn't playing him.

Eddie was finalizing his plan as he made his way to the train station. He stopped by Joe's Mercantile and purchased two pairs of pants, a couple of flannel shirts, chewing tobacco, and some dry goods so he could rough it for a while and watch her. He didn't want to head into town too early.

Surprise was the key to getting Allie back. He needed her startled and unprepared. He purchased his ticket and made his way onto the train heading east. He settled into the back of the train and was imagining Allie on her knees begging to be taken back. The corners of his mouth drew up revealing a row of brown stained teeth. *Yes! I will sit and watch for a while.*

At this point he was unsure if he would approach her in a few days or if he needed to wait awhile longer. Time would tell. He needed to see how comfortable she was and who was around. Just because John said she was establishing a routine, didn't mean he was right. He knew her better than she knew herself. He needed to see her habits. He would know when the time was right.

As the train pulled out the station and began rocking him gently, he drifted off to sleep.

CHAPTER 16

Allie dressed for town. She had to hurry and get this over with quickly before she lost her nerve. Going to town was hard enough. Word spread like wildfire in her hometown and she was already seeing looks on the residents' faces and knew comments were made after she passed. Making her way down to the front room, she grabbed her reticule and made her way to the door. Just as she reached for the door, she heard Ma's footsteps.

"Allie, are you sure you want to do this alone?" Ma had a towel in her hands and she was twisting it into knots, not even attempting to hide her nervousness for Allie.

Allie, let her shoulders drop as she released the breath she was holding. "Yes, I need to. I got myself into this and I am the only one who can get me out." Before Ma could say anything else she slipped through the door and shut it behind her

She was nervous, scared, and feeling defeated. Her emotions were not under control. She lifted her skirts to free her legs as they pumped rapidly beneath her. She failed in her attempts to slow herself down. She knew her ankle was only just healed, but her emotions won out over her thoughts to be careful and not reinjure it.

Running made the trip to town shorter than normal. There was no time to think about what she was about to do. There was also no time left to slow herself and control her breathing before she found herself a good way down the main street. She bent over with her hands on her hips and began taking deeper and slower breaths. When she straightened up, she noticed eyes on her.

Apparently, she had been getting more attention than she thought. Many people were staring at her. The looks ranged from surprise to disgust. Giving a simple nod, she smoothed her skirts and made her way to an empty bench across the street. She needed to rest a spell—even though she knew the looks would continue as long as she remained in the open. She could put on a brave face even if she was crumbling inside. No one could see what she was trying to keep hidden, all would be well in the end.

After sitting for a few minutes, she heard her name called. It was distant at first but getting closer. She peered through the crowd and her eyes landed on Frank. He was quickly making his way to her and took the open seat next to her without giving her a choice. The last time they were together was awkward for her…to say the least. They sat silent for a while as she pondered whether he knew her secret or not. He was a smart enough man. It probably wouldn't take much for him to figure it out. Continuing to sit side-by-side, he spoke first. "How are you?"

That was vague. It didn't give her any information about what he might know. Were they going to stay superficial in conversation or was he moving slowly? "Fine," she answered, equally vague.

"Allie, look. I know I haven't been over in a while. I've been trying to leave you alone so you could think things through. You seemed very upset the last time I saw you. I know you are dealing with things and I want to help. If you want me, I am here for you." His eyes were focusing on the boards at his feet.

Okay, maybe he won't stay superficial. Maybe clearing the air is better. He was a good friend and she knew she could use more of them these days. "I had a procedure done at Doc's that day . I wasn't feeling very well."

"I know. I am a doctor. You don't have to tell me anything if you don't want to. Please know that I understand more than you think, though." His eyes were intensely staring into hers. He reached over and placed his hand on top of hers. He realized where he was and withdrew it quickly. Enough people are gossiping already. He didn't want to add more fuel to their fire.

Allie's reserve was breaking. She could only pretend to be brave for so long and worked at controlling the sob that had worked its way up her throat. All she could do was nod.

Rubbing his palm on his leg and pulling himself up, he turned to her. "What brings you to town today?"

Might as well tell him. She wasn't entirely sure how he would react to her decision, but she thought he would be accepting. "I'm going to speak with Sheriff Griffin about starting the process for a divorce."

"Would you like me to come with you?"

There was no hesitation. He didn't pause to think about it at all. Maybe he already guessed. Not much could get passed him. "No, thank you. You could walk me home if you want, though." She felt like she should give him something to do in return accepting her decision.

"I'll do better than that. I'll take you to lunch first and then see you home." He wouldn't take no for an answer and she knew that. "I'll walk you there and wait outside for you."

She stood and fell into step next to him for the short walk that would change her future.

The court house was a beautiful two-story building with a smaller wing off the back. Large trees circled the building, acting as a shield. There was a grand staircase leading to the front entrance. Allie left Frank waiting out front as she made her way up and into the massive building.

Despite the tree cover outside, bright light filled the inside from the arched windows. Allie made her way across the floor to the front desk and asked for Sheriff Griffin. The gentlemen led her down a long hall, towards the back of the building. The sheriff's office was located here. He used a side entrance to come and go throughout the day. The man knocked on the sheriff's door, announced her, and left them alone.

Feeling nervous, Allie began wringing her hands. "Hello, Sheriff Griffin. Do you have a moment, Sir?"

Paul Griffin stood and motioned for Allie to sit which she quickly did. "Hi, Allie. What can I help you with?" He noticed her nervousness and that made him a little apprehensive. He had known Allie most of her life. This behavior was not normal for her.

Allie began to talk before she had her swirling thoughts in order. "Sir..."

The sheriff interrupted, "Please...Allie...call me Paul."

"Paul..." Allie nodded in acceptance and took a breath. "As you know I am married and was living in Idaho. I am here to talk to you about what I need to do to get a divorce and to let you know that my husband won't be too kind when he learns of my plan. I'm sure he...Eddie...is already unhappy with me. I'm not sure what he is fully capable of, but I know what he has already done. I don't want anyone getting caught between our issues and his temper."

Paul took his seat while he absorbed this information. He was not unfamiliar with this sort of person. Deer Lodge had its fair share of questionable individuals that tried to blend in with the upstanding citizens. The fact that Allie got herself mixed up with one of them bothered him. She was a great girl and had blossomed into a beautiful and respected young lady before she met Eddie.

Paul gently tugged on his long mustache. He was a tall man and could fill a large room with his presence, but Allie had thrown him off and he was struggling to find a quick way to help her. "Allie, do you know that you have to be married a full year with abuse, if that is what has been taking place, before you can file for a divorce?" His brows were raised waiting for her to absorb this.

Her shoulders slumped, and her chin fell to her chest. "I didn't know. It hasn't been a year yet. I don't even know how to prove what he did. Does the abuse have to be for a full year or just the marriage? It started off okay...and, of course, I've been home...away from him...for the last month."

"I think that will depend on the judge." Paul sat tapping his desk. Can you write everything down? The whole story from the first day you met him. Don't leave out any detail, even if you think it's too small to matter. I will try to figure out how to do this." He stood and motioned for her to follow him out. They walked back to the main entrance and through the front doors. "I will also keep an extra watch out. Boys like him tend to get upset when their plans go awry." Frank stood and took the steps two-at-a-time to reach them, "Morning, Sheriff." He reached his hand out and shook Paul's.

"Hi, Frank. You here for business?"

"Nope, just waiting for Allie." He turned and looked into her eyes. "I'm taking this young lady to lunch. That is, if you're all finished?"

The sheriff gave Frank a knowing nod. "You two go have some fun. Frank, will you come find me later today? I have something I'd like to speak with you about."

Frank took Allie's arm and led her down the steps as he called back, "Sure thing, Sheriff. I'll be back this afternoon." He led her down the walk toward the hotel that had a small restaurant in the front corner. "Allie, will you wait right here for a moment?" Frank dashed inside before waiting for her answer. Allie was left confused standing on the walk, but it wasn't long before Frank came back out carrying a basket and offered Allie his arm. "I thought, after this morning, you might like to dine alone. Lunch is in the basket. We can go find a quiet picnic spot and I can return their basket after I take you home.

Allie didn't know what to say. It had been a long while since anyone took time to care for her and Frank seemed to do it every time she turned around. She accepted his arm and placed her free hand around it as well.

CHAPTER 17

Lunch was perfect. They found a spot by the river that was somewhat secluded. The flow of water seemed to make the air feel cooler. March had been warm, but April was coming in downright hot.

Frank opened the basket and pulled out several items. Not knowing what Allie liked, he'd ordered a variety of sandwich makings. This way she could put her own together.

After they ate, they leaned back for a while on the blanket that the hotel provided and talked about the past. The deep past…safe topics, back when they were kids and life was simple. It was the perfect conversation to the perfect meal. Unfortunately, time could not be held still, and she needed to get home before Ma and Pa started to worry. She helped fold up the blanket and placed everything back in the basket before standing and stretching.

"How did your talk with the sheriff go?" Frank had fallen into step with her in the direction of her home.

And with that one question reality came rushing back in gulps that were too big for her lungs to take in. She stopped and bent over—trying to calm herself.

"I'm sorry Allie, I didn't mean to upset you." Frank sat the basket down and stood there twisting his hands not knowing what he could do to help.

She stood up and grabbed his arm to brace herself.

"No! No...it's okay. That question threw me, that's all. I was relaxed with our lunch. Everything felt safe. But now... I'm not sure how it went this morning. Seems I need to be married for a full year and we are unsure if the abuse needs to be constant during the year before I can file or not. I can't go back and wait it out. I don't know what I should do now." She moved ahead of him, her steps growing faster.

Anger built within him. He scooped up the basket and trotted to catch up with her. "How can they do that? They can't put you back in danger. I won't allow it."

Allie stopped mid-step and turned, her cheeks red from exertion.

"You won't allow it?"

Frank heard the deeper meaning in that question. *Oh no, she just went from one abuser who had all sorts of rules placed on her. She doesn't need me talking like that, too.*

"I'm sorry Allie, that's not what I meant. Well, it is, but it's not. I can't explain it really. See, oh I don't know, I feel something. I've never felt like this with any other person except my family. I want to protect you. I want to make you happy.

Allie's lips were turning up into a smile as Frank's face was becoming more and more flushed.

"Stop! Please!" And she began to laugh.

"Well don't laugh at me. I'm telling the truth here and it's hard." He ever so slightly stomped his foot.

"I'm sorry, Frank. I don't know what's come over me. Just seeing you get flustered...well...it was cute." As she said this, she turned her head away from him.

Frank's chest puffed out just enough to be noticeable. He set the basket down and reached for her hands, turning her back toward him. "Allie, I know you are dealing with a lot right now, but will you think about letting me be your beau?" His eyes were searching hers.

Allie's heart was beginning to pound, but then realization slapped her in the face. "Frank! I'm still married. I can't...we can't." She tugged her hands out of his and began to move toward home again.

"Allie, wait! You can't leave yet!"

She spun around. "Frank! Stop! Please! It's not just that we legally can't. I don't know if I can. I used to be so trusting...too trusting. And, look where that got me. I don't know if I can. I want to trust you...I do. I'm scared. And there are some things you don't know. At least...I don't think you know."

Frank stood still letting her talk. Deep down he knew this would be a hurdle he hoped wouldn't be very tall to jump. He didn't know whether to go wrap his arms around her or keep his distance. He decided the latter was a better choice for now.

Allie turned back around slowly and began walking towards home again, leaving Frank behind. He watched her walk as long as possible, only turning and heading in the opposite direction once he couldn't see her anymore.

Allie continued home and headed straight to the creek taking her top layer off and slipping in the cool water. She needed to cool her whole body. The hot outside was bad enough, but now she had a heat burning from within that needed to cool. Maybe the creek would be so cold she could numb her mind. Her tears flowed freely and were washed away every time she dunked her head under the rush of water. She had loved Frank for years, but he always saw her as one of the younger girls, never as a wife. *Why did life do this? A year ago would have been much better timing.* She walked out and laid on the bank letting the sun dry her.

She laid that way for a long while before deciding to dress and head back to help Ma with dinner. Ma would be wondering where she was. This was a long day and she was ready for it to end. Just a couple more hours and she could hide away in her room for the remainder of the night.

CHAPTER 18

Eddie made it to Deer Lodge and decided that following the creek would provide him coverage while he made his way to the farm where Allie lived. It was a longer route, but he didn't want to risk being seen headed that way. He wasn't in town long before, but someone may still remember him. Allie was the town's little lamb and a few heads turned when they found out he had snatched her up. There were a couple of close calls in the saloon right before they tied the knot. *Leaving this town was the best thing I could have done for us. Too many folks wanting to stick their noses into our business.*

The creek seemed low for this time of year. He hadn't really paid much attention to it before, though, so maybe it was just fine. The grass and trees still looked good. These parts have their fair share of fires and the weather sure wasn't going to help them out this year. He knew this area usually had heavy rain in the spring, but it looked like there had only been a few showers.

At least he wasn't a logger. They would be out of

work if the fires took hold this summer. Rail work didn't stop. Areas might have to be put on hold, but there was always another section in another area that needed workers. Train workers could find work pretty easily. Taking this little time off shouldn't hurt him. If his old boss wouldn't welcome him back, he would go elsewhere.

Eddie continued walking, thinking about the other places he could go if that was necessary. Traveling was his joy. He loved to sample the local tastes in liquor and women in new areas. He could move on before he grew tired of it. If only Allie would cooperate, so he had someone doing the work at home.

Nearing the farm, he found a boulder to crouch behind while he kept watch on the house. Everything looked quiet. They must all be inside. It was about supper time and his stomach was not going to let him forget that. He reached into his pack and pulled out some of the food he'd brought along and made short work of it. It sure didn't taste very good, but it did the job. It gave him the strength needed so he could get back to looking for his wife. This first part of his plan had been seamless. Now, for step two: watch her every move to see when the best time would be to confront her and take her kicking and screaming back to Idaho.

Allie helped Ma clean up the dishes and feigned a headache. She made her way up the stairs, donned her nightgown, and wrapped a blanket around herself. Sitting in the chair, she decided to pull out her old diary and read about the good times. She read through the pages where life was simple. She wished she could close her eyes and be magically sent back in time.

Early on, she wrote about her favorite doll and her best friend, the time George Pilchuck, the same George that married her best friend Blinne, pulled her braid and called her a ninny, all of it was mixed into those beginning pages. Back then, those were the rough times, back when a problem could be fixed with a piece of Ma's chocolate cake and a cold glass of milk from their cow, Bertha.

No amount of chocolate cake was going to solve her current problem. Could she endure that life again if she was forced to complete the year, so she could be legally divorced? Would the month she spent here be added to her remaining time? And...there was Frank! Allie had loved Frank since they were kids. She had imagined what life would be like with him. She had even written about him several times in her diary. If she did have to go back and live with Eddie, would Frank wait for her? He had his whole life ahead of him. He had a promising career and an open schedule to go wherever he wished. She was not sure if he would pause his life for her to clean up hers.

Allie was finished looking at her past. It only upset her. Time was marching ahead. While she waited for answers about her divorce, she needed to live her life. In two days it would be Sunday and she decided she had hidden long enough. Church sounded like the best chance to enter back into life in Deer Lodge.

She tried to sleep, telling herself that all would end well, but the negative thoughts plagued her throughout the night. No use pretending, she had a headache now! She truly had one from lack of sleep. Tomorrow, she would go to Blinne. She always had a way of calming her down. Blinne would want to know what the sheriff had to say. It would be good to share with her. Maybe she would have another perspective.

Dawn came a few short hours later. Allie had eventually fallen asleep, but was at a loss as to how long that might have been. She rose and dressed in the same plain work dress she had arrived in and headed downstairs to find Ma in the kitchen making breakfast. Allie said good morning, rolled up her sleeves, and began rolling out the biscuit dough Ma had just prepared.

"How is your head dear?" Ma said, while frying sausage.

"Mmm...still hurts a bit. I didn't sleep well." Allie closed her eyes. The mere mention of the word sleep left her body yearning for it.

"Well, you can take a nap later. When we're done cleaning up after breakfast, you can help me carry some buckets up to water the garden."

This was always a chore for late July and August. They never needed to do it in late April...but here they were. Their well usually contained plenty of water for them, and the garden, before it would run dry in late summer. Fortunately, the well was still providing for them, but preserving what was there was of high importance right now.

"I really hope we get some rain soon. All this heat is melting the snow in the high country so much faster than normal. I already heard talk of some wild fires starting up about two months earlier than normal." Ma wiped her brow on the dish rag and added milk, salt, and pepper to the sausage.

"I do love sausage gravy and biscuits." Allie placed the last of the biscuits on the baking pan and took it to the oven.

Ma had the fire lit and it was warm and waiting for the doughy wonders to enter. Soon the smell matched that of the sausage. That also means that Pa and Drew would be looking for breakfast soon. As if on cue, they entered the kitchen and sat at the table. Ma poured coffee and took it to them, announcing that breakfast would be ready shortly. They sat and talked about the chores already completed that morning that included carrying buckets of water to the crops and animals.

When the biscuits were done, they all made short work of filling their plates and even shorter work of emptying them. This was one of the family's favorite meals. Sometimes Ma would even break tradition and serve it for dinner—and no one ever complained about that. After breakfast, Allie stood to remove the plates and take them to the sink.

"Save those dear. If we don't get started on the watering now, we will be miserable doing it later. It is getting warmer by the second outside." Agreeing with Ma, Allie left the breakfast cleanup for later and headed out front to find her pail on the porch. Ma was right behind her and grabbed her own pail as they made their way down to the creek.

CHAPTER 19

Allie had kept to herself for a couple of days, dreaming of what life could be like with Frank. *The timing was all wrong!* She wanted to be free, or be able to go back in time and not make the worst mistake of her life. Shaking off the thoughts that continued to circle in her mind, she donned her best dress and headed down to join her family for church. She had kept to herself and her small group long enough. She needed to join the community again if she ever hoped they would welcome her when this was all over.

The white double doors were both propped open, greeting her like arms stretched wide in expectation of an embrace. They drew her in and her heart warmed. This building was always more than walls to her. It was a cocoon that was her refuge when she was in turmoil. The stained wood walls made the large space seem small and intimate. She could easily have burst into a song...feeling like she was the only one in attendance. Walking to her family's usual pew, she was greeted by a few members. Just simple hellos and welcomes, — nothing personal. She knew some were staring at her.

She could feel the attention. It unsettled her a bit, but she hoped it was just curiosity on their part. Allie sat as the church bells began to toll and opened her hymnal, ready to join in the praise that would follow once all had arrived.

Church seemed to fly by. It was typical...nothing to speak of that was of particular note. She just relaxed and allowed the general peace of God and the familiarity sweep over her. A social hour always followed. She was uncertain about how this would go and that's what had kept her from coming for so long. She knew that most would be friendly enough, but there were a few that just never could mind their own business.

Allie followed her Pa and Drew to a table and took a seat. She thought—or hoped—that staying by them would prevent most from attempting to poke too far into her life. She scanned the crowd...and locked eyes with Frank. He was making his way to her and she shivered. Anticipation, nerves, excitement...she wasn't entirely sure what, but she decided she would try to figure it out later.

"Hi," he said, looking directly at her as he sat to face them all. Then he tipped his head acknowledging Pa and Drew.

"Hi, Frank. How're your parents?" Pa, replied.

Frank folded his hands in front of him on the table and engaged Pa in a brief conversation, catching him up on his parents and what he had been doing. Then he looked at Allie and held her gaze for a while—unsettling her further.

"Well...I see your ma has taken up a conversation with Mrs. Wimble. I'm going to go grab a plate of food. We might be here awhile. Let's go see what we can muster up Drew." Pa and Drew stood and left without looking back, and Allie folded inward as her shield moved farther away.

"How are you, Allie?" Frank didn't waste any time trying to strike up a conversation.

Of course, he wants to know how I am. The last conversation wasn't superficial. He will probably want to continue where we left off.

"I'm hot, Frank." She choked down a chuckle that was bubbling inside her that she knew he wouldn't understand. After their last conversation she was hot: hot from embarrassment, hot from anger, and hot from this sun! It must be moving closer. That was the only explanation she could come up with for why it felt like the end of July instead of the end of April. She knew the weather was a safe topic...and would stick with that explanation.

Frank sat silent not knowing how to respond. This was not the time or place to get too personal, he realized. So, he sat waiting for her to elaborate so he could decide if he needed to change the direction of the conversation quickly or not.

"The well is drying up and the heat is getting worse. I don't know what this means for the rest of summer. Ma and Pa are a bit worried about it, but they try not to show it. I may have to spend some time down in the ice house just to find some relief." She looked down at the table and hoped he believed this was what she originally meant.

With a slight sigh of relief, he joined in her topic of choice "I have heard of some fires already...over in Idaho. Seems a bit early, but they are not in the way of anything and no one is real worried about it now. We have seen some summers with more rain than dry days. Hopefully, we'll have one of those."

"Yes, we can hope for that." She began twiddling her thumbs wondering what to talk about next. "Have you seen Blinne recently? I thought she might be here today, but I haven't spotted her yet."

"She is nearing the end and I'm sure the trip in would be too much for her to do right now. I was going to go check on her this week. That baby could come any day." Glancing around to make sure no one was within ear shot he found another subject "Remember...Paul asked me to come back after our lunch by the river?"

Not the topic she was hoping was next on the list, but she was curious as to what Paul wanted to tell him. "I do. Did you get a chance to speak with him?'

"I did." But before he could say more, Gladys approached him from behind and sat with purpose.

"Hi, Frank...Allie." She made eye contact with both and then focused on Frank. "How are you Allie? I'm sorry I haven't made time to come and see you, but you know how it is. Life is busy. Frank, how are you? I've come calling a couple of times, but your mother told me you were out each time.

Allie attempted to hide her smirk as Frank, ever so slightly, rolled his eyes. "Yes, I have been busy helping my father at the bank and catching up on the doctoring side of things here." Frank locked eyes with Allie before turning to look at Gladys. She had on a yellow dress and not the pale subtle kind. *She might be the sun and the reason this place is so darn hot. That dress could blind a person!* Turning back to save his eyes from permanent damage, he asked Allie if she would enjoy taking a short walk.

"I would love to Frank, but it seems that Gladys might enjoy your company more right now." She darn near giggled knowing what she just did to him.

Gladys pulled herself more upright and agreed that she could use the exercise after sitting so long at church. Frank's expression was perfect. Sure, she felt somewhat bad about the predicament she just put him in, but she needed to stop the direction he was leading their conversation. Sitting smack dab in the middle of the church social was not the place to discuss such matters. Some of these women had sharp ears and what they didn't hear they would fill in, leaving her unaware of what gossip might start spreading about her, and Frank, for that matter.

Frank hesitated while he glared across at Allie, who fought the urge to laugh out loud. He rose and held his arm to Gladys, while asking if she would care to join him on a brief walk. He looked back at Allie when he said the word *brief*, trying to convey that he would be back shortly and didn't want her to leave. Gladys, of course, agreed in an overly excited tone and grabbed his offered arm. They made their way towards the tree line as Mrs. Wimble and Ma were approaching.

Mrs. Wimble spoke first. "It is so good to see you again, my dear. I heard a rumor that you had an accident. A few ladies in my women's group saw bruises when you first came back to town and I did notice some color on your face. Whatever that was, it looks all healed up now. I sure hope it wasn't more severe than that. Your ma assures me that you are very healthy and just relaxing at home for a bit."

Allie looked to Ma who had a just-smile-and-say-as-little-as-possible look on her face.

"Yes...well...I am here, and I am fine now. Thank you for your concern, Mrs. Wimble. You just missed Gladys and Frank. They headed over there on a walk." As she glanced in the direction they had taken, Allie spotted Pa making his way back with his plate loaded down. Knowing him, he probably already ate some of it, too. *At least this conversation will be short...Mrs. Wimble won't stay long once he arrives.*

"I did not. Frank is such a nice man. I hope he stays around for a while. Poor Gladys was beside herself when he moved away. Looks as though she might get her chance with him after all." Mrs. Wimble turned in their direction to monitor their moves as she continued singing Frank's praise.

"Hello, ladies!" Pa boomed as he set his plate down and took his seat.

Mrs. Wimble turned and paused. "Hello to you! Oh! Hello, Andrew! Uh...yes...did you hear that? Someone called me. I must go and see what they need. Pleased to see you all again. Do take care."

Ma and Allie chuckled together for a moment as Mrs. Wimble rushed away before Pa asked, "What was that all about?"

Allie sat, and Ma just shrugged...but they both knew it was Drew's presence. Since the accident, he made people nervous. They didn't know what to say or do around him anymore. It irritated Allie, but for now, she would be thankful for not having to deal with Mrs. Wimble anymore today. Most likely, no one would stop over here again and that was fine with her. She'd been uncomfortable in public enough for one day. She hoped they would leave before Frank had a chance to make his way back over.

Ma must have understood Allie's feelings as she encouraged them to finish and get on home. At Ma's request, the men made short work of the rest of their meal and they were off—with Allie in the back of the wagon where she could be alone with her thoughts.

Drew was catnapping. This was, no doubt, due to the piled plate of food he had just eaten.

Frank hadn't made it back to continue their conversation, but Allie knew he would find her soon. She just hoped that next time he would wait until they were in a more private area. Overall, church was good. There were looks from some that she couldn't interpret, but nothing too upsetting for her. Of course, word had yet to spread about her hope for a divorce. She may have to go into hiding for a while once that news broke. She closed her eyes and decided to let tomorrow worry about tomorrow. She would take notes from Drew...and use this day to rest.

CHAPTER 20

Allie carried the last bucket up from the creek. Watering the vegetable patch was exhausting work. Every year they did this job, but it was usually only for a couple of weeks to a month before the fall rains returned and water began filling their well. She had already been carrying water for longer than they usually did all year, and it was only a couple of weeks into May.

Of course, their well wasn't dry, but they hoped to prevent that by adding this chore earlier. The weather wasn't cooperating and seemed to be stuck in the same pattern over the last several weeks: hot, dry, and relentless! That's all it seemed to know.

"Maybe it forgot what to do?" She thought out loud, using her apron to wipe the sweat that was trailing down the side of her face. Then she chuckled as she realized she was talking like the weather was alive and could be convinced to change. Apparently, it was beginning to get to her—and not just the plants that seemed to die a few more each day.

Looking across the field, she spotted Pa and Drew.

They were doing the same job, but their work required carrying the water farther. Each bucket added a little more to the animal trough. Pa had talked about creating a path for the animals to drink directly out of the creek, but decided to continue with the buckets. This way, the creek would remain clean in case they ended up needing it for the household. The people living downstream would appreciate it, too.

While she was making her way back around to the front porch, Allie thought she saw something move out of the corner of her eye. Turning, she placed her hand above her brow to block the hellish luminous orb. Nothing was in view, but her eyes felt sunburned and everything seemed to look blurry, making it hard to see much beyond the first few feet in front of her.

Allie continued to walk inside as someone ran up the steps behind her, grabbing her around the shoulders. She screamed and whipped around quickly, but her eyes wouldn't cooperate. The sun was so bright outside walking into the dark house made everything look black.

Her hands flew to her face in a well-practiced move to shield what might be coming. Then she heard Frank's voice in a soft soothing tone that quickly changed to a chuckle. Suddenly, the front door banged open and the chuckle was replaced with voices. Everything was swirling around her. She could hear multiple voices, but was unable to tell who belonged to them. Falling to the floor, she placed her hands on her ears and attempted to block them out.

"Drew! Drew!" Frank attempted to distract him before Drew could follow through with his raised fist. It hit him square in the jaw just as Pa was making his way into the house. Pa put his body between Frank and Drew so no further punches would be thrown.

"Now, what is the meaning of all this!" Pa's voice boomed through the small room getting everyone's attention. Allie remained on the floor, but lowered her hands. As her eyes began to focus, she began to understand what just took place.

Frank spoke first while rubbing his jaw. "I startled Allie and that made her scream. I guess Drew heard her and came running to her rescue."

Pa spoke next. "Why would you do a thing like that, Frank?"

Allie's head cleared and she began to follow the conversation.

Pa gently shook Drew to get his attention. He had remained in the same position staring at Frank.

Frank began to explain, "I'm sorry! I didn't realize...um...Allie put me in a bit of a situation a couple of weeks ago that I am still trying to undo. I was just doing a little payback is all. I didn't think it through, I guess." He bent down and helped her to her feet. "You okay?" He held her gaze trying to read her eyes.

Allie's face broke into a smile and she nodded her head. "What do you mean still undoing the situation?"

She placed her hand over her mouth attempting to stifle her giggle.

"That little walk you sent me on with Gladys turned into her finding any reason possible to drop in at my house and ambush me when I return…almost daily. It seems that was all the encouragement she needed for me to become her prey."

Not able to hold back anymore Allie let out a loud cackling sound that she could tell unnerved Frank more.

Pa noted the turn of events and the abrupt change in emotions.

"Come on, Drew," he called out as he began walking out the door. "Everything's okay." Not turning back around, he called out, "Frank, please remember to think next time you're around my daughter. I don't need a lovesick young man causing all kinds of ruckus round here. I have work to do."

Allie's and Frank's eyes would have popped out of their heads if they weren't attached. They were both silent for a long while, not quite knowing how to recover from Pa's words that still hung in the air.

Frank spoke first, while Allie tried to recover from her father's brazen comments. "Well, I think I'll go see what Doc's up to. He's been using me lately for second opinions and catching me up on the town folk. He's decided, since I'm here, that he's going to take a vacation for a couple of weeks. I'll be running the practice while he and his wife visit family." Frank turned and began walking out.

"Frank! Wait!" Allie quickly tried to gather her thoughts. "The last time we spoke you were going to tell me about what the sheriff talked to you about, but we were interrupted."

He slowly turned and motioned for her to sit as he took another chair. "Do you know where Reno is?"

Nodding, she replied, "Vaguely. I know it is south of here...in Nevada."

"Paul seems to think that might be your best bet...going there, that is. File for the divorce there. Seems they are granting divorces like it's nothing—no big deal. One catch, though...you must live there for six months, but it's a guarantee. You won't have to depend on the mercy of a judge." Frank sat quietly as she processed the information.

She folded her hands in her lap and focused on her breathing. *Moving to Reno was a lot to take in. She didn't know anyone there. Could she live all alone?*

"I will have to think on it. My first thought is protection. No one is there. What if he follows me? I would end up back where I started." Her eyes became distant and out of focus as she pondered the possibilities.

"That's why the sheriff told me instead of telling you...so I could help you figure out if it was an option for you." He stood to say good-bye to her. He knew she needed to absorb the information for a while. "If you need to talk, I'll be at Doc's during the day for the next two weeks. The schedule is busy, but I will always find time for you." He took a step out the door before turning back to add, "Oh! And Blinne had a baby girl. She asked me to tell you she would love for you to come see her soon."

Allie didn't move as he made his way out and closed the door behind himself. She continued to sit for a long while before realizing how much time had passed. Ma had asked her to prepare supper for them tonight while she was visiting with a neighbor. Pushing all thoughts aside, she rose to make her way to the kitchen.

CHAPTER 21

Eddie had been watching Allie and her family for a while. His camp wasn't far away, and he stayed hidden in the brush. He hated camp life. Cooking wasn't an option as the smoke would tip someone off to his location. He didn't have much food left and, judging by the way his clothes were hanging from him, he clearly wasn't eating enough.

The last time he was only here a short while and he doubted anyone would recognize him. But he stayed to himself and away from town, just in case. Going in, getting a bath, some decent food, and maybe a game at the tables would be heaven. But he wouldn't take the chance of running into the few that might recognize him. He was tired and hungry, but at least he wasn't cold. That was one positive if he wanted to think that way about it.

Everything was dry and brittle making his movement difficult when he got close to the house. Every footfall had to be placed very carefully or the noise of the crunch underneath could tip anyone off that something was there. All the stillness and crouching led to a very sore back and legs. Grumpy couldn't begin to describe his current attitude. He was ready to be finished. Things were looking like he might be able to come out of hiding and take what was rightfully his anytime now.

Eddie was thinking of just how he would come out of hiding and daydreaming about his trip back home when he accidently shifted and broke a stick with his foot. Allie, was just outside the house and turned to look. His heart stopped. He was sure she had heard him...or smelled him. He was ripe from weeks of hiding out. But, he breathed a sigh of relief when she turned back to the door. Just a few seconds later a man came running up and he heard Allie scream. Through the open door, he saw the commotion that followed.

Eddie had come to gather information...and now he knew that Allie and her family were not completely comfortable. Suppressing disappointment, he continued to watch quietly from his hidey-hole. He'd hoped enough time had passed that everyone would have their guard down. Judging by their behaviors, this was not the case. He began to reform his plan. He hadn't anticipated needing to drag this out longer, but he was patient. If he didn't wait until the right time, he would be caught before he was able to get her back to Idaho.

As the commotion settled, he was already thinking about his options. He was hot, miserable, and hungry. Not being able to move on to the next part of his plan irritated him to no end. Staying and continuing to camp was not an option. He didn't even want to think about it. He didn't want to continue being miserable. The only option was to head back to Idaho for a while. Then he could wait out Allie and her family in some comfort.

His thoughts wandered to Pearl. Her company would help pass the time while he waited for everyone here to get back to their routine. Thinking of Pearl left a smirk on his face. He could slip back to town and catch the next train. Tonight, on the train, he would dream about clean clothes and a meal prepared by someone else.

CHAPTER 22

The wet cloth Allie placed on her neck to make the walk to Blinne's home more bearable was drying...and she was only half way there. The walk back home later in the day would be worse, she thought to herself.

Seeing Blinne's baby was bound to bring forth varied emotions, but the alternative would be sitting at home going back and forth between what to do about Frank. She trudged on, making her way over the top of the hill. Pausing to enjoy the view that opened from the woods, she took a breath and tried to calm herself. She could see their house down below. It was small and bursting with love. Birds were chirping from their nests in the trees. It was a happy sound. One day...maybe soon...she could also be as happy and content. Putting one foot in front of the other, she made her way down the other side of the hill and walked up to the front door.

Blinne was singing from behind the door, adding to the surreal feeling of joy from the little house. This was a big contrast to her melancholy mood. Allie knocked, and the singing stopped. The door opened and the bright smile on Blinne's face was just as bright as her yellow dress. "Oh, Allie! I am so glad you came. Come in, come in!"

Allie stepped over the threshold and gave Blinne a tight squeeze before walking to the table to set her hat and washrag down. "Well, don't make me wait, let me see your angel."

Blinne held up one finger and gave a slight giggle before going to the bedroom. Allie took the opportunity to sit at the table and take a few more calming breaths before she came back. When Blinne returned, she had a bundle of pink wrapped in her arms. She held her out and let Allie take her. Allie stared at the sleeping little doll. Blinne stepped away and began rambling on about the birth and first few days of being a mother. Allie had no idea what she was saying...she really wasn't paying attention. She couldn't help herself. She was in awe of this tiny person—so perfect and sweet. Sadness also crept deeper into her soul as the seconds ticked by. Sadness for what she had lost...forever.

Babies could be loved by anyone. She could be an aunt-like figure to this one...but she longed to be a mother. To feel a baby moving inside her would bring her such joy. Faintly, she could hear her name being called.

"Allie! Allie! Are you listening to me?" Blinne came and placed her hand on Allie's shoulder jolting her back to reality. "Oh, Allie! Here, take my hankie. I'll take her for you."

It was then that Allie noticed her cheek was wet. She was crying. She took the hankie with one hand and kept her other wrapped securely around the pink bundle.

"Oh, my! I'd like to hold her a while longer, if you don't mind. I'm just so happy for you, Blinne. All you ever wanted to be is right here in this house...and my arms. Does she have a name, yet?"

Blinne nodded. "We just picked it out yesterday...Lena Rose."

"Little Lena...Lovely Lena...Lady Lena! It's beautiful...just like she is." Allie took the back of her finger and made little circles across Lena's cheek.

Giggling, Blinne commented back, "Well...she will *behave* as a lady, but royalty we are not!"

Both girls began laughing and Allie was feeling a bit lighter. She felt her heart had opened a bit...and Lena was the cause. She could get used to this feeling—this overwhelming feeling of protectiveness and love for someone else. Maybe being around a baby is exactly what she needed to get over the loss of her own baby. Life does move on, after all. Ma's words came back to her. But before she could dwell on them, she pushed them aside...for another time.

"How are you doing, Blinne?"

"I'm tired and sore." Blinne gingerly sat down next to Allie. "I knew the delivery would be hard, but no one can prepare you for it. It is intense, and you can't really come up with any words that match that intensity," she sighed, further stressing her point.

"Well, you look wonderful! Your skin is glowing."

Lena started to stir and make little mousy sounds.

"Thank you, I don't feel that way, though. She must have realized I sat down. She seems to know when I start to relax. That is always when she decides that it is time to wake up and nurse." Blinne held her hands out silently asking to take back her daughter.

Allie reluctantly handed her back over and stood brushing her hands on her skirt. "Well, what can I do to help you out then?"

"Oh, Allie! That would be such a blessing. George will be home in a while...and hungry. He's been fending for himself for lunch, but I know it would mean a lot to him if dinner was ready." Blinne settled herself in the rocking chair that her father brought over a month or so ago. The same chair that her mother had used to rock her little ones. "There is flour in the bin and vegetables down in the cellar. George milked Tootsie before he left this morning. I think you can find enough for a potato soup."

"Well, now, you just sit back and enjoy Lena. I'm going to make the best potato soup you ever tasted."

Allie fetched the ingredients and got started. Sure enough, she found what she needed with no problem.

With the weather so warm, no fire was started, and she was not about to start one in the house on a day like this. Good thing there was a pit built out back for cooking outside on these hot days.

She gathered up the wood and started the fire. Thankfully this pit was completely contained. There was no risk of having an ember spread the fire. Not everyone took this precaution, she thought to herself.

Heading back inside to grab the pot, spoon, and knife, she glanced at Blinne—so engrossed in Lena she was unaware of Allie. She longed to know what Blinne was feeling, but she would have to accept that she would never fully know.

Stepping back outside, she put salt pork she'd found in the barrel into the pot to brown. Then she made short order out of cutting the vegetables and plopped them into the pot. She sautéed them for a while and finished cooking the pork before she piled it all up to one side of the pan and tilted it to let the fat from the pork run to the other side. She added flour to the pork fat to make a roux before pouring in the gift from Tootsie. All that was left was to stir it occasionally to make sure it didn't scorch on the bottom of the pot.

Allie was hot, but at least this part was finished. The soup would take a while to cook so she decided to make some fry bread to go with it. The Indians in these parts had taught the settlers how to make it. She took flour, milk, baking powder, and some salt and mixed it all together. Then she broke off chunks and flattened them out like patties. Once the soup was closer to done, she would fry them up and they could dunk them in their soup. Not the traditional way to eat them, but she didn't have time to make regular bread.

She wiped her brow with Blinne's hankie and sat back on her heels. Somehow, she would move forward. She could feel herself being pulled in that direction. God was calling her to move on. Was it with Frank? She wasn't sure yet. Going to Reno seemed like the only option. But, going alone would be challenging. She rushed into this mess and now it was up to her to fix it.

"Hello, Allie," George boomed as he walked closer to her.

Startled, she looked up before replying a hello.

"How is Blinne doing?" He came closer, kneeling next to her.

She wiped her brow again and told him about their visit while stirring the soup. "You're a little early from what I was expecting, but I can fry this bread up pretty fast and you two can eat."

"Thanks for helping out. She has been so tired and I'm getting tired of fending for myself. I want her to rest, but I'm hungry. I don't want her to know that though. She is busy, I know. And life will resume soon. Are you staying? I can go set the table." George stood.

"You know, I think I will finish up here and leave it for the two of you. I'm sure you would like the time together and I need to get back home before this heat turns me into a puddle. Of course, the ground might appreciate that!" She grabbed the flattened dough and began frying it in the hot lard.

"Thanks, Allie. You are more than welcome to stay...but it's your decision." George went inside to say hello to Blinne and set the table for two.

Allie finished frying the bread and took the food inside. She said goodbye to George, Blinne and, of course, Lena. She went out the back to put out the fire. Before she began her walk home, she stopped at the trickle of a creek that ran out back and cupped her hands to wet her mouth. As she began her journey, she knew she would need to do the same from their own creek. Something needed to be done about this heat or trouble would be coming in some form. Only God knew what that would be.

CHAPTER 23

June began with no change in weather. There was some rain here and there...if you count mists. Most of the time it didn't even dampen the ground. The water seemed to evaporate in midair and never made it to the soil. Maybe that was all an illusion, to further the intensity of the sun. Maybe it did fall all the way to the ground only to be sucked up so fast it couldn't be seen.

The sun was once a welcoming beacon in the sky following the brutal winters. Now, it was quickly becoming an enemy of all living things. The land was turning into a desert before their eyes. Day chores were exhausting, but nights brought no rest because it was too hot. The air was suffocating.

Despite the heat that made Allie constantly want to find relief in the ever-shrinking creek, she needed to walk to town and look for some work so she could save enough money to get to Reno. There were only a few places in town she could try. Deer Lodge was a small but growing community. Going back to the restaurant where this whole mess started was always an option. But it would be considered only as a last resort.

Being reminded of how this all started did not sound ideal. Moving ahead with life and learning new things was more desirable. That would allow her to focus on her future, instead of reliving the past every day. Mentally making a list of places to check while taking in the majestic mountain views in the distance made the walk short.

Doc's office would be first on the list. It was the closest to her so that made the most sense. She couldn't forget about the pharmacy just down the street from Docs office, Powell County Post, the local newspaper, and, of course, the bank that belonged to Frank's family. That was on her list just above the restaurant.

Frank would be there, she was sure of that. Seeing him today might not be wonderful if her day didn't go as she hoped it would. Frank hadn't been around since the incident with Drew. She didn't know if he was rethinking his feelings towards her or waiting for her to recognize her feelings toward him. Well, she already knew that. She'd known since she was a silly school girl, but her life complicated matters and he didn't need the mess that she would bring into his.

Realizing where she was, she took a deep breath and walked into Doc's office. He was standing at his bookshelf with his back to her.

"Dr. Leman?" Allie stood with her hands clasped in front of her and her hand bag hanging from her wrist.

He turned, closing the book resting in his palms, and removed his spectacles. "Ah, Allie! What can I do for you today? Are you feeling well?"

"I'm feeling fine, thank you. I do have a couple of things I wish to discuss with you though. Do you have a moment?"

Doc was intrigued. Allie was speaking more formally than usual. Something was up, and he was about to find out. "I do. This heat is not bringing many people my way these days. Would you like to sit a spell?" He gestured towards the two waiting chairs against the wall and she obliged.

She angled towards him. "I understand that you and my father have worked something out regarding the bill from my procedure. I would like to take that burden from my family and be responsible for paying it."

Doc sat quietly for a moment. He knew the financial strain on the family and this drought was only making that worse. Taking responsibility for oneself was honorable, but Allie had no means to provide for herself. "Allie, I'm not sure I understand. Your pa and I have come to an agreement that is suitable for the both of us. Maybe you could do something to repay him and let us handle this."

With effort, she kept her face steady and controlled the quiver in her voice. "My family has done more for me than any should. I created this situation and I want to finish it myself. Now...I can't pay you today, of course, but I am currently looking for some work to be able to set my life right again. Which brings me to my other topic...do you have need for anything I might be able to help you with?" Allie bit the inside of her cheek.

"Oh, Allie! You know I would be pleased to hire you, if I could. My missus helps with cleaning the office and keeping my paperwork up to date. And with patient visits dwindling down right now, my time is opening up, allowing me to take on more of what she's been doing. I wish there was something, but...maybe in the fall? You could check back with me then, if you haven't found anything." Doc stood and walked back to the bookshelf to replace the book he was still holding back on the shelf. It was a signal to Allie that it was time to look elsewhere.

"Thank you for your time Doc. I will check back in with you regarding my bill when I find something." She was already leaving as she finished the sentence.

One down, but several others remained on her mental list. Doc was one of the nicer and more understanding people in town, but that didn't mean he was the only one who might have something for her.

Doc remained standing at the book shelf, looking out the door as Frank walked out from the back room. "Hey, Doc. I'm finished back there. I heard your conversation with Allie."

"I suspected you could hear it. I should have told her you were there, but she caught me off guard. I feel for her—I do. I wish I could do something."

"Let me pay her bill," Frank blurted. Doc whipped his head up to stare at Frank. "I'm working for you for a couple of weeks so you can go on vacation. Instead of paying me all my wages, hold back what is needed to cover the bill, please." Frank set his jaw making it clear he was not going to budge on this issue.

"You sure Frank?" Doc looked quizzically at him. "It wasn't just a standard office visit. I can't go into the details, of course, but it is a sizable bill."

"I am more than sure, but don't say anything to Allie just yet, please. I want to tell her once it is paid." Frank stepped out through the door to see if he could still get a glimpse of Allie walking down the street.

"All right, Frank. You have a deal." Smiling to himself, Doc walked into the back room to check on Frank's work.

Frank caught up with Allie as she was walking into the pharmacy. He knew why she wanted money and he wished he could help in some way. He decided to follow her and see if she was having any luck. Meeting a doctor in a pharmacy shouldn't tip her off to his nosiness, anyway. As Frank approached the door, Allie walked right past him. "Hey, Allie. How are you?"

She spun around quickly putting her facial expression in check.

"Frank! Good to see you. I'm in a hurry today. Sorry we can't catch up. I have to go."

He wondered why she was agitated. He didn't push the issue, though, and further upset her. "All right, I'll see you around sometime, then."

Allie spun around and walked quickly off the main street and onto a side road. She needed to calm down before she went to the next business. She could understand why she wasn't hired if there were no openings or business was down, but blatantly telling her she was a married woman and not hirable because of said marriage made her steam! How was she supposed to get out of said marriage if she wasn't hirable because of it?

Oh...she was mad all right. It shouldn't surprise her, though. Most of society felt that way. Her job now was to work solely for her husband and maybe take in mending, or other meaningless side jobs that paid a pittance—to assist her husband. As a married woman, working to support herself was frowned upon and, in some circles, completely forbidden. Luckily for her, not everyone thought that way. Mr. Ashton, the owner of the newspaper company, had a different view. And that was her next stop.

Walking up the steps and through the doors, she was more cautious than she was earlier in the day. Not knowing if she would be accepted, pitied, or slapped across the face does that to a person. She had Doc's pity, giving her hope of work in the fall. That might just have been to make himself feel better, though. She was slapped across the face by Mr. Richter to remind her of her place. Would Mr. Ashton be accepting? She could only hope. Approaching the empty desk, she tapped the bell that sat on top next to a little card that read *Ring for Assistance*. Then she waited.

"Yes? Can I help you?" Mr. Ashton appeared out of the back looking a bit disheveled.

Allie stood up straight and tried to appear confident. "Hello, Mr. Ashton. I was hoping for a word with you, if you can spare a minute of your time?"

"Why, hello, Allie. How are you?" He gestured for them to move to his office and she followed him.

After removing a pile of papers Mr. Ashton motioned for her to sit and he took the seat directly across the desk from her. "What can I help you with today?"

"Mr. Ashton, to be frank with you, I am looking for a job. Something, anything that will pay a decent wage." She held her breath waiting for whatever was next.

He folded his arms and sat quietly for a moment. "Your timing is impeccable my dear. I normally do not hire the gentler sex as this work can be a bit rough and physically tiring but, as you know, this heat has made extra work at home. My young boy employees have been called back to carry water and such to help their families. My son and I are sinking trying to do it all. Now, I know you won't be able to do the more rigorous parts of making the paper, but I may be able to use you for some things around here. Cleaning up, running errands, and even delivering the local papers are things I think you could handle just fine. That would free up our time to do the actual writing and printing. I could only pay you about fifty cents per week to start. If you can handle the job, I might be able to do a little more later." He leaned back in his chair and waited to see how she would react to that.

It was an offer. Not the full open arms of accepting her regardless of her gender, but still an offer. She couldn't refuse it. "Thank you so much, sir. I would love the opportunity." Just as she was accepting, young Mr. Ashton walked in waving a telegram.

"Just in, close to 100 fires are being reported all over Idaho and Montana. Says the cause is everything from campers, loggers, arsonists, and even the trains themselves. The U.S. Forest Service is asking for men. They need strong men they can train quickly to squelch the fires before they get too big." He looked up and noticed Allie. "Oh, I'm sorry. I didn't realize you were with someone. Hi, Allie. How are you?"

"Fine thanks, your father and I were just discussing work. And, I was just accepting a position. I can see that you are busy though so, after I am told when to report, I will leave you to your work." She stood, turned toward the elder Mr. Ashton and waited for his response.

"How's tomorrow sound? We could use the help soon to get this place in shape. We might not always need you all five days of the week, but for the first week, we will…just to sort out all of these papers and get this place cleaned up. Paper goes out on Wednesdays, so if you work Tuesday to help with last minute items, Wednesday for deliveries, and Thursday to clean up and get ready for the next issue that would help us greatly." He stood and took the telegram from his son.

Allie stood and thanked them both for this opportunity. She felt so light hearted, she could have skipped her way out and down the stairs, but she contained herself until she was alone on her way home. Finally, a break that made things look up. Sleeping tonight would be much easier.

CHAPTER 24

Eddie had been back home for a while and hadn't found work. His boss didn't seem too happy that he ran off, and fired him as soon as he came back. To make matters worse, John was getting edgy waiting around for his payment. Now with the fires starting, workable land was shrinking. Everyone wanted to blame the trains. All right, they did throw sparks, but how else was work going to get done. Apparently, his time was up in Idaho and he needed to move on to another area that he could be anonymous in. Allie was supposed to be here to move with him though.

Eddie felt edgy and knew he needed to leave. He packed up some provisions and decided it was time to head back to Allie. First, he needed some funds before he could make it all the way to her, though.

Maybe he could find some odd jobs along the way to bank a little before taking her back and righting this marriage. Everyone around here knew him and wouldn't hire him. Fortunately, he could cross into Montana and find something there, but he wouldn't stay long. He couldn't just breeze through and pick up

Allie, but he would be closer and able to watch her awhile. And, he could stockpile some money.

When he took her again, they could travel a greater distance from her family. Maybe if he put more space between them and her family, she would be easier to handle. His next step was taking shape and his edgy mood was turning into a more composed and collected feeling. He needed to keep this feeling. It made plotting and planning much easier than when he was agitated.

Taking one last look around the shack, he put his pack on his back, stepped out, closed the door on this phase of his life, and began thinking of the next one— with his controlled and disciplined wife. He began walking towards Montana with a smirk on his face.

Allie's heart was soaring with the birds and her steps were light as she made the familiar trip back home. She had a plan and a means to achieve it. It wasn't until she was almost home that she realized the significance of the telegram. It planted her thoughts firmly back on the ground.

The U.S. Forest Service was a fairly new agency created in 1905 under President Roosevelt. The appointed leader of this new agency, Gifford Pinchot, was fired in January. A man by the name of William Greeley took over and he had his work cut out for him. The general feeling that the department was unnecessary, and a financial waste was rampant, at least in these parts.

The railroad companies and logging industry didn't see the need to reserve and preserve so much land. Boundary lines were not off limits for them. They used their monies and power to take what they wanted and asked for forgiveness after the fact. This country was big. The land and trees would not and could not be filled up and used up completely. There was too much of it for that to ever happen. At least that was the current theory floating around, despite the fact that was exactly what happened on the Eastern coast. Allie was unsure who was right regarding this issue and had decided a while back she didn't want to take a side.

The number of fires reported sounded devastating, but this was big country. They had fires every year and many times you couldn't even tell when or where they were. Most of the fires that occurred yearly were remote and the land would recover before anyone would stumble upon that ground.

Fires could just as easily destroy homes and towns, like the 1908 fire in Big Timber that sits east of Deer Lodge. That fire wiped out one third of the town—all from a spark thrown by the train.

With the ground this dry, this was certainly a cause for concern. The papers had reported that the U.S. Forest Service first tried to contain then stomp out fire before it could destroy. Their recommended procedure was to dig big trenches to create a fire line that would prevent the fire from moving forward, then set intentional back fires to move in the direction of the original fire and burn up the path between. They claimed this would prevent the fire from pushing forward. While those actions sounded great on paper, it had never been done on a large scale. Whether it would work was questionable. This might be the test year. She shook the dreadful thoughts aside and pushed forward.

Arriving home and telling Pa the news of the fires was first on her list. Telling him about her job and plan could and would wait. Going to Ma first on that decision and hoping Ma would tell Pa for her would be best in her opinion. Pa was intimidating, and Ma was the go-between and buffer. At least that was the route she aimed for most of her life.

He was carrying more water to the animal troughs. It seemed carrying water was all anyone did these days. Hopefully the rains would come before the creek dried up. It had never happened before, but watering before July had never happened, either.

Pa, like usual, didn't seem too fazed by the news of the fires. He kept his hard shell on to protect those around him from worrying about things they couldn't control. Ma fed off his attitude regarding situations. If Pa seemed calm, the others followed suit.

With that task out of the way, it was time to head inside and get the talk with Ma behind her. One could never tell how that would go. Better than telling Pa of course, but whether she would find full support or merely acceptance remained to be seen. Ma knew she was an adult and could make her own choices.

Before she reached the front door, she could hear singing. Ma was in a good mood. That meant it was the perfect time for telling her. Allie opened the door with a smile on her face and renewed energy. "Ma?"

The singing paused. "Yes dear, I'm in the back room," Ma replied, then began to hum.

Allie made it to the back room before Ma reached the chorus. Ma was putting the clean sheets back on her bed. "Let me help you!" Allie jumped right in on one side opposite Ma. "You seem in a great mood today."

"Ah, yes. It's another beautiful day! Drew's having a good day and that makes your Pa happy. The well still seems to be holding for us. And the pastor's wife, Mrs. Shirley has asked me to teach a needle point class instead of asking Mrs. Wimble, like she has in the past. The look on that woman's face will be etched in my brain for a long while." Ma returned to humming while she finished the bed.

No wonder Ma was in such a good mood, Allie thought. Anytime anyone can put Mrs. Wimble back in her appropriate place is a good time. This also made this a great time to share her news. "I had a meeting today at the newspaper with the senior Mr. Ashton. You are now looking at a working daughter." Allie stood with a smile spread across her face.

Ma dropped the pillow she was holding and rushed

over to wrap Allie in a hug. "That is wonderful news. Pa and I could use a little extra help...like before."

And just like that Allie was brought back down to earth. She could no longer keep her head in the clouds feeling that she could take on this world. Of course, her parents needed help and would expect her to provide it. That was the way before she married. If she was staying here, she needed to help. "Yes, Ma. I will give a portion of what I earn to you and Pa. But, I need to save some for myself, too."

Ma slowly backed away and waited for her to provide more information.

Allie folded her hands and collected her thoughts before she told her of the plan. "I'm not going back to Eddie."

Ma interrupted, "I know that and don't want you to. I saw what he did to you. You're lucky...we're all lucky...you're still alive."

"I'm going to divorce him, Ma." Before Ma could interrupt again, she sped on. "I am going to save up and move to Reno. I can divorce there with no questions asked. I just have to be a resident for at least six months." She put her head down as a silent sign of showing she was finished.

"How are you going to live there? We don't know anyone there. I can't go with you. Allie, have you thought this through?" With a huff Ma turned and walked out of the room toward the kitchen.

Allie rushed behind to keep up with Ma's pace.

"I'm not sure about those details, yet. I am taking things one step at a time. This is too big to plan out all at once. The first step was getting here. That I did—and did well. The second step was finding a job, so I can earn money to move. Now, I have the job and can begin saving, with permission from you and Pa, of course."

Adding that last part would set some things right with Ma—even if she wasn't serious about asking for it. She wanted their blessing, however would do this regardless. "Once I have enough saved to support myself for a month or so in Reno, I will move there and begin looking for work to support myself the rest of the six months I need to be there."

Ma busied herself washing dishes to distract herself while Allie finished sharing her plan. She handed Allie a towel, so she could dry. Finally, Ma responded.

"Life cannot be all planned out like you are trying to do. Things come up all the time that destroy our well-made attempts at planning. I wish you would pray about this and wait. Wait for God to answer you." She placed a hand on Allie's shoulder. "His way, His answer will be the right one. Yours may bring more pain and trials than you think. You are jumping into this like you have done your whole life. Think about that. Ever since you were a little girl you would dive head first before waiting for Him to guide you. Why did you even marry Eddie in the first place? Think back. Was that God's plan for your life or did you see an easy out for all of us? I know the answer to that, but do you? Your good intentions have and may cause pain again for more than just you." She left Allie frozen, holding a glass in one hand and a towel in the other.

Allie wanted to cry. She was more confused now than ever. Ma didn't give her an answer. She expected her to give herself one. She thought she already had, but now she didn't know what was right. She was right back where she started. No, that wasn't right. She had a job. She was earning money and money led to options. What those options would be wasn't clear, unlike the glass in her hand. Why couldn't she just look through this glass and see the answers?

It was so clear. It was clean, unlike her. Her life was muddy, and she had caused it all. Cleaning this up would take more than a scrub in the wash tub like the glass held. She needed to see another perspective. Blinne was out of the question. She was too busy now, and it wouldn't be right to burden her with this.

That left Frank. *Oh boy*, she thought as she pulled herself up from the table. Their relationship was up and down these days. He wanted to help and would push, and she would run the other way. Then he would back off completely for weeks at a time. Reaching out to him would encourage his feelings to grow. This felt like a bigger decision than moving to Reno.

Do I need to seek out God for this too?

She was so confused. Going to sit by the creek was

the only real decision she could make without questioning it. The only thing she knew for sure was the fact that she was in trouble.

CHAPTER 25

It didn't take long sitting by the creek for Allie to realize she did need to talk to Frank—for better or worse. That realization didn't stop her from procrastinating though. She had gone into work the first day and the day after that and the next. Before she knew it, the week had past and she had successfully avoided the looming conversation, and the even more dreadful decision she had to eventually make.

She would see him at church and could let him know she wanted to talk with him. Talking there would not be private enough, even if the topic of following God's wishes instead of her own was appropriate conversation given the setting.

Her Tuesdays, Wednesdays, and Thursdays were now full. That left only Monday and Friday for chores at home. She could legitimately put the conversation off another week and, by doing that, put off thinking about it all together. That idea was appealing. Besides, she was on her way to church. She should be thinking about bigger problems and how to help other people instead of selfishly thinking of her own issues.

Allie sighed silently. Her problem was a big problem and affected so many others. She wanted to push it out of her mind, but she was reminded of it everywhere. Home was a constant reminder of why she was there. Work kept reporting on fires and the railroad reminding her of Idaho. She was more confused now than ever before.

The ride to church went by fast. She was so busy not thinking about her predicament that she lost all track of the time. Before she knew it, she was walking through those doors, following behind her parents, with Drew at her side. She forced her head down and walked to their family pew automatically. She could feign a headache and maybe Pa would decide to head straight home instead of staying for lunch. She decided to sit with her eyes not focused on anyone or anything and hope that her parents would assume something...anything...so she wouldn't have to lie.

Lying was wrong and she hated doing it, and to do it in this building was worse. She could go through the motions but be inattentive enough that, maybe, Ma would at least pick up on something being off. She could hope at least. *Is it a form of lying to let people make assumptions based on false appearances?* She pushed that thought aside as the pastor directed the congregation to open their Bibles to Matthew 7:21.

As she read the verse, she felt she wouldn't have to pretend. Her stomach flopped and that headache that she was thinking of pretending was beginning to become reality. *His will! Today, we have to hear about*

His will! She silently screamed those words.

He would not be making this easy for her. Maybe she could put her fingers in her ears like she used to when she was little and didn't want to hear what the boys at school were saying. No, that would only make this situation worse! It would draw the attention from the entire congregation.

If only she could muster up a fever, so they could leave right now. She had tried to do that on a few occasions when she was young—but never succeeded. That was an impossible mission that just wasted her time and effort. Scooting down in the pew she resigned herself to sitting through the perfect torture that only the Father could provide.

Frank was sitting several rows behind Allie. He had arrived a bit late and didn't want to disrupt the service that was already underway, so he took an open seat towards the back. It didn't take long for him to find Allie. It was easy, as she was sitting is the same pew as always.

Allie was a hard nut to crack these days. He had watched her from afar for a while this past week and she seemed to be in turmoil. Her moods changed quickly. Today, she appeared to be either in mental anguish or had some physical issue. Not pain—more as if something was irritating her. If she kept wiggling and slouching further down in her pew, she'd certainly have a rash or chaffing, Frank thought.

If she was trying not to draw attention, it was doing the opposite for him. He wasn't hearing a word the pastor was preaching. His own voice was louder in his mind. He couldn't shake thoughts of Allie. He had it bad. He wanted her by his side. Wanted to hurt those who caused her pain. He was never a fighter. These feelings were completely new to him. They didn't sit well either. He was a man of healing, not hurting.

Something needed to be done about this. Living with his heart held in someone else's hands—thoughts that seemed to change his whole character—was not what he had in mind when he came back home. He came back here to relax and think about his future. His work future. Work was so important to him that women, especially just one woman, hadn't been a part of his thinking. He used to be focused and driven. Now he felt like mush. Trying to make simple decisions was tiring these days.

Maybe coming back wasn't the best idea for him. Maybe he should have just jumped head first into another doctor position somewhere new. This was big country and doctors were scarce. He could move many different places and hang out his shingle, but...something brought him back here. Initially he thought it was to see his family. He wasn't so sure now.

Everyone around him stood and he realized he had mentally skipped the whole service. Another odd behavior for him. This was very frustrating. Hopefully no one would want to talk about the sermon. If he found Allie, and kept Drew close, maybe no one would get close enough to strike up a conversation.

Why anyone was frightened of Drew was beyond understanding, but for today, he'd take all the help he could get. Finding Allie wasn't difficult. She was trying to hide behind her father without looking too obvious. It was obvious, though. And the look on her face was extremely readable. She didn't want to be here…and didn't want to talk to anyone.

This couldn't be more perfect for him. He could sit with her and talk about nothing. That meant not talking about the sermon. No one would be the wiser. He could stay for a while, leave, and put this whole Sunday behind him. He was covering for Doc starting tomorrow so he needed to rest up anyway. He was excited to get back to his real work and he needed the distraction. Hopefully, it would be enough of a distraction that he could move on from all this nonsense.

As he made his way closer to Allie, he noticed she was slipping further and further behind her pa. That was very interesting. Was she avoiding everyone or only him? He quickened his steps.

"Hello, Sir." Frank held his hand out to Allie's pa. The handshake was exchanged firmly, but friendly. "Would you mind if I accompanied Allie on a stroll?" Frank fought to contain his smirk.

Say no…say no! Allie was desperately trying to send the silent message to Pa. Instead, he consented to Frank's request. This left her feeling betrayed for some reason. Stepping out from behind her father, she nodded to acknowledge Frank. Looking at her father, she tried to keep her discomfort from showing.

Frank held his arm out and she hesitantly accepted it. Then they were moving...away from her security net. It was just Frank. She had been alone with him many times in the past. *Why was it so different now*? She didn't really need to ask herself that question. She knew the answer months ago. But, she was questioning everything...and the frustration was building.

Neither spoke for a while. They just walked...and walked some more. Not really going anywhere but going everywhere—to avoid anyone else who might try to approach. It was all very odd. Frank was not usually quiet, but today he was speechless. Maybe he was just waiting for her to start up a conversation, so she tried.

"Your day...how...you are...oh..." Allie bit the inside of her cheek to stop herself. Her words came out jumbled and that made Frank stop cold and stare at her. She tried again. "I'm sorry. That didn't come out right, did it?" *That was a question. So, he had to talk now.*

"To answer your question...as jumbled as it was," he began, shaking his head. "It's an okay day. I've been distracted, thinking about this next week...working for Doc and such." He ever so slightly turned his head away, hoping he wouldn't have to elaborate on the "and such."

Why did he even say that? She wondered.

Frank paused, briefly. *Do I need to reverse this conversation?* He didn't want to be talking. He wanted to find out what was going on with her. "You're usually not flustered. Something bothering you?" Taking her hand, he turned her to directly face him.

She dropped his hand and began wringing hers. "Can't say that it is. All seems well to me." She turned her back to him and acted as though something caught her attention.

Frank was not fooled. "Allie, look at me, please." He straightened up as a sign of not backing down.

Allie slowly turned back around, but still refused to make eye contact. "Shall we sit?"

She began walking away from him, but he caught up in two strides. The quicker this was over, the better she would feel. She stopped midstride and sat in the grass, or what was once grass, instead of walking to the nearby picnic table. The former grass was brown thin sticks that poked and irritated her. *Everything is irritating these days, why not this, too?* She gave a defeated sigh.

Frank sat down next to her with a puzzled and concerned look on his face. His forehead was wrinkled, and lips pursed just a bit. He didn't talk, though. He knew her too well. Sit quietly and patiently and wait for her to speak. *If I speak first —and guess wrong—she could run with that and we'll never get to the truth.* He reached into his pocket and pulled out a penny. He put it in his palm and held it out to her.

Allie stared at his hand as he cleared his throat. Her mind started spinning. *How can I avoid the inevitable?* She could offer to get him something to drink...and then run. Looking in the distance, she noticed several women cleaning up the food table. *Is lunch over already? What happened to the time...again?* So many thoughts were running together in her head.

Heading over there would put her face-to-face with Gladys and her mother. They were apparently leading the cleanup today. She could see them giving orders to the other ladies. Sinking a little further into the itchy grass, she reached out and took Frank's penny.

"All right...since you're buying!" She attempted a bit of humor...but knew she'd failed. "Really...it's the same problem. Except this time, I made a decision. But, when I told Ma, she clearly pointed out that I needed to reconsider."

That wasn't as hard as she thought. Maybe she was overthinking everything. Resolved to bare it all on her own terms she set the penny on the ground before she continued.

Frank remained quiet and noted the difference in her behavior. Allie always held the penny until it was time to either hand it back or keep it. Now, it sat before them on the grass and he was unsure what that meant. This was not the time to focus on it though. He needed to hear every word Allie said. This change could only mean something important had...or was...happening.

Allie turned to face him a bit and started again. "I decided I was going to move to Reno, get the divorce, and move on with my life."

That caught his attention. He wanted to pause and talk about what that future life looked like for her, but she had already moved on.

"Ma not so subtly pointed out that I was, perhaps, doing the same thing I always have, leading my own life instead of being led by God. The same thing the sermon was about today, really."

Frank tucked that little bit of information away in the event a patient brings up today's sermon. Then he refocused on Allie.

"I never thought about that before. I knew God's plan was the right plan for us all. But, I never realized that by making a choice for myself without seeking His guidance first, I wasn't putting His way first. Take marrying Eddie, for instance. I thought God placed him here to give me the future that I wanted: to be a wife, a mother, and take the burden off my parents. I guess he was a gift from the devil. He tempted me, and I bit that fruit. Now, my whole life is a mess and I don't know what I'm supposed to do. Waiting on God could make my situation worse before it gets better. I don't know if I can handle worse."

Allie folded into herself. Crying would have given her some relief after spilling all of this to him, but there were no tears. No anything, really. She felt numb.

The penny still sat glistening in the sun before them. Frank didn't know what to do. This was a situation that had never played out before. Maybe staying neutral would be best since she clearly didn't buy his opinion from him.

"I couldn't give you a direction before and I can't now. I wish I could make this all go away for you."

Before he felt the need to say anything more, Allie's family pulled their wagon over to the side of the road next to where they were sitting. Frank and Allie stood expecting to say good-bye to one another.

Pa called out. "I just wanted to stop and ask if you will walk Allie home when your talk is finished, Frank. We have to be heading back, but that doesn't mean she has to right away."

Pa never even asked her. Allie just stood there, unsure how she should feel. She was an adult, a married adult, at that. But, somehow in the few months she'd been back home, life had reverted back to how it was when she was a child. Decisions made for her. Maybe her emotions were just getting the better of her. She was all over the place these days.

"Sure, Sir. Not a problem. I'll have her back soon."

Frank waved as the wagon pulled ahead. Ma made eye contact with Allie and didn't remove it until she was forced to by a bend in the road that took them out of sight.

What had just happened? Allie was now more confused than ever. Her Ma wanted her to let God make her decisions, but that clearly looked like they just did it for Him. *Maybe this was all His plan. How will I ever know?* Pushing those thoughts aside, she looked over at Frank and found him looking at her.

Allie dropped her head and Frank reached out and lifted her chin back to meet his eyes. "Like I said before, I wish I could take this all away, but I can't. No one can." His eyes were locked on hers.

Most everyone had left the lunch. Thoughts were circling her mind like birds circling prey. Each one taking a turn to dive in and have a say. She felt smothered and alone all at once. Everyone was choosing for her, but no one was solving her biggest dilemma. She wasn't a child. She was an adult who had made adult decisions. The man she loved was standing right before her. The only man she ever truly wanted to spend the rest of her life with...and he was just out of reach. She closed her eyes and before she knew it her lips were pressed to his. Then her eyes flew open.

Frank let the kiss happen. He probably shouldn't have, but it felt so right. Too right! Allie stood stock still in front of him with her lips on his and her eyes in shock. He broke the kiss and took a small step backwards. Taking her arm, he began to lead her slowly in the direction of her home. Although he enjoyed that kiss—and wanted more of them—anyone could have seen it. And that wouldn't help anything. To make matters worse, Allie looked completely torn. Her mind was fighting with itself. His mind was fighting with itself. He better get her home soon, or he wasn't sure what might happen.

They were moving more quickly, now. Allie was so confused—and her mind was adding more reasons by the second. She had to put a stop to all this madness and let her mind lead her actions. As she came to a halt, her arm tugged on Frank and spun him around to face her.

"Wait, please. I can't keep doing this. I'm going crazy."

"Allie, please don't. You ran from me the last time we started this conversation. I need to run from you to protect you this time." Frank tried to leave, but she pulled the arm she was holding closer.

"Protect me? Why is everyone making choices for me...then telling me they can't make the biggest choice of all? I can't be pulled in two directions anymore. I get treated like I'm a child, then told to make grown up decisions. When I do decide, I'm told it's incorrect. I'm tired of deciding. I just want to feel and do. I want to be free from Eddie, so I can act on my emotions with us...with you. I have wanted you for a very long time. And, now, when you want it, nothing can happen because I messed up. I'm so stupid. Why do I ruin everything?" She leaned against the back of a tree they'd stopped under and crossed her arms as a sign of protection.

Frank could not believe his ears. *She has wanted me for a very long time.* "What does that mean? Long? As in months...or years?" He stood right in front of her, making it clear he wasn't moving until this conversation was talked out.

"Years," she replied, her voice barely a whisper.

Frank's shoulders dropped, and he closed his eyes.

"You are not stupid, I'm the stupid one. If I had known this and hadn't been so rushed to start my life as a doctor, maybe this wouldn't have turned out this way. Maybe you wouldn't have had to meet Eddie in the first place. Oh, I messed up big time."

"Now what do we do?" Allie's sorrowful eyes met his and begged for an answer.

His mind went blank. His heart was thumping loudly, drowning out all other noise from his ears. Following Allie's earlier impulse, he leaned in and kissed her—more fervently than she had and she accepted the kiss. This wasn't right, but he couldn't stop himself. His control was lost.

Allie melted into the kiss as it deepened. It felt safe and right. It felt as though the earth itself was again spinning the way it should. None of her problems were spinning around with it. They had all been spun out of her head. Until they came raging back in, like they were blown in from a fire burning so close she couldn't escape the heat.

Placing her hand on his chest, she gently pushed, but Frank only pushed back with his lips. She had to stop them before this went too far. Except it had already gone too far. She was married. With that realization, she pushed harder and broke free from the kiss. Stepping slightly to the side, Frank reached out and caught himself before he fell into the tree.

"Oh, Allie, I'm so sorry!" Frank sat down with is back propped against the tree and placed his forehead on his arms that were folded on his knees.

Taking deep breaths trying to calm her own heart, she sat next to him. "Don't be sorry, Frank. We both wanted that. It's just wrong timing. I need help and I don't know what to do or how to find it." She put one of her hands on top of his. She needed some physical connection to him and that seemed like the safest choice.

They sat that way for a long while, listening to the gentle breeze blow through the leaves on the tree above them before he spoke.

"You need Him," Frank pointed up to the sky as he spoke. "Only He can help you. Anything that anyone else says will be the wrong choice. He is the only one who can fix this without causing more hardship." Frank looked her in the eyes. Both had tears building.

"I don't know how...what to do to hear him." She looked down, slightly embarrassed by the admission.

"Talk to Him, ask Him. He will give you an answer and you will know when He does. Until then...be patient. Know that He has you." Frank lifted her chin to look directly at Allie. "He has us!" Pausing briefly to reflect on what he just said, he added, "It seems I need to take my own advice."

He stood and grabbed her hand to pull her up. Wrapping her in his arms would feel so right, but it really wasn't. She wasn't his...yet. If he wanted that, he also needed to seek God and be patient. Otherwise, a wedge would be placed forever between them.

"Let's get you home. Are you ready for that?" He looked her in the eyes, knowing that she could say anything, but her eyes wouldn't fail to tell him the truth.

She closed her eyes, not allowing him to see her soul and nodded. When she opened them, her expression was that of resolve. She needed to be truthful with God first. Once her life was right with Him, she could be free and open with Frank. The problem was...she still didn't understand how to do that. But, she wouldn't bother Frank with it. She needed to figure that out on her own.

He hoped that her expression meant that she had listened and decided to stop fighting with herself and God. He would have to accept that and respect that she wasn't ready to share everything with him yet. He needed to respect her...and himself. Waiting for God's help would lead to that. Placing her hand in the crook of his arm, they began their quiet journey to her home.

CHAPTER 26

Everywhere Eddie looked there were trees. It all looked the same and it was easy to get turned around. He knew he'd been lost a few times—probably walking in circles. If he hadn't stumbled into a couple of towns that seemed to just spring up out of nowhere, he might have been lost forever.

His plan had been to follow the train, but there were many places where the landscape wouldn't allow that. Sometimes the foliage was too dense to push through. Other times, there were great ravines that added several miles to his journey. He was forced to go off the path and try to find his own way through all the trees...trees that towered to unimaginable heights. Some seemed as wide as they were tall. Green was no longer just a color for him. He was disgusted by it. He couldn't remember any time in his life that he despised a color before. He didn't understand how they could still be green with no rain. It seemed to him they should all be brown. Some were, of course, but not all. Trees were the constant in his life right now: trees, isolation, and lack of liquor.

He could scream...and no one would hear him. He wanted to scream. Whiskey was calling him—or maybe he was calling it. It didn't matter. He was out and that meant he was dry. Dry made him irritated. Dry made him feel. The briar bushes he was pushing through made his skin hurt and itch. Whiskey was good—and needed—on any trip like this. At least he was warm. Hot rather would be a better word. Whiskey could help a man stay warm on cold days and colder nights, but that wasn't an issue in June. The summer usually started off warm, but it had already been warm for months. Summer was just beginning by calendar measurements. It was already shaping up to be the longest summer of his life. The sooner he found some work to save some cash to buy some whiskey—and go get his wife—the better he would be.

Finding work was futile. He asked around in every town. The same story always followed. The heat and drought were causing less work. People were having a difficult time finding enough work for their employees. Some places were cutting back on shift hours. All of it spelled trouble for him.

If Allie were still around, he would have been gone from this area long before it completely dried up. He could have already been enjoying his time in a new town with new people—where no one knew his story. It could have been a town that was cooler, wetter, and had barrels and barrels of whiskey. A place with new girls. The ones back in Grand Forks had lost their charm. They were predictable. He needed excitement. Something new and different.

No girls. No whiskey. No food to speak of. Wretched heat! This must be Hell. That's what this is! I've up and died on the trail. And now I'm being punished for all my wrong doings.

"What about punishing those who did wrong doings to me?" He yelled up to the sky as he shook his fist. The sky was pale blue and hazy. It looked as if it were a dream floating up there. *That's it, I'm in Hell and Heaven is a dream.* He needed whiskey or Allie. He'd take her over whiskey. He could slap her around a bit and calm his rough edges. She was so good and proper. He'd spit on that. People used to think of him that way before he decided to become the person he wanted to be.

Hell, or not, he had to keep going. At this point, he'd take any kind of work there was. Maybe not for long, though. He had his standards. Just long enough to get him stable to move onto the next place. He had to push forward. He couldn't go back now. He skipped out on John. If he went back, he'd be expected to pay up. He couldn't be put off any longer. He could see it in John's eyes the last time they talked.

Eddie knew when it was time to jump ship and it all came together that day for him. He had outstayed his welcome and knew not to push it. When things began to turn downhill, they rolled faster and faster. One person upset with you will quickly lead to more. He didn't want to mess with that.

The folks in Grand Forks were a fun bunch to be

around, but they also had tempers to match. He had seen a few of those tempers from time-to-time, but never turned toward him. Going back would surely be his undoing. So...pressing forward it was. To where? He really didn't know. As long as he was headed in the general direction of Deer Lodge, he was satisfied. He knew right where Allie was. If he could ever get to her, he could take her with no issues to speak of.

That sat well with him. He needed to stay focused. This was a mission. With or without whiskey, he would see this through. Then he would make sure she never got a crazy harebrained idea of running away again. No! When he was finished, that girl would know her place and wouldn't stray from him again. He began whistling as he pushed through more brush.

CHAPTER 27

The front door to Doc's office hadn't had a rest all day, and Frank was loving every minute of it. Just as he was finishing with one patient, another was making their way in. Doc was a well-respected man and doctor in these parts and it showed by how busy he was. Of course, some of his clients were not of the people kind, but Frank seemed to be holding his own in that area as well.

He had some experience working with animals in the logging camps. Horses, oxen, and mules were the primary work animals, but dogs and chickens were common as well. They were usually treated for injuries not illness. Here it seemed to be reversed. Many animals were coming in with intestinal issues. It was easy to speculate there might be an underlying issue. Something for him to investigate later.

Frank's next patient was already settling into the waiting area. The smaller animals were carried right in the front door by their owners. The larger ones stayed outside, thankfully. He never knew when he walked out to greet his next patient if it would be one with feathers, fur, or flesh. He didn't have time to check the schedule and familiarize himself with their charts beforehand.

Washing his hands quickly and scanning the exam room to make sure everything was tidy and ready for the next patient, he stepped out to see who was next.

"Oh! Good morning, Sir. Or is it afternoon now? I've been so busy today, it seems I lost track of the time." He reached his hand out and waited for Allie's pa to stand and accept it.

"Afternoon...but just barely, Frank." As he shook Frank's hand, he pulled out an envelope from his back pocket. "I have a payment here for my account. Could I leave it here for Doc?" He held out the envelope expecting Frank to take it.

Frank ran his hand through his hair. "Ah...well...I think you should probably wait and bring it when Doc and his wife are back next week, Sir." He did not want to tell him that the bill was already paid, or basically it was anyway. After this week of working it would be. No, he was a proud man and Frank knew that he wouldn't accept his money. *If Doc tells him it'll be better.*

"Well, if you think that's best, I sure can do that. Would you write a note to let him know that I was here and will pay next week? You can put it in Allie's file where the balance owed is." He stuffed the envelope back into his pocket.

"Will do. Thank you, Sir" Frank stepped over to the

table that held the schedule to scratch a note onto a piece of paper.

"Thanks, Frank, I better head back home. Nothing is watering itself these days." He grabbed his hat from where he'd left it on the chair behind him, put it on his head, and moved towards the door.

Frank looked up from the note he was writing. "Take care, Sir. Tell Allie and...well...everyone I said hello, please."

Allie's pa continuing out the door and snickering. "Will do, Frank. Will do."

Shaking his head, he finished his note and walked over to the file cabinet that sat in the opposite corner from the overstuffed book case. He hadn't opened this cabinet before. Helping Doc with the patients was one thing, but this wasn't even Doc's area of expertise. Mrs. Leman, Doc's wife, handled all of this for him. Doc was a fine doctor but, like Frank, he couldn't stomach the accounts.

One glance into the cabinet showed that Mrs. Leman was an organized person. The files were categorized into two sections: paid and owing. Then they were organized alphabetically by last name. It didn't take much time to find Allie's, even though it was filed under her maiden name. That was probably because that's how most around here knew her.

Most people hadn't met her husband before they married and moved away. Those that did had only a brief week or two of history with him. No one knew his capabilities. Pushing all of that aside, focusing on the task at hand, he removed her file from its resting place and spread it open on the open drawer.

Mrs. Leman was very thorough. She not only had the total amount owing, but she had an itemized list of what procedures were done. Frank dropped the note in and shut the file quickly, but he wasn't fast enough to miss confirmation of what he had speculated all along. All the dots had come together, and he now had proof of his speculation. Allie had miscarried, and Doc had to finish the process her body didn't manage on its own.

Suddenly, he felt as if his shoes were made of lead. He couldn't move. It all made sense. He didn't want to think that had happened, but all the signs pointed to it before. He wanted to unsee what he just saw. *Now what?* He couldn't tell Allie, but he couldn't keep his knowing from her either. *Could anything about this summer just be easy?* The door behind him opened and in walked a very familiar voice.

"Hello Frank. How are you today?" Gladys came bustling through and made her way directly behind him.

Closing his eyes, he quickly said a prayer asking to make this quick and send her away. That was a rude thought, he knew, but desperate times called for desperate measures. *Turn around and face it.* He forced himself to comply with his brain.

"Good afternoon, Gladys. What brings you here

today?"

Holding a brown paper sack out and fixing her doe-like eyes on him, she increased the pitch of her voice. "I brought you a little lunch. I know you've been working hard and I want to make sure that you're taking care of yourself."

Frank had to figure out a way to stop her advances, but he didn't know how to do it nicely. Maybe the truth was the only way to go. Not the full truth that would stop it all at once, but small truths to shut down each one. Maybe after a few rejections, she would get the big message and stop trying.

"Thank you so much for your generosity and kindness, but my ma already saw to my needs. I must be getting to it, too, as right now is my only break in the day." He tipped his head and moved towards his bag he brought with him this morning.

"Well, I suppose, since your ma already provided, I could eat this and join you for lunch then." She smirked and took a seat against the wall.

How was she always one step ahead of him? He forced himself to unclench his teeth. "All right, if you wish, but I haven't much time until the next patient. He took the seat next to her and opened his sandwich. Fortunately, he was able to eat a bit in silence. *Maybe she only wants someone to eat with and there isn't another agenda.*

He was just about finished with his sandwich when

she seemed to be working up the nerve to talk about something. She kept opening her mouth to speak and then stuffing it with food again. *It's a bit amusing to watch, at least. Lunch isn't completely ruined.* Just as he was popping the last bite into his mouth the door burst open to reveal an out-of-breath and much worked up woman.

"Where's the doctor? We need a doctor." The lady was panting and bent over trying to catch her breath.

Frank stood and brushed the remaining crumbs from his mouth as he swallowed the half-chewed bite of sandwich...willing it to go down so he could talk. "I'm here! Please, come take a seat. Would you like a glass of water?" He was motioning her to sit.

"No, hurry! Please! My boy...it's my boy! He was walking beside me when a wagon broke loose from the horses and came over right on top of him." She spun around and headed back the way she came.

Frank followed quickly behind, leaving Gladys to herself. *Lord, when I asked you to make it quick, I did not wish for a child to be injured for it.* He looked up as he ran and made a mental note to ask for forgiveness for that one later. That lady was quicker than he'd guess from her appearance. He was working to keep up. It didn't take long before he saw a crowd had formed ahead of them.

He saw many familiar faces in the group and directed the first few men to keep everyone back. The boy was sure to be frightened and having all these people around wouldn't be helping it any. After securing the area, he knelt next to the boy, who looked to be around 5 or so, and began his initial exam.

"Son, I'm going to move you around a bit. You just let me know if anything hurts okay."

Frank began at the boy's head and proceeded down to the abdomen. First, he made sure there were no injuries to the most vital areas. The boy was writhing in pain and frightened, but he didn't change his behavior in any way to indicate the source. Moving on to his arms didn't reveal an injury, either. One leg was beneath the other, but not in an obviously out-of-place position. But, when he attempted to move them apart, he knew he'd found the issue. The boy yelped, and his mother's cries intensified.

"It looks like we have ourselves a broken leg. I'll need to take him to the office and remove his pants to be certain first though. Ma'am, will you step back, please? I need to get some of these men to fasten him to a board, so we can transport him back easier?"

Frank gently touched her shoulder to get her attention. She nodded and backed away after she kissed her son's forehead. He needed this to be as easy as he could make it. Setting a leg isn't pleasant for either patient or doctor. Trust earned now would help when setting the leg. Having her boy see that she trusted him was a big start.

It didn't take long for the men to fasten up a platform suitable to do the job and in no time, they were rolling him on it and headed down the street. Moving him onto the board was painful, but it was nothing compared to what was going to take place back at the office. He was relieved he didn't see Gladys. He needed to focus all his concentration on this boy. Having her here wouldn't help.

"Okay, men, please, leave him on the board and place it on top of the exam table. I'll need one or two of you to stay to help hold him. The rest of you can go work on getting the team and wagon put back together and fixing this problem so it doesn't happen again. Thanks for all your help today."

As the men followed his orders, Frank was rolling up his sleeves and washing his hands. Walking over to the boy he held his hand out and introduced himself.

"What's your name, son?"

The boy didn't shake his hand, he probably didn't see it. His eyes were scrunched tightly closed. He did manage to squeak out that his name was Thomas.

"Alright, Thomas, here's what we need to do."

The boy's ma was making her way in and Frank motioned to a chair for her to sit on. She did, and started wringing her hands, but remained silent.

"First, I need to cut off your pants, so I can see better. Your ma is right over there, son."

He used his eyes to point to her direction. Then he grabbed his scissors and began quickly cutting away. It didn't take long to confirm that his leg was fractured. The bone felt like it was broken in two.

"A clean break. Nothing we can't fix." Frank sounded as chipper as he could for all in the room.

"Ma'am, I am going to write you a prescription for some medicine he will need when we are finished here. I'll do that now and you can go fill it while I tend to him."

He moved to the desk, scribbled out the note, and handed it to her. She silently took it and after another look at her son, she ran out of the room. He was relieved to have her gone. What he had to do would hurt and he didn't want her to try to intervene. The men that stayed were well known by Frank. He grew up with them.

"Clyde, will you go find some straight sturdy sticks please. Make sure they're about...oh...this long," Frank requested, showing the length to him with his hands.

"Bill, I need you to go get acquainted with young Tom, here. You're going to be helping secure his trunk and arms while I work. He needs to like you."

Bill immediately walked over and started telling jokes to get him to relax a little. Bill had always been good with kids. Frank knew this and that's why he chose him for this job. Clyde returned with a handful of very fine sticks.

Frank instructed Clyde he would be securing Tom's other leg. Any grown man should be able to control a five-year-old boy, but when a body was under this much stress, they could have more power than anyone would realize. Frank wanted to be safe.

"Tom, I have to do something now that is going to hurt. I need you to be brave for me, okay?" Frank looked him in the eyes and waited briefly for the boy to find some bravery.

"Okay, I'm going to count to three. I need everyone ready. Tom, you just relax and know it will feel better soon."

Frank positioned himself and began counting. It was all over in a blink. The bone cooperated, thankfully. Tom screamed, but quickly calmed back down. Clyde and Bill were able to keep him still and backed off a little when Frank was finished. They stayed that way for a bit while they made sure that Tom had calmed down enough so he wouldn't move. Meanwhile, Frank was preparing the plaster mixture.

Now that everything was quiet, he could hear movement out in the other room.

"Clyde? Will you tell whoever is out there that I am busy and will be for a while? They are going to need to reschedule." Clyde willingly obliged. His face showed that he needed to calm down a bit himself.

Frank wanted to keep Bill talking with Tom a little longer. His attention was making a great difference.

Working as quickly as possible, Frank applied the plaster cast. Tom's ma returned and went straight to her chair. After a few moments, she was relaxed enough to come stand next to Tom and stroke his hair. Bill took that as an opportunity to quietly step out of the room. Before he left though, Frank stopped him and made sure he wouldn't go too far. Clyde and Bill would need to carry Tom home. Applying the cast didn't take nearly as long as it used to, but it still was a process that required a bit of patience. When he finished, he secured it all with the sticks that Clyde had brought in earlier and wrapped it all in a soft cloth to keep the sticks in place. This way the cast could dry and harden thoroughly, and Tom could head home instead of waiting here until that point.

The cast stretched well above and below the break to make sure once it had dried it couldn't shift. Instructions were given to Tom's ma, and Clyde and Bill were called back in to help get Tom moved home to his own bed. He would be able to get up with crutches in a couple of days, but resting was the best thing for him now.

With that emergency finished and the exam room clean again, Frank was able to get back to his day. Looking at the schedule book, he saw where Clyde had moved a couple of appointments to later in the week. He only had a few more people to see before he could head home. He loved the rush of adrenaline when emergencies occurred, but he was always tired afterward. Heading home was all he wanted to do, and he was glad that would be happening soon.

Frank welcomed the next patient and got back to work. The day continued, and everything went smoothly. It wasn't until Frank was locking up that he remembered the information in Allie's file. Dread settled in and he decided to push it all aside for now. He needed to sleep first and think on this with a fresh brain tomorrow. Home and sleep, and maybe some of Ma's fine cooking, that was all he needed right now.

CHAPTER 28

Working three days a week and doing all five days of chores at home in the remaining two was exhausting. It was paying off though. She had already received her first pay. Mr. Ashton gave it to her before he ducked back into the printing room, where he spent most of his time.

After giving some to her parents, there wouldn't be much left to tuck away, but it was more than she had a week ago. She was working on the next chapter of her life. What that chapter would look like was anyone's guess at this point.

She had spent some time reflecting on what Frank had said, but she wasn't sure how to go about it. The last time she remembered truly speaking with God, she had been angry. She realized she was still angry. Blaming God for putting her in this mess was easy, but as Ma pointed out—not too subtly—Allie's finger might not have been pointing in the correct direction. Should she have pointed that finger at her own chest instead? It was all too confusing to work out in one afternoon.

She had just finished sweeping up and putting the broom away when the senior Mr. Ashton walked in.

"Allie, I'd like to talk with you in my office if you have the time. I know you're ready to head home, but it will only take a few minutes."

"Sure! I'll be right there, Sir."

Mr. Ashton turned and headed for his office behind the frosted glass door. She took off her apron and brushed off her dusty skirt. She hung her apron next to the broom in the cleaning closet and headed for his office.

"Please sit," Mr. Ashton boomed, as he was going over some papers cluttering the top of his desk. Allie did as he instructed and waited for him to speak.

"Allie, I just wanted to let you know that we appreciate all that you are doing around here. The place looks great. You're doing a fine job," he paused.

"Thank you, Mr. Ashton. I am really enjoying it here." Allie sat up a bit straighter, welcoming the praise she didn't expect.

"Yes...well..., I do need to let you know that we have been getting reports of possible layoffs all around this region. The railroad, mine, and timber industries are being forced to halt operations in some locations due to the fires."

"I see. I fail to see what this has to do with me

though, Sir." Allie started fidgeting.

Mr. Ashton stood and walked to stare into a picture hanging on his wall. "If those reports turn out to be true, I may have to let you go, so I can help at least one man out. I could give him your job. It doesn't pay much I know, but many men are going to be desperate for anything to help take care of their families. You have your pa and ma to look after you. I know you'll fair well, but I need to do what I can to help others."

Allie couldn't breathe. She knew this was all too good to be true. She wanted to get up and run from here, but she remained quietly in her seat.

Mr. Ashton turned and saw her rigid posture and expression. "Ah...now...Allie, I'm not saying you don't have a job right now. This is only if the number of layoffs they are projecting actually happen. Maybe we will have a storm roll in that douses all the fires and we won't need to worry about this. Put it out of your mind for now. I just wanted to give you some notice should the need arise, but I can see it upset you. Go ahead and head on home. I'll see you next week."

Allie stood and gave a brief nod before turning and fleeing into the fresh air. She needed to breathe. The walls felt as though they were closing in on her. Unfortunately, she couldn't take very long to compose herself. Gladys was making her way towards her. This was the last person she wanted to be with right now. She would rather be alone...but anyone was better than this.

"Allie! There you are. I've been looking for you for a few days now." Once Gladys reached her, she looked Allie over—moving her eyes but not her head. "Well, are you all right dear? You look pale." Her voice changing to concern, but her appearance anything but. She put her arm around Allie and guided her to the closest bench.

That was Gladys, a tornado that woman could be.

"Yes, I'm fine. It's just so hot these days. I'm not sure what's better, sitting out here where the sun feels like it's cooking you or sitting inside where it's so stuffy you can't breathe."

"There are many things these days that take one's breath away aren't there?" Gladys raised her eyebrows and looked at Allie who was confused by what that meant. "What are you doing outside of the paper? Did you bring them some news to print?" She smoothed out her skirt and focused down the road.

"No. Actually, I am an employee for the paper now. Nothing big but doing something that is mine. It feels good." She didn't mind telling Gladys that. Whatever she said would be spread through her circles and on to her ma. Then her ma would spread it even further. But she was proud of this information, even if it might only be temporary.

"Ah, that's nice. Well, I must be off, but before I go, I have something of yours." She stood and reached into the pocket of her skirt.

"You do?" Allie was very perplexed. *What could she have of mine?*

Gladys had something small in her outstretched hand and dropped it into Allie's open palm. "Seems you left this behind after church services." When Allie glanced back up, she could see the unpleasant look Gladys had aimed toward her. Then Gladys said, "Keep away from Frank. I saw what you two did...very ungodly...and on church grounds, nonetheless. You are a married woman! I shouldn't be required to remind you of that. But I feel it is my place as a Christian and an upstanding citizen of this fine community. We do not treat your kind very well in these parts, *Mrs.* Coghill. Take your money somewhere with people more forgiving of your situation or seek forgiveness from the Lord and change your ways. Now! Frank and I are becoming close and your hands and lips *will* remain off him. You will not taint his reputation with your loose behavior any longer." Gladys turned briskly, leaving a bewildered Allie behind.

Looking down into her palm, she saw the penny. It must have been the one that Frank gave her on Sunday that they left behind in the grass. That means that Gladys—most likely accompanied by her mother—saw them kiss.

Gladys thought he paid me for the kiss. Wait...did she really only think I was worth a penny? She has some nerve.

Allie's stomach rolled. This day had gone from bad

to worse and was about to get downright ugly. She could see Frank making his way towards her...with Gladys still in sight.

Clutching her skirts to lift them above her feet she began to run. She ran as quickly as she could, but she could hear footsteps pounding behind her. If he was going to be so insistent, she needed to find some place private. With them both running down the main street, they were beginning to draw attention. She ducked quickly between two store fronts and slowed her pace. Keeping her back towards him she calmed her breathing and forced down the knot that formed in her throat.

Frank placed his palm on her shoulder. "Allie, why are..."

"Frank, we can't do this now," she blurted out to silence him. "A scene has already been made. There is something you don't know, and I will tell you in private. But, we can't be seen together in public again." Then she was running again, leaving Frank standing confused in the shadows of the two buildings.

When he turned, he saw Gladys standing in the sunlight looking in on him. Pointing his finger and walking towards her, he began to spit out the words, "You! What did you say to her? I saw you talking to her back there and now she's upset about something. Leave her alone. She doesn't need you interfering with anything." He spun around to follow her as Gladys began yelling back

"Frank, wait. I didn't say anything to upset her." Raising her voice further she added, "If she's upset, it's her own fault. I only gave her something she left at church last Sunday. Really, I am just being helpful." She huffed as Frank was moving farther and farther away.

Frank could care less what she had to say. He needed to find Allie and straighten out whatever this was. Gladys was not going to mess this up for him. Fortunately, he knew where to look and headed straight for the creek behind her house. That was her place when she wanted time alone.

Hopefully, he could calm himself down on his way. He was in a rage, but he didn't even know why. Allie was upset and that made him upset, but for what he had no idea why. She needed him level-headed, though. Both upset was not going to help either one.

It wouldn't take long to get there, running all the way. But when Frank arrived, she was nowhere to be found. He stopped at the creek edge just below the big tree where she usually sat. He scanned up and down the water hoping he'd find her wading, but the water was too shallow, and wading wasn't possible now. There had been no rain. Things needed to change quickly, or this would be a life-changing summer for folks in these parts. He didn't want to think of all the problems the dry land could cause. He had his own immediate problems, even if he didn't know all the details just yet.

"Frank? Is that you?" Allie's ma hollered from the

back of the house.

Frank had just dipped his hat in the creek and was putting it on to cool his head, "Yes, Ma'am. Just looking for Allie. Do you know where I might find her?"

Allie's ma was standing on the porch with her arm raised to shade her eyes from the sun. "She left here this morning...went to work. She should be back soon. You could wait here for her, if you like."

Frank decided not to share that Allie wasn't in town anymore—and she was upset. Allie could tell them what she wanted when she wanted. That wasn't his to tell.

"Thanks, but I think I'll head back into town and meet her another time. I just finished my week up at Doc's and thought I'd stop in to see how she was doing. I'm sure I'll run into her soon. You take care though."

He started to head back in the direction he'd come when she hollered back, "You want me to let her know you were here?"

Frank paused and turned around. "No, Ma'am. It's all right. I'll see her soon enough. Thank you though."

Allie clearly wanted to be alone. He needed to respect that—no matter how maddening it was not knowing what had happened. He decided to take the long way back to town, so he could think a while without any interference.

Gladys said she'd found something Allie left at church. He didn't know what that could be, but it gave him something to ponder while he was deciding what next to do. Maybe his own ma could shed some light on all of this. She understood women more than he did.

With the answer of his next step made, Frank felt more confident in how to move forward. Surely his ma would know what to do. Maybe this was all just a silly girl issue. And, maybe, he had nothing to fret about. He felt hopeful that all of this was just a slight hiccup on the path to their future together. He needed to cling to that hope.

CHAPTER 29

Talking with Blinne put Allie at ease. She was always the level-headed one in their friendship. On the outside Blinne appeared to be full of life. People expected her personality to match her fire-red hair. She was calm and collected though, and able to look into a situation and see details that Allie never noticed.

One of those details that Blinne pointed out to her was that both she and Frank had wonderful reputations here. On the other hand, the reputation Gladys had made for herself left much to be desired. She was known for spreading false words about town and this, most likely, would be added to that long list.

Of course, if anyone else saw the kiss, they could back up her story. Most people—those that mattered anyway—would not believe that Allie was leaving her faith behind and relying on other means to provide for herself. Nor, for that matter, would anyone believe that Frank would partake in that behavior.

Blinne also pointed out they would need to weather whatever storm this might bring. Gladys still had her followers, despite her reputation as a gossip. They would play this game as long as they possibly could. Staying clear of Frank was important to shutting this down as quickly as possible. That's why Allie was on her way to get a note to Frank to meet her at George and Blinne's.

If anyone saw them together there, it could be played off as pure coincidence. Everyone knew Allie and Blinne were close friends. She could be there helping and visiting her friend when Frank shows up on his doctor rounds to check Lena and Blinne. Getting all of this in the open with Frank—and his agreement to the plan—was her first priority.

Doc Leman was back from his vacation. Hopefully, Frank wouldn't be there, too. She could stop in and see how he and his wife enjoyed their trip. Then, casually, she could ask him to give Frank this note...and head back home. That was the first step of the plan, anyway. She was on her way. The walk was a familiar one to her. The temperature was not. The end of June meant that summer was just beginning—officially, that is. Summer had been here for a couple of months already. With the weather so off-kilter to the calendar these days, maybe fall would come early. *One could hope!* She was making her way around the corner to Doc's office.

Stepping inside, Allie noticed a new addition to the office. Sitting next to the schedule book was a pitcher of water with some tin mugs stacked up. Apparently, Doc saw the need to hydrate those who came trekking in from this heat. She walked everywhere, too, not being fortunate enough to have the wagon when she needed it. Pa needed to have access to it whenever he needed it. *And the horses don't have to work in this heat on my account!* Pa worked them early in the morning and late at night. The horses could rest in the shade during the heat of the day.

Grabbing the pitcher and a mug, she helped herself and sat down to wait for Doc. She could hear someone working. With the first cup of water down, she stood and refilled it before retaking her seat. The water wasn't cold, but it did feel heavenly sliding down her parched throat. *This could possibly be the best idea he's ever had!* She was sitting quietly, thinking to herself, when Doc came through the door. He appeared alone and was carrying a bowl full of used rags. Allie stood before speaking. "Hi, Doc!"

"Well, hello, Allie. What brings you here today?" Doc stopped his forward movement and waited for her reply.

"I was just wanting to see how your trip went." She hoped she didn't hesitate too much and sounded convincing enough to make him believe that was her only reason for being there. She walked over and set the mug down on the table—some distance from the stacked ones.

Doc shuffled his feet a moment before asking her to hold her thought for a moment.

"Let me take care of this bowl first. Then we can

catch up. My last patient needed some teeth pulled. I was just cleaning up after that mess. The mouth tends to bleed more than other areas."

Doc stepped outside, and Allie retook her seat, thankful that the bowl was moving farther away from her with every second. Blood tended to make her stomach churn a bit. Since it was already dancing around nervously, she didn't need to add to it.

Doc was taking his time. That increased her nervousness. She needed this to go along quickly...and be gone before Frank returned. Talking this out with Frank was a must, but she couldn't do that here. She also knew that if he saw her, everything would be a bit awkward. That would further complicate things. She didn't want to be seen with him by anyone. Even if they were in the company of Doc, who could vouch for their behavior. That is, if he ever returned. She stood and began pacing the little room as she waited for Doc.

When Doc returned, he explained that he had walked the rags back to his house for his wife to tend to. Doc lived in town—just around the corner—so the trip was short. It had seemed a long while to Allie while she was waiting. Now that Doc was back, she realized it really hadn't taken long at all.

"So, you came all this way to hear about my trip, did you?" Looking questioningly at Allie.

Apparently, she couldn't hide the truth from him very well, but she still needed to try. *Let him think what he wants.* She couldn't tell him the truth, but he could speculate all he wanted. She knew he wouldn't spread his speculations around. "I was in town running some errands and thought I would stop in to see you." *Not technically a lie!* She justified her means to herself.

"Well," Doc sat and motioned for Allie to join him. "Our trip went rather well. It's good to see and catch up with family and know all are doing well. A very pleasant trip indeed."

Short and sweet. This wasn't going to be dragged out, Allie thought, trying to come up with something else to say. "I'm glad all went well." She tried to hide her anguish. *That was all I could come up with?* The conversation needed to be dragged out so the note to Frank appeared as a side reason for coming. Luckily, Doc seemed to have something else to discuss.

Standing and walking over to his cabinet he pulled out a file and shuffled through some papers. "I would like you to take this to your father, please." He walked back towards her and held the paper out for her to take. "I would, but I have too much work to catch up on. Having Frank here was a blessing, of course, but some of my patients chose to wait to be seen."

Allie reached for the paper but failed to understand what was written on it. It didn't make sense. Her pa was going to make payments on the tab, she knew. She had given them a large portion of her own earnings—but that was only a small fraction of the total bill. *Ma and Pa could not have paid all this amount already*. She didn't know their exact finances, but knew they were just getting by—with the time of year, lack of rain, and crop issues. If any crop survived, it wouldn't be sold until harvest. That money would be needed to live on for the year, and buy what was needed for planting next year. The drought was causing more hardship than her family had ever dealt with in the past. This was new territory for them all.

"Doc, I'm sorry. Of course, I will give this to him, but I'm not sure I completely understand what this means."

"It means it's paid. Nothing else is required." He crossed his arms in satisfaction leaving a slight smirk on his lips.

"This is wonderful news, of course! I'm just not sure how it's possible." She pulled the paper to her chest and clung to it with a feeling of hope for the future. She wouldn't need to save for this! "Thank you, I will take this to him right away." She didn't wait for him to comment as she turned and flew out the door. She reached the outskirts of town before she realized she hadn't left the note for Frank. She stopped in her tracks...and knew she needed to turn around. She hoped Frank would still be out. She took a chance the first time. Adding a second trip only increased the odds of running into him. She needed to make this fast.

Allie headed straight back to Doc's office at a brisk pace. As she made her way around the last corner, she spotted Frank at the end of the street. His back was toward her and he was in a conversation with someone. She could see a skirt peeking out from beyond him but couldn't identify her. She turned from him and pushed through the door quickly. Doc was making notes in his schedule book and looked up, pencil still in hand, when she entered.

"You're back. Is something wrong?"

She held the note out for him. "No, nothing is wrong. I just forgot to ask you to give this to Frank."

Doc set the pencil down. "He'll be here any minute. You can give it directly to him."

She knew she was starting to panic and just dropped the note on top of the schedule book.

"I need to get home and talk to Pa. Thank you, though. Tell Frank I said hello, please."

Her exit was so quick, she left the door slightly ajar. As she made her way down the steps, she glanced quickly in the direction she had seen Frank. He wasn't there, but Gladys was close by and wearing a dress the same color as the person who had been talking to Frank. She put her head down and moved out of town as quickly as possible. Getting home was all she could think about. She had to focus on the task at hand. She didn't want to think about why Frank and Gladys were talking.

At least, she was trying not to think about it, but her brain had its own ideas about what to think about on this walk back home. Gladys was front and center in those thoughts. She needed to talk to Frank. She hoped he would follow the instructions in the note. It would drive her mad to speculate on whether Gladys was just flirting more with him or if she was telling him anything about what she saw.

Arriving home, Allie immediately sought out Pa. He was in the barn pouring more water for the animals. Everything revolved around water these days. Drew was in the corner brushing down one of the horses.

"Hi, Pa!"

"Oh, hello, dear. Did you have a nice walk to town?" Pa didn't look up as he began to check on the animals. The chicks were quickly turning into pullets and he could more easily see which would be hens and which would be roosters. The roosters could be sold or traded.

"I have something for you. Maybe you know more about it than I do, though." She held out the paper and waited for Pa to wipe his hands on the towel that he carried in his back pocket.

He reached for the paper and Allie watched his face for clues. First, his brows furrowed together, then they shot up on his forehead. "Did you pay the bill?" He looked up at Allie and waited for her answer.

She shook her head. "I thought you would know about this."

"I have no idea. I went to make a payment several days ago while Doc was gone. Frank said to hang onto it, so I could talk to Doc about it when he got back." *Frank!* He decided that might need further investigation.

Fr...ank? She hesitated mid-thought on his name as understanding dawned. Not wanting to tip off Pa, she made a mental note to add it to the list of items they needed to discuss.

"Well, I'm not sure how it all worked out, but that is one item no one needs to worry about anymore."

"Yes, yes!" But his mind was clearly elsewhere. "Tell Ma I will be in shortly for dinner? I need to finish up here and wash up first."

Allie knew that this was a way to dismiss her. Pa was curious and wanted time to think. She hoped she would have a chance to meet with Frank before Pa beat her to it. She wasn't sure if Pa would be willing to let this pass. Giving Frank some notice would help.

"I will! And, I'll go help her get it ready."

Allie left Pa to think. She needed to do the same, but that would have to wait. The meeting with Frank couldn't come soon enough, but she needed to be patient and wait it out. There was never a shortage of things to occupy her time. She would get a lot done while she was waiting.

CHAPTER 30

The sky was not its normal bright blue on the walk to Blinne's. The sun was hiding behind the clouds. It was still warm, but the clouds brought hope that they might see rain soon.

The closer she came to seeing Frank again, the more conflicted she felt. Allie had pushed through her work at the paper and kept busy at home over the last several days. She thought she was ready to confront the situation head on and push Frank away to protect him, but she didn't know if she could go through with it.

Only two people really knew her heart: Frank and Blinne. Pushing one away could rip her heart open again. She needed to rely on God, but she was still struggling with how to do that. She couldn't shake the feeling that even meeting with Frank was taking matters into her own hand. She couldn't think of another option to shut Gladys down, so the fire that was her life smoldering around her wouldn't spread further. She needed to keep pushing forward.

Blinne knew she was coming, so instead of

knocking, Allie let herself in. She had arrived before Frank as was the plan. She hoped Frank would follow the instructions in the note.

"Good morning!" She picked up the broom and started in. After all, she was supposed to be here helping Blinne.

"Is it still morning? I've been up forever it seems." Blinne was sitting in the rocker with Lena in her arms.

"Blinne, you don't look well. Are you all right?" Allie set the broom down and walked over to her.

Blinne forced her eyes open. Just trying to form thoughts was difficult. "I just seem to have a slight cold. I'll be okay, but Lena has it, too. I've been up all night with her."

Before Allie even touched Blinne's forehead, she could feel the fever. "Blinne, where is George?" There was no response. "I'll be right back. I'm just headed to the well to get some water."

She left the drowsy Blinne and quickly returned with the bucket of water. Blinne was fast asleep. Allie set the bucket down near Blinne. She seemed unaware when Allie took Lena from her arms. Still holding Lena in one arm, Allie retrieved the rag from the table, dunked it in the bucket, and tried to squeeze it out the best she could with only one hand. Looking down at Lena, she was unsure what to do next.

Holding a baby was all she ever did with them. She

didn't grow up around babies, so she didn't have any first-hand knowledge. She pulled the rag off Blinne and was dipping it back in the water when a knock came on the door.

Leaving the rag in the bucket, she opened the door to a wonderful sight. Frank had come. The reason for his visit had left her mind. She grabbed his arm and pulled him in. "Thank you! Oh! Thank you! They are both sick and I don't know what to do."

Frank took Lena from Allie and started examining her. He unwrapped the blanket that swaddled her and put his ear to her chest and back. "She just seems to be a bit stuffy. Can you put some water on the stove and get it to boil? Then we can get her near the steam. That should help open up her nose a bit. We just need to open it up a bit and she should be fine."

Allie immediately set to work, thankful for something to do. Frank found Lena's cradle nearby and gently placed her in it before going to check on Blinne. He examined her and went back to the bedroom. Allie wasn't sure what he was doing as she kept busy with her task. When Frank reappeared, he walked back to Blinne and gently lifted her in his arms and carried her back to the bedroom. Blinne didn't wake during all of that.

Allie started the fire and put the kettle of water on top of the stove before walking toward the bedroom. She picked up Lena and held her while she stood in the doorway and watched Frank work. He must have felt her presence. His back was to her, but he spoke knowing she was there.

"She has a fever, but I don't think it's as serious as it could be. Lena is sick with no fever. I think Blinne is just overly exhausted. She needs to rest, and I'll stay to make sure the fever doesn't spike, but I think her body is just tired and can't fight the basic cold."

Allie shuddered with relief and gave Lena a little squeeze before stepping back out into the main room. She sat in the rocker that Blinne had been in and reveled in the beauty of little Lena's bright blue eyes looking up at her.

"Your momma will be just fine, little one."

Lena cooed back, making Allie smile. The two sat there like that for a few minutes. Each one staring into the other's eyes. Allie's heart was open, ready and waiting for the love of her own child that would never be. Little Lena's love was melting her heart. She yearned for a child in her future. In that moment, with the wonder in her eyes as big as saucers looking up into Allie's, all felt right with the world. Hope was found. Life continued onward and good times were to be found in the future. Maybe not with her own flesh and blood, but she knew she would not let the tragedy that occurred from her mistake ruin her future.

Where there's a will, there's a way! She rocked a bit faster as her heart also quickened its pace knowing...somehow...some things would work out. *Lena doesn't need a mother, thank goodness. But other children do.* A sound from the back startled her out of her thoughts. Allie stood and made her way to the stove where the water was beginning to boil. George walked in through the back.

"Hi, Allie! How are you today?" He grabbed himself a mug from the cupboard and came over to tickle Lena's toes.

"I'm okay, George." Allie let out her breath and then inhaled sharply. "I'm okay, but Lena here has a bit of a cold. She's going to be okay, of course," she added quickly. "That's why we're standing here near the steam." George held his hands out to take his daughter and Allie obliged. "The steam is supposed to help her breathe easier."

"Where's Blinne?" George's face was a mixture of concern and confusion.

"Come with me, please."

Allie led the way to the bedroom. George's face paled when he saw Frank kneeling by the side of the bed next to his sleeping wife. George handed Lena back to Allie and cautiously walked over to the side of the bed opposite Frank.

"George. I'm pretty sure she is going to be fine." Frank stood as he tried to reassure him.

"What do you mean *pretty sure*? What's wrong with her?"

"I think she just has the same cold that Lena has. But, with taking care of a new baby and getting sick, her body was simply too weak to fight it without a fever to help. She should pull out okay as long as we let her get plenty of rest and keep this fever in check."

"Is there anything I can do?"

Frank walked around and stood next to George. "Of course. If you want to stay with her and keep changing the cool rag on her head, you may. That was all I was doing right now."

George nodded and sat down next to her.

"Just don't get your body too close. I don't want your heat driving up hers, and holler if you need anything. I'm not leaving yet, but I'll be just outside the door." Frank grabbed Allie's elbow and gently turned her towards the door and nudged her forward. "Let me take Lena and I'll work on getting her nose cleared. Would you start something for them to eat later?"

Allie handed Lena over, after she kissed her forehead, and nodded in reply to preparing a meal.

"Thank you, Allie. She will need to build up her strength once this fever brakes," Frank explained, as he walked Lena over to the stove and made a tent with a towel placing himself and Lena under it. Allie headed to the cellar to see what she had to work with.

When she returned, Lena and Frank were both still under the towel. She heard Frank giggling and Lena was making little sniffing sounds. Allie set down what would become a meal on the table and began peeling potatoes and carrots. Frank pulled the towel off and used it to wipe Lena's nose.

"Works like a charm those tents. The steam helps loosen what's stuck in there and Lena began sneezing. I think she will be good for a while." He put Lena back in her cradle. As he stepped back into the kitchen, he asked Allie, "What can I do to help you?"

Allie was taken back a bit. Even her own pa didn't help in the kitchen.

"I suppose you can grab a knife and help peel." She watched him work and realized this wasn't his first time. He was peeling faster than she did. "I guess living alone has made you learn some skills men normally don't need."

"Actually, my ma taught me before I left. She knew I needed some basic skills when I headed out a few years ago. I can sew, too!" Frank watched as Allie took that information in. She looked confused at first before breaking out into full laughter. "All right, so I can't make my own clothes. I can sew up a hole though. It's not perfect or pretty, but it does the job.

Allie thought for a moment. "I guess sewing is not too far off from doctoring. You did sew me up. It probably is similar."

"You're right. I was a bit ahead of the others in my class because of my ma's teachings. I work better on skin then on cloth, though."

He wanted to get to the reason for this meeting, but he didn't want to push her too fast. She was broken, but mending. The healing needed to continue. Still keeping the conversation light, he knew they would eventually talk about whatever she needed to discuss.

"You know...ever since you set me up with Gladys, she has been relentlessly pursuing me." He was smiling, she was not. He thought that would be a safe subject. Her reaction led him to believe that Gladys must play a bigger role in this meeting than he initially thought. He knew, based on the last conversation with Allie, that Gladys had said something to cause her distress. Gladys was usually just the messenger of bad news or gossip, though. Apparently not...this time.

Allie set her knife down and wiped her hands on a cloth. "Gladys is the exact reason why I called you here. Do you remember our time after church a few weeks ago, when we were sitting in the grass after everyone left?"

Frank was thinking back and reveling in the memories of their lips connecting. The timing was all off, but that didn't mean he didn't like it. "Yes, vividly."

She blushed, understanding what he was commenting on. "The penny was left behind, and we were not alone."

Frank was rapidly trying to piece together that information with what he already knew. Gladys had mentioned she gave Allie something. "Please explain."

She wrung her hands. "Well, it seems Gladys, and probably her mother, witnessed our display. After we left, she must have gone over and found the penny. She thinks I was paid for my, ahem, services." She let Frank finish the puzzle to decipher the full meaning.

His face went from confusion, to dawning, to angrier than she had ever seen him before.

"That not only questions your behavior, but mine as well! How does she think doing that would help her cause? She has no chance with me, but she doesn't know that yet. If she spreads this, we will both suffer ridicule and condemnation." He began pacing.

"Sh!" Allie moved in front of him and forced him to stop mid-step. "We don't want to wake Blinne. Wearing a path in their floor is not going to change this predicament, either. We need a plan."

"Yes!" His mind was spinning, and his eyes were darting around the room. "I will handle Gladys!" He began pacing again.

Allie sat at the table and let Frank pace away. "Frank, you can't just handle Gladys. Her mother is also aware, and I'm sure they have already begun spreading rumors."

Frank stopped and stared at Allie. "Yes, I can. I know exactly what will get them both to be quiet. I can beat them at their own game." Frank walked over to Allie and took the seat next to her. "Oh, Allie, you have enough to worry about. I'm sorry that this has been added. Let me handle it." He looked into her eyes with his jaw set in determination.

Allie sat quiet for a moment. Her eyes moved to the table and her hands that were folded on top of it. "Will you handle it the same way you handled my medical bill?" She looked up at him.

It was Frank's turn to sit quietly now. He took a deep breath. "Yes."

Lena began to stir. Allie pushed herself up from the table and walked over to pick her up.

"Frank, I know   you meant well, but I wanted to take care of that bill. My pa was working on it and I was going to pay him back. I need to take care of myself. I can't go from one man to another right now. I need to stand on my own two feet and focus on myself and God. Besides, my pa wasn't exactly happy when he found out. He is a proud man. He takes care of his family."

Frank stood and walked over to Allie. "I'm sorry. I know how you feel, really, I do. I want to take as much of this away as I can, so you can heal faster. I'll speak with your father. Allie, I love you."

She stared blankly at him. She knew his feelings but hearing them was wonderful. As she was opening her mouth to reply, George pushed open the door.

"She's awake, Doc."

Frank immediately rushed in and Allie followed stopping at the threshold. He was examining her again. "Fever's gone. Oh, thank God. Allie, please bring Lena over here. I'm sure she is hungry." Allie did as she was told and then walked out of the room to give Blinne some privacy. Frank followed shortly after. "Allie, I'm going to go. I have some things to take care of."

She knew what he wanted to do and wouldn't stop him. There was no use trying. "I'm going to stay and finish this meal. I may clean up a bit around here, too, before I leave."

"Bye, Allie!" Frank froze looking into her eyes.

"Frank, part of what I wanted to say to you is we need to lay low for a while. We can't be seen in public for now, at least until this rumor dies out. I don't want to feed whatever has been started."

"I understand, although it will be hard for me to do." He placed his hand on her cheek and gently touched his lips to hers before making his way out and closing the door. Allie stood there for a few minutes. Her lips were warm, she touched them, burning this memory into her mind. She could hear the happy little family in the bedroom. Someday, maybe she could have that. She held onto that thought as she went back to her work.

CHAPTER 31

Frank knew he needed to cool off before he spoke with Gladys. Talking with Allie's pa would have to be first on his list...to give himself more time to calm down. He left George and Blinne's knowing that Blinne would be fine. Her fever broke and she appeared to have regained some strength when he handed Lena to her.

As he made the trek to Allie's home, he hoped that putting some distance between the two of them could help calm them both. His emotions were stirred up and he needed to think with a clear head. Reaching the last crest, he could see the small dot ahead that was the house with a bigger dot to the side that made up the barn.

The weather had changed a bit over the last few days—turning to hot and muggy. The sky was dark and talk of thunderstorm possibilities were being spread like wildfire in town. There wasn't much you could do to prepare for the possible outcomes of those, but Frank was sure that he would find Allie's pa in the barn doing whatever he could to be ready for anything.

Allie's pa was a proud man and a hard worker at that. The only time Frank ever saw him sit idle was in church. He sat so still it looked like he'd figured out how to sleep with his eyes open. The benches were so uncomfortable, but he never showed any sign of discomfort. He was a tough man and that didn't settle Frank a bit. He knew he'd crossed a boundary, but he hoped that the line he crossed was not solid black where Allie's forceful father was concerned.

Making his way to the barn's big double doors, Frank tried to figure out the best way to start the conversation. Nothing sounded quite right, though. So, he decided to let the words flow however they came out. *What will be, will be!* He pushed through and blinked his eyes to adjust them to the relative darkness inside.

"Frank, I'm glad you stopped in. I need to have a word with you." Pa walked over to Frank and wiped his hands on his pants before holding out his right hand to offer a shake.

Frank shook it. "Yes, Sir. I spoke with Allie a while ago and knew I should come and explain myself."

Pa crossed his arms on his chest and widened his stance. He remained quiet and let Frank talk.

Frank hesitated, hoping that he wouldn't have to be the first to dive into this, but realized quickly that if he didn't talk, a staring match would ensue.

"Sir, I paid Allie's doctor bill."

Pa remained unfazed. He already knew...or had suspected it. He continued his stance while Frank continued.

"I should have spoken with you first. I wanted to help, and I saw a way I could." Frank rubbed the side of his face and looked down at his feet.

"You shouldn't have done that. She is not your responsibility, son."

"I know, Sir. But, it wasn't much trouble for me to do this."

"Well, I'm glad you have money to pay other's debt. That must feel real good," Pa looked annoyed.

"No, no. It wasn't like that. I didn't pay in terms of money. Well...not in the sense you're thinking anyway. I worked it off when I covered for Doc while he was on his trip."

"I see," Pa rubbed his beard. "Well, that does change things a bit. What are your intentions with my daughter?"

Frank didn't know if it changed things for good or bad, but he continued to stay still and quiet. The question threw him. This was not the direction he envisioned this conversation going.

"Sir, may I be clear with you?"

"Oh, please do. I really dislike beating around the

bush!"

"I love her." Frank let that hang there.

Pa shook his head. "I suspected that. What do you plan to do about it?"

Frank turned and walked to the pig pen. Staring down to talk to the pig was not as intimidating as speaking directly to Allie's pa.

"I don't know, Sir. I've been waiting. I know she loves me, but she is married. I'm not going to ruin her reputation or mine." He turned and faced Pa. "...or the families', for that matter."

Pa gave a brief nod and let Frank continue.

"I can see a future together, but I know we need to wait until God plays out the current marriage."

"I'm glad you are waiting on Him. Allie has always followed herself first. She has gone from one mess to another in this life. I'm hoping this will finally make her slow down and realize that patience pays off more in the end then rushing to a decision. I don't know how this marriage is going to play out. Can't say that I like the man, but the law is on his side right now. I have to trust in God to make this right."

Frank let the words he heard sink in. The man's faith was so strong. Allie came home broken and bruised and this man remained calm and patient. Frank was ready to seek blood in the beginning, but this man showed no sign of wanting revenge.

"Sir, I hope someday I grow to be the man you are. I'm not sure how you remain in your faith so unwaveringly."

"No one ever said I never wavered. I'm still a man. I would love to make Eddie feel the same pain that he caused Allie...and us. I don't know the whole story, though."

Frank was confused by this. Was there more than he knew?

"I'm sorry, Sir. I'm not following."

"Eddie's story, Frank. I don't know his story. Only God does. Allie's strong. She takes after her mother there. Eddie is very weak. I'm not sure what happened to him, but there is a story there. Not to say that it's okay...what he has done, but I need to trust in God that He will sort all of this out in a better way than I can.

"He knows us all in ways that we can't even know ourselves. He's been with us through it all. His way is the only rightful way. If I stepped in, I would only mess things up even more for Allie. I don't know how long this will take or if Allie will need to suffer anymore, but I need to sit back and patiently wait for Him. God will fix this—if Allie lets Him."

Frank nodded his understanding and continued to listen.

"The law has some changing to do. Women need to be better protected from men like this. Unfortunately, that won't happen quickly. Again...all in God's timing for this, too. So many have suffered. I knew this before, but seeing my daughter that way broke my heart. I wanted to do the same to Eddie. The way the law sees it, though, I'd be the one in jail and then I wouldn't be here for Allie. If she stays here, I can make sure she stays unharmed. I can defend her, as long as I don't harm Eddie. If Allie wants to stay with us, I will allow that. I will stand between her and him if I have to. I can't prevent him from seeing her and trying to sort this out, though. She will be protected, and it will be done within man's law...and God's."

Allie's pa hung the horse tack on the wall. "You have my permission, by the way."

Frank was puzzled by the last statement.

Pa chuckled. "If Allie becomes a free woman, you have my permission to pursue your feelings with her. Only—when she is free, though."

"Yes, Sir. Thank you, Sir."

Frank shook his hand and said his goodbyes. He had something else to attend to today. The doom he felt walking here to speak to this strong man was replaced with joy, pure elation, as he left.

He had never taken the time to really talk to Allie's pa before. His outside appearance was formidable. He was someone that was not easy to approach. Seeing this side of him was inspiring. This was a man worthy of looking up to. His own pa was, too, but not like this man. He was secure in his faith. He fully relied and trusted in it. Even with all the trials in his life, he knew where his focus should be. Maybe the trials helped make him stronger. Frank's pa had a pretty easy life. He didn't want for much when he was growing up and was able to provide the same lifestyle to his family.

Frank hadn't really understood the struggles of others until he lived in the logging camp. Living among those hardworking people made him see how they had not had it as easy. It made him understand their need to seek something that was numbing. Drink was common among the camp workers. Not all partook, but he had begun to understand why some would. Maybe this is some of what Eddie had been through.

Still didn't make it right, but it wasn't for Frank to judge. There was so much in this world he didn't understand. The more he saw and realized, the less he knew. Thoughts swirled in his head as he made his way to town to find Gladys. Thinking about her didn't make him as angry anymore.

The conversation with Allie's pa was now making him wonder about everyone's story. He didn't really know Gladys. Sure, he didn't like her ways, but why was she that way? Was she just a mean-spirited person, or did someone or something make her hold bitterness? He didn't know much about her. Growing up together, he never sought information out. She ran in different circles than he and Allie. He always thought her to be cruel. Other than attending the same church and knowing Gladys lived in town, he didn't know much of her parents. Well, Mrs. Wimble had a reputation much like her daughter, but Mr. Wimble was a mystery.

Frank was glad he chose to talk with Allie's pa first. Yelling and setting Gladys straight might not help. That might only make her push harder. He could clearly see this now. He did need to have a word with her, but he could do it more gently.

Town was dead. No one was on the streets. Everyone was busy at home with the drought. No one had money since crops were failing. He hoped they could all survive this summer and next would be better.

Gladys shouldn't be too hard to find without a crowd in the way. There were a few places he could check for her. The only place he wouldn't go was her home. That would only stir up more gossip for them instead of squelching it. He had to meet her in a public place. If he couldn't find her today, then he would try again tomorrow.

He was glad he'd a chance to calm down. His earlier conversation gave him perspective he hadn't considered. He needed to approach this conversation calmly and with a clear head. It was the only way that wouldn't cause more trouble. Frank didn't want to think about the possible results he might have faced if he'd gone to see Gladys first.

Frank checked at the restaurant in the hotel

and the one that Allie had worked in before—with no luck. There were only a few patrons between both eateries. That made the search quick. From there he searched the pharmacy, church, and Doc's...to see if he had seen her. He hadn't and gave him a curious look.

Frank realized he shouldn't have mentioned anything to Doc, but he knew Doc wouldn't say anything to anyone. He wouldn't check the bank. He didn't want his pa to rope him into staying and working the books all afternoon. That left the Women's League Chapter House (still under construction), the Memorial Library, a couple of dress shops, the school, and the college. Of course, there were other places of business, but he couldn't see why she would need to frequent those. They were set up more for the men folk.

This could be a long day with all these options to check. He organized the options from most likely to least likely and began his search—starting with the dress shops. Fortunately, he found her in the second. These shops always unsettled him. There was fabric piled up everywhere, many dresses on display, and too many women. Of course, too many women was a relative term.

Just a couple talking about fashion made him crazy. He never bothered with fashion, instead dressed in what was comfortable for him and readily available. Since his pa was a banker, he and his ma did dress with the fashion. They made sure that he had what he needed and didn't push him into dress that didn't suit his needs.

Growing up with the farmer boys, Frank dressed closer to the rest of the group. He was very thankful for that. He only stood out because his clothes were cleaner and not mended. That helped him remain friends with everyone. And now, it helped him blend in with the logging bunch. As a doctor you need to be clean, but not unapproachable.

Gladys was behind a screen being fitted. He knew it was her, though. That voice was unmistakable. He decided that waiting outside for her to come out would be a better option than calling for her. There was a bench not too far away that allowed him to watch the door. He would go relax outside while she finished her business in the shop.

Stepping outside and taking a seat, he breathed a sigh of relief. He was glad to be out of there—and without having to speak to anyone. No one had seen him enter. The employee was in the back, assisting Gladys. Without many people in town, there were no other shoppers. That also meant that Gladys had all the attention and didn't need to wait. When she walked out after a short while, it didn't surprise him. She was carrying a bag draped over her arm. Frank rose and jogged to catch up with her. "Gladys!"

She stopped and turned. Her lips rose at the corners of her mouth. "Frank! Hello. How are you?"

"Good, good. Do you have a moment? I need a

word." Frank had stopped in front of her.

Gladys's face turned to puzzlement. "Yes. What's on your mind?"

"Here, we can keep walking while we talk. You lead the way." He turned to walk on the street side of the walk and let her set the pace. After a few steps he began, "I need to be straight with you. I know that you have feelings for me, but I do not for you."

Gladys stopped and turned to face him, "Frank, I'm sorry...but I'm not following."

Wiping his hand down his face he thought of a nice way to continue, "You have made it obvious that you would like more than friendship from me. I need you to know that I don't"

"I see." Gladys switched the arm that was carrying the bag. "Thank you for clearing that up, Frank." Her lip started to quiver, and she turned to hide it. "I must be going now, I'm running late." She began to walk as quickly as possible.

Frank caught up with her. "Gladys. There's more."

"I'm really sorry, but I'm late." She didn't stop but continued down the walk.

"Gladys!" He was talking as quietly as he could, but he still needed her to hear. "I didn't pay Allie for any services...nor did she pay me. I'm not sure what you saw and thought, but it wasn't what it might have appeared to be."

With that, she stopped. "Really? I saw you kissing a married woman. I saw money exchange hands. Please, explain what I saw, Frank."

"Gladys, look at me, please." She turned although reluctantly. "Thank you. It was a penny, you know that. I paid for her thoughts. It is something we have done for years. 'A penny for your thoughts.' I'm sure you've heard that expression. We act that out. Then she usually pays me for my advice with the same penny."

"What about the kiss, Frank. That was inappropriate and at church, no less!" Gladys stomped her foot to add to her point.

"You are very right. We had a moment when neither of us was thinking. We have both agreed that it can never happen again...as long as the situation remains the same."

"I see. You love her then?" She lifted her chin to help brace for the blow.

"I do...and I think she loves me, too." He felt pity for her. He could see she was hurt. Maybe there was more to Gladys than he first thought. The hard, mean shell she put on was starting to shatter.

"Thank you for clearing everything up. If you'll please excuse me." She turned to leave.

"Please! Wait!" She froze.

"I'm not sure I want to hear more right now, please."

"I understand, but this part is important to me." She kept her back turned to him but allowed him to continue. "I would appreciate it if you would not say anything about what you saw. We know we were in the wrong and it won't happen again. Spreading that information will only hurt us. And, it might make her situation worse than it already is."

Gladys was quiet for a moment. Her breathing was deep. When she finally spoke, it came out a bit struggled. "I understand Frank. I won't hurt you." She picked up her skirt with her free hand and, as quickly as she could, left him standing alone.

Frank let out a breath he didn't realize he'd been holding. Hurting her was not on his agenda. Before today, he didn't think Gladys could be hurt. He couldn't think of a different way to do this. He hadn't realized there was more to her than she usually allowed to show. Whatever he'd have said would have hurt her.

Knowing that this business was taken care of should have calmed his nerves, but now he was concerned for her. He couldn't do anything, of course. She would see that as interest. He could pray for her, though. That was something he'd never done before. He had prayed for many people, but never Gladys...or others like her. He needed to go do something to take his mind off all this. Maybe helping his pa with mind-numbing accounting work was just what today called for. Pa would appreciate it. He could make one person happy today.

Turning directions, he headed to the bank and pushed thoughts of Gladys aside for now.

CHAPTER 32

Still not able to find work, Eddie was beginning to lose hope. The weight he'd lost from lack of food forced him to continually hike up his pants to keep his backside covered. Desperation was setting in. He thought he was somewhere around Missoula, based on the rivers he was trying to follow. If he could walk a straight line instead of going in circles he would be closer to Allie by now.

He tried his best to follow the train tracks. For the most part the tracks followed the river and he could walk across the train trestles instead of swimming. The river was low in most places. At least the drought was good for something, he thought.

Making navigation harder, the wind was pushing smoke in his path from the various fires. Sometimes the smoke was so thick he couldn't see twenty feet ahead. The flames weren't visible, but the smoke came and went with the direction and speed of the breeze.

Finding his way around cliffs and through thick brush in the smoke made him lose his way many times.

And finding the tracks proved difficult as well. Once he did find them, he had to guess which way was east.

I need a drink. He'd been completely sober for a long while now and his head didn't like it. He couldn't think straight sober. He kept pushing forward hoping there would be work for him when he stumbled into Missoula.

Eddie crested the top of a hill and paused to see what he could make out further ahead. The trees and brush were thick. That made it nearly impossible to see any distance ahead, but he thought he saw a portion of the trolley bridge. He hoped so. That would mean he *was* close to Missoula.

That raised his hopes and gave him the strength to pick up some speed. He almost ran down the other side of the hill. He was normally slow in his gait, keeping an eye out for critters. These mountains held some dangerous creatures. Many snakes called this area home, but the only one to be fearful of was the rattlesnake.

Eddie knew to make noise and pay attention, so he could hear them before he got close enough to have one cause a problem. Black widows were also found in these parts, but they weren't seen as often. His main concern though wasn't a creature. The native greenery posed more of a problem.

Most were poisonous, only if eaten, but there were a few around that caused a nasty rash. Poison oak and ivy were two of those. Running down this trail might not have been such a great idea. He realized he was pushing right through some plants that he would regret soon enough. He slowed his pace to be more careful—and hoped he wouldn't discover a rash later. He was almost to the bottom. Unfortunately, that meant he ran through most of the brush without thinking. Time would tell.

As Eddie made his way across the bridge and into the main hub of town, he became part of a large crowd. A train was parked at the station. He assumed most of the people were either arriving or leaving. He headed toward some men who were having an animated conversation. He needed to pick up on any talk that would provide him leads on work.

The group contained five men of varied dress. One man was dressed in clothes suggesting a business owner. He was holding a newspaper. The other four wore work clothes that suggested occupations ranging from farming to coal mining. The man with the paper was shouting and more men were circling around. As Eddie got closer, he didn't like what he heard.

The man was shouting that three or four thousand railroad workers were being laid off due to the fires. *How am I supposed to find work when that many others are also looking?* He scratched his head as his rumbling stomach reminded him that he needed something to eat.

Eddie edged closer to the man as he began

highlighting points in the paper.

"Says here that the electrical storms have kicked up too many fires. They are laying off men due to crop failure from the drought. They've banned man-made fires to allow those fighting the wild fires a chance to get the upper hand."

The man was holding the paper up and Eddie was able to read the date—July 10th. He tried to keep track of the days, but that proved harder than navigating.

Another man from the crowd shouted out. "They're takin' away all the land to control us. And now they think they can control nature, too." Another man joined in. "They're worried about us starting fires. They're doing it...on purpose! They say starting 'em will prevent larger ones. Calling 'em back fires." The crowd all started hollering at once.

Eddie couldn't tell who was saying what. He knew that the word "they" meant the government. They started taking land in the early 1880s and now had a sizeable chunk known as the National Forests. These forests consisted of millions of acres across the middle and western United States. No one around here understood why they needed control of any land...let alone so much of it. These parts were enormous, and no one believed anyone could use it all up like Roosevelt said. The firing of Pinchot, the main fighter and Chief of the Forest Service, by President Taft gave people hope that some policies would be reversed. No changes had happened yet. Government was just sticking their nose into industry's business, as far as he could tell.

Eddie backed away and started sizing up the town. He didn't want to be considered part of the group that was growing unruly. The law would probably be showing up soon. He couldn't find work in any of the usual places, so he'd need to look elsewhere. Only problem was he didn't know where. This town had all the business one would expect in a town of its size. He generally found work as a laborer. If he could find a family that needed a farm hand, he could manage that easily. He didn't have the know-how for restaurants or other business work. It would be hard to find work on a family farm. Especially for an outsider that no one knew.

He had a couple of coins jingling in his pocket and decided to cross the street and see what he could find to eat. He could also ask around for work possibilities. *Time to turn on the charm!* He wished he could have a bath. He smelled...but that couldn't be helped.

He walked into the diner and waited for his eyes to adjust to the dim light inside. There were many open seats. He took one in the corner, so he had a good view of the entire restaurant and could also see out the window. He wanted to watch what happened to the crowd.

A menu was slapped down on the table in front of him. "Can I start ya off with coffee?" The brunette stood next to his table waiting for his response.

"No, Ma'am! Glass of ice water would be mighty fine in this heat." He wanted to ask for a whiskey on the rocks, but didn't want to get his drinking reputation established this early. He also needed to make his money last as long as he could.

"I'll be right back with that. Have a look at the menu. I'll take your order when I get back."

She took off and Eddie appreciated the view of her walking away. She seemed a bit rough around the edges when she spoke, but her dress made it obvious that she was all soft curves underneath. Maybe he could come up with more reasons to get her to come over...just so he could watch her leave.

He opened the menu and looked for the cheapest meal. Stretching what little coin he had left was a priority. Scanning the menu, he saw his favorite meal, biscuits and gravy. It wasn't the cheapest option, but his mouth watered regardless. *Ah, to hell with my coins*. He tried to calculate what he would be left with if he ordered this and decided it didn't matter. He needed a pick-me-up for his sour attitude. Alcohol would be better, but this would get him going in the right direction. The lovely, sassy brunette was headed his way again. Setting the water glass down, she looked him blankly in the eyes. "Have you decided?"

Eddie folded his menu. "I'll have the biscuits and gravy, Ma'am." He flashed the brightest smile he could muster, and his stomach rumbled loud enough that she broke her melancholy look and stifled a chuckle.

"I'll try to put a rush on that. Sounds like you're pretty hungry." She used her hand to cover her mouth.

Time for the puppy dog eyes. Maybe she'll feel sorry and I'll get a soft place to sleep for the night. He looked right at her with the face that had won over many girls.

"I'm sorry that was not polite. I'm mighty hungry. Haven't eaten in a while." He was following her face for clues to see if she would bite. Her apple cheeks fell as her smile faded. *Hook!* "I've been down on my luck...what with the layoffs happening. No one has been hiring for a long time." Her forehead wrinkled and her eyebrows drew together. *Line!* "My wife and kids took sick several months ago. Kids pulled through and are with my sister while I look for work. Wife didn't make it, though." He looked down and paused to reinforce his sad mood. He was apparently managing quiet well. She took a seat across from him and put her hand on top of his.

"I'm so sorry for your loss. My husband met the same fate about a month back. I've been working here and trying to keep the house running. It's proving to be mighty difficult." Her face reddened as she realized what she had just revealed to a complete stranger. "I'm sorry, I shouldn't burden you with my problems when you have so many of your own." She brushed her hands on her apron. "I'll go put in your order and bring it out to you as soon as it's ready."

She turned, and he kept the somber look on his, so

no one could tip her off to his act, but that didn't prevent him from enjoying the view of her backside. He'd been on the trail for so long, his appetite for a woman had increased as much as his need for food. He just needed to wait. He should know if his plan worked by the time he finished his biscuits.

It wasn't long before she returned with a heaping plate of biscuits and gravy...and a side of bacon. Then she put a second plate down with a slice of pie. He wouldn't get his hopes up just yet, though. He kept the sad look and added a bit of panic to his voice, as he said, "I can't pay for all of this, Ma'am. It sure does look mighty good, though." He eyed the plates with pure hunger. A lustful look crossed his face as he stared down at the heaping quantities before he pasted the sorrowful face back on.

"You eat up. It's on the house." She had an eager look on her face and her chestnut eyes were shining with some mischief. He dug into his food in earnest before abruptly stopping with a mouth full of food and a sheepish look on his face. "Oh, don't stop on my account. Please, eat up while it's hot." She began to fiddle with her hands and looked like she was about to say something.

Eddie took a gulp of water. "It seems like you want to say something. We've both been through enough, it sounds like. Feel free to share whatever you need. Sometimes, it's nice to talk to someone who knows, you know?"

She nodded and gathered the strength. "Well...oh...this sounds so forward. I'm not normally this trusting, but I know what you must be going through. I don't have children, so I can't quite understand that, but I know how it hurts, losing your spouse, I mean." She swallowed a lump forming in her throat and fidgeted with the end of her apron. "I'm struggling to keep up with work at home and you don't have a place to hang your head. Maybe we could help each other." She let her thought hang in air while he sat silent.

Sinker! He had the perfect quizzical look on his face. She would think he was weighing his options before he spoke. "That would help me out for a while, but I do need to find something that can provide me with funds."

Her heart began to race. She needed help and this man seemed like he could provide that. "I can't pay you, of course, but you would have a place to sleep and plenty of food to build your strength up while you look for work." She looked at him with a pleading stare. "Oh, I'm sorry I even mentioned it. It's a terrible idea.

"No...no it's not. I see where this could help both of us. But...do you have separate sleeping quarters, Ma'am?" He was playing the perfect gentleman.

"Oh...of course. Yes. I'm sorry if you felt that implied anything other than strictly two people helping each other out of a terrible situation." Her head fell, and her face was bright red.

He chuckled inwardly. "That sounds fine. Better than fine...it sounds wonderful to this tired and hungry body." He looked down at his plate.

"Here I am talking away, letting your food get cold. I'll leave you to it. We can discuss details after you've finished." He nodded his head and dug his fork in, enjoying her walk away from him again.

Devouring his food did not take long at all. Eddie pushed his plate away after using his finger to swipe up the last of the gravy. She—he still didn't know her name—was coming to remove his dishes. Her coming would also mean she would leave again. He didn't think he could grow tired of watching that. "Ma'am?"

"Ma'am? Oh, dear. We haven't even been properly introduced and I have you moving in. That doesn't say much for my manners." He gave her a soft, sad smile. "I'm Helen." She held out her hand and waited for him.

He held her hand delicately as he introduced himself. "Names, Eddie. Very nice to meet you Helen."

Her heart skipped a beat. *This isn't right! I'm still in mourning.* Her Ben was everything to her. Such a good man. *I need to keep Ben's memory close.* She hastily removed her hand from Eddie's. "I'm off in two hours. If you meet me back here, we can head to my place and get you settled."

"That sounds fine, Helen. Thank you for everything you're doing. This means so much to me. Please tell the cook that was an excellent meal."

Eddie stood and slightly bowed, hoping she would take that as a cue for her to do her walk away again. She complied. He stayed a couple of seconds to admire the view before he took his leave. If he wasn't so stuffed he would jump up and click his heels. His luck was turning around. If she had some whiskey at her house, he might kiss her.

Maybe that wouldn't be such a good idea so soon. He needed to keep up appearances until he had her full trust. *Now...what shall I do for the next couple of hours to pass the time?* He chose a direction and headed into town. Spotting an establishment for men up the road, he knew exactly what to do while he waited. Not paying for his meal and having a roof and regular meals coming meant he had some spare change. *Oh, things are looking up!* He began to whistle a tune.

CHAPTER 33

Allie had already delivered most of the papers on the route. She was having a hard time breathing and focusing on the job, but she needed to finish. The headline on the front page in bold black letters read "Railroad Layoffs." She didn't need to read the article to know what that meant for her own job. She would be laid off to allow some man the opportunity to support his family.

Her boss had yet to speak with her, but she figured that would be happening before she left for the day. She needed to sit and take a break. Finding the closest bench, she perched herself and decided to read the rest of the paper. She ignored the front page. It made her heart pound in her ears. Flipping through the remaining pages didn't reveal anything new. The standard reports were the same as they'd been for a while...covering the drought. Wells were failing. Crops were failing. And, now...jobs were failing. Winters were rough in these parts, but she couldn't help but pine for that season to come sooner rather than later.

The back page caught Allie's attention. This was

the classified section of this paper. Not much had been posted in the help wanted ads, lately. But today...there was one that screamed to her. They were already advertising for her position, before they even gave her the news that she didn't work for them anymore. To make matters worse, they were paying more—double—what they were paying her. Worry turned to anger faster than she could control it. She wanted a word with her boss...now! She knew though that she needed to finish her route first. Her anger renewed the energy that the front page had drained away. Finishing the route would not take long now. And, indeed, she had it done in record time.

Only a half hour later, she marched up the steps to the paper. Bursting through the front door, she called for Mr. Ashton. No one came. She raised her voice and called for him again. His office door opened, and he stepped out, shutting it behind him

"Now Allie, what's the meaning of this ruckus? I have a meeting going on in there." He approached her and crossed his arms mimicking her stance.

"I saw the paper—front and back!" She spit the words out and waited for him to explain.

Unfolding his arms, he placed his hands on his hips and cocked his head. "Now we talked about this. And, I was going to tell you today...just hadn't gotten to it yet.

"We talked about being replaced. We didn't talk about the raise you would be giving someone else," she huffed.

Dawning crossed his eyes and he softened his posture a bit. "Yes, I'm sure that was a bit of a shock. The position is open for someone to provide for their family. You have your pa to help you. I need to offer a bit more to help whomever I hire. I won't hire someone who doesn't have kids. I want to help a family, and this is how I can do it."

She turned her head and blinked to fight back the tears.

"Allie, times are tough for everyone right now. We all need to do our part to help those who need it." He reached out and put his hand on her shoulder.

She inhaled sharply. "Yes! I understand clearly, Mr. Ashton. Thank you for the opportunity you gave me, even if it was short. I will clean up in here and head home when I'm finished." She turned to busy herself.

"Thank you for understanding. When you're finished, please find me and I will pay what you are owed. You have been an exceptional employee and I thank you for your hard work" He turned back to his office to rejoin his meeting.

Allie wanted to get out as fast as she could. He was going to pay someone double for the same job because they would have children. She would have had a child. Would he have paid her more if she did? Would she ever have children? She couldn't think about that right now.

Finishing the sweeping and placing the broom back in the closet, Allie rapped on his door to let him know she was leaving. Mr. Ashton cracked the door just wide enough for her to see him. He handed her the coins due and gave her a sympathetic look. That made her boil. She didn't want or need sympathy! She needed a job. She was right back where she started! All she wanted to do was go to her spot on the creek. She wanted to place herself in solitary confinement. Otherwise, she wasn't sure she would be able to control her actions around others.

Stepping out into the glaring sun, she glanced both directions and noticed a familiar figure down the road. She closed her eyes and took deep breaths hoping to keep her composure. If he saw her, he would want to come and talk. She didn't need that right now. She decided to keep a steady pace through town and not draw attention to herself. Once out of town, she could run her energy off making her way to the creek.

Thankfully, walking through town was a good choice. Frank didn't attempt to approach. She wasn't even sure if he spotted her. He'd been in a conversation with another gentleman.

It was too hot to run, but Allie didn't care. She would have the creek to cool her off. So, she ran...and ran...and ran. She made it to her serenity spot at the back of her house. She turned in a circle and didn't see anyone. Her outer-most layers of clothing were on the bank. And, before she knew it, she felt the relief of the cool water. The creek was shallow, but she could sit and splash the water around to cool off. Her nickers would soak up the water and keep her cool for a while once she climbed out to dry off.

She sat there thinking for a while about the events that had just taken place. The more she thought about it, the more enraged she felt. If she had a child! If she was born a male! If she hadn't married Eddie! If...if...if! The *ifs* would drive her mad. She needed to pull herself out of this. Her thoughts were interrupted by the snap of a twig and an all-too-familiar male voice calling her name.

Panic clawed at her throat. She was half naked. Her pa would consider this full naked if Frank saw her. Without moving, she hollered from her spot in the creek. She hoped her voice would stop him—and no movement would keep his eyes away from her specific location.

"Frank, I'm here. Please stop! Turn around until I tell you!

"Okay," he shouted back sounding confused. He did what she had asked and waited until she said he could turn back.

She very quickly donned her dress and made her way up the bank. After perching on her favorite tree, she hollered at him to approach.

Frank walked over. He'd tried to make sense of all the splashing he'd heard. The situation slowly dawned on him when he saw her dress becoming wet as the seconds passed. Her hair was dripping and hanging limp around her face. A mischievous smile turned up at the corner of his mouth.

"You take a little swim, did you?"

"Shut up! Shut up! Shut up!" She covered her mouth to stifle a giggle.

"By the looks of your dress, I can see why you wanted my back turned. The few dry spots should be soggy shortly!" He pulled up and sat down beside her, breaking out in full laughter.

"Shut up!" The anger was returning to her voice.

"Whoa, now! No sense getting upset at me. I didn't do anything wrong." He drew his brows together and gave her a long stare back.

She gave a curt, "Sorry." Then she drew her knees up and hugged them to her chest.

"Now...do we have to go through all this penny nonsense for me to get to the bottom of what's eating at you? Or, can we do this a little more grown-up like?"

She harrumphed! His question irritated her further.

"All right then!" He reached into his pocket, pulled out a shiny penny, and held it out to her.

Allie looked at the penny and turned her back to him.

She was sure a stubborn one, but he usually got, at least, a word or two out of her. This complete silence treatment (not counting her childlike noises) was new. She seemed to be testing his patience on a regular basis these days.

"I can be a patient man. I'll just sit here. You talk if you want, or don't. I don't mind."

They sat there silently for a while. Then her patience finally wore thin. She wanted him to leave and she knew he wouldn't without talking first.

"Fine, if you must know! I'm not sure why you are so nosy!"

"Hey! No reason to be rude!" He tried to match her mood.

"Sorry." She turned so they were side-by-side, but she wouldn't look at him. Staring at the creek felt better. She tried to envision the coolness of the creek...washing over the hot rage inside her.

"Three thousand men have been laid off."

Frank was confused. What in the world would make her so angry about that? He was saddened to know so many lost their employment, but what did that have to do with Allie. It didn't affect him.

"I heard that. Talked with a few folks in town today and they were all abuzz with the stories."

"The articles should read 3001!" Her hands were repeatedly opening and closing...making and releasing her fists.

Frank was still confused. "Did someone else lose their job? Do you know more than what was in the article?"

"Yes...ME! I lost my job to help provide a job to someone else."

Allie was not making sense to him. She seemed irritated with his questions, but he didn't care. He would ask them anyway.

"Your paper job? Why would that help someone else?"

Allie stood and began pacing. Her dress was dripping all along the bottom hem.

"Mr. Ashton decided to let me go so he could hire someone who needed it more. Seems a family man is more important than my needs."

Frank scratched his head. "How is your job going to help a family man?" He blushed realizing how that sounded. "Sorry."

She brushed his comment away. Even though it was irritating, she knew what he meant. "Mr. Ashton placed a help-wanted ad in the paper and doubled the wage...for the same job! I don't want children to starve, but why didn't he pay me what he is willing to pay a man?" Her knees buckled under her and she crumpled to the ground, quietly sobbing.

Frank moved to her and placed his hand on her back. "I'm sorry, Allie. Mr. Ashton is just trying to help. I'm sure he didn't mean any disrespect by it." There wasn't anything he could really do for her. He knew her strength and knew she would pick herself back up. After everything that she had been through already, this would not break her. Knowing that didn't help her, though. She needed to know it for herself. "Allie, have you talked to Him about it?"

Knowing who he meant, she paused to think over the day. Had she reached to Him for help at all? Should she? He didn't seem to care how her life turned out. Look at the mess that was all around her. He could have stopped any of the events that had brought her to this place...but He didn't.

"You should talk to Him. He cares about all of us. Wants the best for us." Frank was rubbing circles on her back trying to comfort her as best as he could.

She looked up to the sky. "Why? Why should I? What has He done for me? My life is a mess and He could have intervened at any moment to change it...but He didn't."

Frank pondered her questions. She spoke the words to him, but her eyes stared up also directing them to God. This was a big moment for her. He could feel it. Silently, he closed his eyes and said a short prayer for wisdom.

"He does care. He isn't a puppet master, though. He wants us to come to Him freely...opening ourselves up for Him to take the reins. He won't force Himself upon you. I am a patient man, Allie, but He is the most patient of all. He sits back and waits. We mess our lives up. We make decisions without seeking His way first. We direct our lives down slippery paths. He waits until we come to a place where we can no longer go it alone. He sits back and cries when we cry and laughs when we laugh...but doesn't step in until He is asked." Frank held his breath. He hoped this was enough. He was a physician, not a pastor. This was out of his comfort area. He was ready to move the conversation in a different direction.

Allie sat silent for a long while, trying to absorb what Frank had said. It wasn't the first time she had heard the general message. Frank, himself, had even said something similar the day they kissed. "I know what that means, but how do I do it?"

She knew she was fighting it. The idea seemed complex and irrational. She was tired of doing it her way, though. The walls she had built to protect herself were ready to crumble, but she was very perplexed. *How do I pass those reins off to Him?*

Frank looked to the heavens with Allie.

"You just tell Him. You have an honest conversation giving Him permission. Then you walk away from your thoughts. Busy yourself to the extent you must to do that. Let Him work. He'll let you know when it's time for you to do something." Frank knew this, but a more complete understanding washed over him. As he enjoyed the peace that came with the knowledge, he hoped that she was also feeling it.

"I'm going to leave you to it. I don't need to be privy to your conversation. You come to Him on your terms when you're ready. He's waiting for you." Frank stood, and left Allie soaked with creek water...and bathed in the words he'd showered on her. He left so God could take over...and do what He does best.

Frank left so he wouldn't try to dive further into the conversation than his knowledge and abilities allowed. He preferred working on the flesh not the soul. The flesh was black and white. You could touch it, see it, and watch it respond to your actions. Soul work involved diving into places only that person knew. It required a steady faith in things humans could not fully comprehend. Allie needed to take the next step herself. He couldn't help her any more.

Allie sat silent for a long while after Frank left. She wanted to cry, scream, and shake her fists to the sky, but that wouldn't help anything. A child-like fit never solved a problem. It did create more though. Closing her eyes, she started quietly, "God, what do I do?" A simple sentence with a big expectation. She let that hang for a while before she added, "Help, please."

She hoped that was enough. That was all she had

the strength for as she stood and made her way to the house. Frank said to first ask and then make herself busy. There was plenty of work to be done around the farm. She quickly rolled her sleeves up and dug into all that needed doing. She focused her mind on the task at hand...and left her worries with her prayer by the creek.

CHAPTER 34

Just when things were looking the bleakest for Eddie, everything seemed to turn on a dime. He camped in the barn and took care of some odds and ends around the place that needed some attention. He was minding his Ps and Qs to gain her trust. Now he didn't need to. He had found himself a job. It wasn't ideal work, but it would do for now.

The previous Sunday, more than 3,000 men were laid off. Now, the government had hired 3,000 men to join in the fight to protect the timber lands. Eddie had knowledge of the area, so he was hired on the spot. He wasn't sure what he was supposed to do, but he could pretend and collect his pay for as long as needed. The best thing about this work was it was easy to get lost in the vast wilderness. Once he had enough money in his pocket to settle somewhere else, he could just disappear. He could head down to Deer Lodge, grab Allie, and be long gone before anyone realized what happened.

Life sure had a way of righting itself. He had found this to be true more than once. Roping Allie in was his next step. He needed her back. Keeping his focus on her would help him through the next few weeks. He hated the thought of having to head back into the woods. He had just come from there and preferred what a town could offer a man.

Eddie knew he should just be happy that he had employment. So many were struggling right now, and he didn't have to be one of them. He didn't know where he would be assigned yet, but that would come shortly. All the men were told to gather at the train depot with whatever belongings they wanted to carry. That was where he was now—with the only belonging he wanted. He had done some snooping when he was alone during the week. Helen's late husband had a stash of whiskey. If he nursed it, it would last a while. He had it tucked into his pants. It would become his close traveling companion.

There were hundreds gathered with him. All, presumably, for the same reason, to get their orders and instructions. A train could be heard in the distance and a man was hushing the crowd. Eddie pushed closer so he could hear. With this many men it was a challenge.

From what he could gather through the noise, he was headed northeast. That was the direction he had just come from. He would board the train and it would take him closer to the fires. Then he would have to go deeper into the woods by foot (or horse if he could find one) to meet up with the other men in his assignment group. *Isn't this just hunky-dory. I make it closer to Allie just to end up further from her than I am now.* He shook his head and gave a snort. At least his pockets would be headed in the right direction even if his body wasn't. He had made the journey this far once and he could do it again. He had to.

Up and leaving without a proper goodbye was disappointing. Eddie had worked hard all week to gain Helen's trust. Eventually, he had hoped to end up in her bed. Now, that wouldn't happen. He had a place to hang his hat and food to fill his belly for a week. That would have to be enough.

The train whistle blew. Soon the train chugged its way between the man that was giving the instructions and the gathered group. This would be the train he would board to head back. He hoped he could avoid John. That was one man's path he didn't want to cross. Really, it was the only concern he had when he realized where he was going. It was big country. Maybe once he got there, he could request another location and be shipped out quickly. He could try, anyway.

Boarding the train had a somber feeling. The men were quiet and moved slowly. Some womenfolk were gathered to send off their men. Others were like him, alone. He imagined many were terrified, not knowing what was ahead. He had his liquid courage. If he could make that last, he would be just fine.

Stepping onto the train he made his way to a seat. This train was filling up fast and would be crowded with all the cars overloaded. He hadn't stayed up on the news about the fires, only knew there were many. Judging by the number of men here, he knew they must be more widespread than he'd thought.

Eddie hoped he wasn't getting in over his head with this job. The government said that the fires could be controlled and snuffed out. He figured there would be some kind of training before he set out to face the red devil. If he was lucky, maybe he would work the few weeks needed and not have to go head-to-head with the actual flames. One could, at lease, hope.

He laid his head back and closed his eyes with that thought. No sense worrying about something you couldn't change. He would face what tomorrow would bring tomorrow...and not a minute sooner. He was just starting to doze when the train started moving. He wasn't sure where they'd be when he awakened, but he would enjoy the ride as much as he could. This work was bound to be grueling. Sitting here with nothing to do but sleep could not be taken for granted.

Eddie was in and out of sleep the whole journey. This was not a normal passenger train, even if it appeared to be. All aboard were heading into what they were being told was "the storm." They didn't stop at the train depots along the route. They pushed through as quickly as possible to bring help to those places already in the depths of hell. The hell that was being experienced by these souls would be nothing compared to what was headed straight for them all in just a few short weeks. Eddie didn't plan on staying long enough to find out what continuously dry conditions and hotter

August days would bring.

From the names on the stations they were speeding through, he realized they were not headed to where he started. They were on a northerly course and would most likely be stopping at Hope, Idaho. Those forests were not as well known to him. He had worked in the area to the south of there, but they were bound to be similar enough. It was a longer ride than he thought they would be taking yet they were making good time. He was relaxed, knowing that the chance of running into John would be much smaller than he originally thought.

The whistle interrupted his thoughts as it signaled the next station. This was where they would leave comfort behind and venture into the open woods. By the time the train slowed and pulled to a complete stop, all the men were standing. It was black outside, and nothing could be seen through the windows. Night had come while Eddie slept most of the day away. His stomach was loudly commenting on the lack of food offered to anyone on this leg of the journey. If that was any indication of the treatment they would receive for this work, he wasn't so sure he wanted to do it. The whiskey helped keep his head calm and clear. He had nursed the bottle to keep his spirits up.

The train doors opened, and the men charged off—grumbling about their hunger. Apparently, he wasn't the only one who neglected to bring provisions. He waited his turn and joined the line headed up the aisle. Stepping down from the train, he noticed a man holding a lantern and speaking to them. He tried to get close enough to hear, but the crowd was so large the man's voice didn't carry to everyone. He did understand, though, they were being told they'd be getting some food and sleep and would be meeting back here tomorrow morning.

Where he was supposed to go for food and sleep was still a mystery. He decided to follow the crowd. That seemed like the best choice. Many of them were headed to what he could now see were lodgings. He was out of money, so he decided to move to the side and sleep with is back to the wall of the building. He hoped the sounds of the others in the morning—when they made their way back to the depot—would wake him. It wasn't comfortable, but he figured that's how it would be from here on out. He wasn't sure of the time and didn't know how much time they would be allowed for sleep. He settled in and closed his eyes, praying it would be long enough.

It felt like Eddie had just shut his eyes. He heard grumbles and footsteps pounding down the stairs around the corner. His stomach had given up on food. It was silent. He stood and made his way with the crowd headed to the depot. The strong smell of cooking bacon grew as they came closer. At first, he thought he was imagining it. His mind was playing tricks on him, but then he could see the long line of women making bacon and eggs. He joined the men getting in line.

While he was waiting, he heard the ladies were from a local church. Feeding the crowd of men was their thank you for helping them fight the blazes. He was thankful he could get something to eat, regardless of the reason. He devoured his full plate faster than he intended. All the men seemed to eat with the same gusto, so he couldn't really fault himself he supposed.

As they were finishing, the speaker from last night reappeared. He had a group of men with him. They were wandering through the crowd and dividing up the men. Eddie was put into a large group and told to step back twenty paces to further separate themselves. Once they were all divided, one of the men stood before them and gave them their orders.

Eddie's group would head further north to battle a fire that was thought to be six miles long and a couple of miles wide. They feared it would reach the lake and more men were needed to help the two hundred or so already fighting.

There wasn't any training or advice given—just the location. They were heading straight into the mouth of the dragon. Eddie figured it must be simple work. They just needed bodies and muscle. If no training was required, it must not be difficult. Those thoughts reassured him since he had no idea what was really in store for them.

The men were loading up in wagons. They were told that the wagons would take them as far as possible, but the rest of the journey would be on foot. It would be a while before they made it to their destination. Eddie decided to sleep, even though he wasn't tired.

Nothing else to do—and he didn't want to be forced into conversation with the other men. He would be in the middle of nowhere camping with a group of men. There would be many opportunities for talking. He wanted to put off the inevitable as long as he dared possible.

When Eddie woke up, he didn't think they had reached the fire, but there was a layer of smoke all around. A group could be seen up ahead and he figured this would be their stopping point. He was correct on that assumption. The wagon came to an abrupt stop.

After the initial jolt, the men were told to get out as quickly as possible. With barely enough time to climb out, the wagons left them to fend for themselves and walk the rest of the way. The small group ahead was making their way to his group. More wagons were pulling up and dropping off their loads of men.

The men approaching were covered in soot and their clothes were torn in multiple places. Handkerchiefs covered their faces. Eddie pulled his out and did the same to block the smoke. A man moved in front of the others and started yelling for all the men to gather 'round. *This must be my new boss*, Eddie thought, and positioned himself at the front of the crowd this time. He wanted to hear everything this man was going to say.

The man introduced himself as William Brashear. He told them which direction they would be going. Eddie didn't know these parts well enough to recognize the landmarks he mentioned. They would start digging a fire line when they arrived.

As the men moved out with William leading the way, he was relieved to hear that they would not be fighting the fire directly, but instead, clearing a dirt path to prevent the fire from traveling further towards the nearby towns. Seemed simple enough. And that was the general belief—until they arrived and started doing the work.

It didn't take them as long as he'd hoped it would to make it to their new place of employment. Eddie wished he could drag the arrival out as long as possible. Since that wasn't going to happen, he rolled up his sleeves and began clearing the thick brush that he worked hard at avoiding on his original hike to Missoula.

The work was already proving grueling. It was scorching hot. The sweat that formed evaporated before it could trickle down, and the smoke was so thick, breathing was work in and of itself. He knew he was close to the fire, even if they couldn't see the flames.

The sooner the line was cleared the sooner they could move to another location to do it again. He hoped the conditions would improve as they moved. That hope, and his whiskey, were keeping him going...until he could escape this new hell. He had to remind himself that he signed himself up for this.

CHAPTER 35

It was Sunday, and Allie was in church. She still didn't know if she had an answer from God. Maybe this was the place she needed to be for Him to send her a message. Frank was behind her. She could feel him staring a hole through her. Only Frank would do that to her here. She wouldn't turn around, though. He would need to wait to get her attention after services.

The congregation was instructed to open their bibles to Psalms 37:7; Rest in the Lord and wait patiently for him: fret not thyself because of him who prospereth in his way, because of the man who bringeth wicked devices to pass. And there it was. She realized she had her answer. Not the full answer she was hoping for, but something to hold on to for now. Closing her eyes, she silently told herself and God that she would continue in patience. She would not act, she would sit back and continue to wait. She sighed and hoped that after today she would understand something about what she was waiting for. Was it a voice? A vision? A sign? She had no idea. Her faith would remain steadfast for as long as it took.

After the verse was read and the sermon given, she thought she did have a better understanding. He wasn't going to tell her what she needed to do. He would be the one to act. Maybe that meant she would find a way to earn more money... or Eddie would show up on her doorstep and force his way back into her life.

Whatever happened...that would be her answer. She hoped it would be favorable for her, but she wasn't going to question the ways of the Lord. The final song ended. People began setting up the shared meal.

Allie knew Frank wanted to talk to her. She hoped he would wait for a private moment. She moved in the direction of her mother and the other ladies so she could help. It was their turn to keep the bowls of food full. That would keep Frank from diving into whatever he wanted to talk about. The line formed, and people began filling plates. Frank was towards the front of the line and stopped in front of her.

"Hello. Come find me when you're finished please." He gave a small smirk.

Allie gave him a look back, hoping to show that she wished him to remember about not wanting to be seen in public. Was that taking matters into her own hands, though, or letting God do His work without her interference? She mulled that over for a while. She supposed she could act as though they were just two acquaintances catching up, just like everyone else did on Sundays. Pushing that thought aside, she grabbed the almost empty bowl of rolls and replaced it with a full one. Then she topped it off with what remained in the last bowl.

The line was shrinking. That meant she could dish up her own plate. She was hungry. She spooned up a variety of salads and some chicken and found a seat close to her father. He was sitting with some of the other men folk. She was at the opposite end of the table. There were more empty spots close to her and she hoped Ma, who was still serving, would join her.

Frank came and plopped himself down instead. He had already finished his pile of food. She didn't see him make his way back for seconds. But since she saw his first plate, she suspected he couldn't possibly have room.

"Last time I saw you, I had some news to share, but I forgot about it when you told me about yours." He sat with his hands folded and a smug smile plastered across his face.

Allie had taken a bite and only cocked her head to the side in response.

"Well, I shouldn't say all of it here, but I can tell you something I overheard."

Allie was thankful for his discretion and worked to swallow her mouthful. "You have my interest. I could sure use some good news. And, judging by the way your face is lit up, it must be great.

"Well, most of it is great...and the rest could

become great. Not sure how it will turn out yet." He snickered a bit. "You look pretty hungry. I'll let you finish up first while I go see if the ladies need my help with anything." He stood and strolled away whistling as he went.

Allie harrumphed as she purposely shoved another bite in her mouth. How dare he string her along and then walk away! She didn't care if it wasn't ladylike as she continued shoveling in her food. She needed to finish up. Then he would tell her his so-called great news. Great news was hard to come by these days. Just knowing there was some raised her spirits.

She had grabbed her chicken leg and was tearing a bite off with her teeth when her mother approached. "Dear, please! People are staring!"

Allie looked around and saw Pa and all the men around him with eyes large staring down the other end of the table. Some were chuckling under their breaths. Her cheeks flushed with embarrassment.

"Honestly, Allie!" Ma took a seat across from her. "I don't know what has come over you! This is not how you were raised!"

Allie swallowed a large hunk of chicken and barely managed to avoid choking. "Sorry, Ma. Frank said he had some good news to share with me and he won't tell me 'til I'm finished eating." She grabbed her fork and began eating more politely.

"Ah! I bet I know what that might be. Your Pa!" She

looked down the table and smiled at him. "He told me some things the other day."

Allie was plumb confused now. Frank had good news...and her parents were in on it? What might that be? She stood and picked up her plate intending to take it to the tub to be washed.

"Allie! Where are you going with all that food still on your plate?" Ma slapped her hand on the table.

Allie reluctantly set her plate back down and retook her seat. "Sorry! I just wanted to be finished so I could talk to Frank."

Ma giggled. "Don't go wasting good food, now. Fill up and then talk. The news won't be any better coming sooner than it will be later."

Ma stood and sauntered over to the table where the ladies church group was in a lively conversation about the upcoming summer festival. There was a meeting scheduled next week to begin planning. Allie was planning to attend to see how she could help this year. The wells were drying up, the crops were failing, and the ever-growing potential of a disastrous fire was threatening.

Everyone needed to look forward to something. Watching her manners, she slowly finished her meal and felt thankful that Ma slowed her down. Indigestion would lessen the effects of this great news. She quickly cleaned up her end of the table and deposited her plate in the wash tub. Then, she searched for Frank.

Allie scanned the group but didn't find him. Deciding to walk the perimeter to get views from different angles she moved at a leisurely pace making a casual sweep of the crowd. When she noticed two individuals by themselves talking by the base of a large oak tree she realized that must be him. And the person he was speaking to could only be Gladys.

Allie's heart fluttered. Did Gladys have something to do with the good news? She highly doubted that. It was more likely the good news was being replaced by bad with every word they spoke. Pushing the feelings of doom aside, she decided to continue her walk in their general direction to see if Frank would notice her. She didn't want to make it apparent that she was trying to get his attention. Their wagon was parked in the ideal place for her to set her steps towards. If Gladys said anything she could feign collecting something left in the wagon. When she was halfway to the wagon, Frank spotted her.

"Allie! Hey! Wait up," Frank called, as he quickly caught up with her and matched her pace.

She continued her walk to the wagon to keep up appearances and he followed.

"So, about the news," he began. She braced herself for the possibility that it wouldn't turn out to be good. "You know how you told me about losing your job at the paper?"

She hesitated slightly. "Yes."

"Well...I've heard that roughly the same number of men laid off have recently been hired to fight the fires. So, I went to the paper."

"You what?" They both stopped midstride and she glued her unblinking, frightened eyes on him. "I thought you said I wasn't to act. I was to give this all to God and sit back and wait."

"Yes! You were...are!" His hand swiped down the side of his face. "God did act. In this portion of the problem, anyway. The same number of men were hired. Your job is being removed from the paper...and you have it back."

Allie was silent. She didn't know how to feel.

"That's not even the best news for you." He waited for some response from her before he continued.

She swallowed the lump in her throat. That seemed to be all she could give him, so he continued.

"I pointed out a few issues. You not only have your job back, you start tomorrow! And, you will be paid the advertised wage." Frank dropped his hands and stood stock still waiting for her to respond.

"Tomorrow is Monday. I never worked on Monday before." She was excited and confused all at once.

"Mr. Ashton wants to change the schedule. You'll be working Monday, Wednesday, and Friday. He says the work can pile up a bit on your days off for you, instead of having less to do by Thursday."

She was elated. *This might help Ma a bit more, too. She could stay caught up if she wasn't gone three days in a row.* Allie turned and finished the walk to the wagon. Placing her hands atop the wheel she focused on breathing.

"Allie?" Frank came up behind her. "I was just trying to help. Are you alright?"

She wiped the tears falling on her cheeks with the back of her hand and turned to face him.

"I'm more than alright. God has answered. I'm not sure how it all worked, but that is wonderful news. I'm going to be okay. At least for now. I can help Pa and Ma again and keep saving—in case God's answer is for me to go to Reno." She lowered her head and silently thanked God before voicing her thankfulness to Frank.

"Allie, there's more news. And I can share it since we are somewhat alone." The side of his lip was inching up. She raised her head and looked him in the eyes. "I talked with your pa after I left George and Blinne's."

She couldn't imagine how that would be good, but Pa did seem to be in a good mood lately. Maybe it was good news, too.

"At first, he wasn't too happy with me, but we came to an understanding. He gave me permission, Allie."

She was confused. "Permission for what?"

"You! To begin a relationship...when your current marriage comes to an end." He waited expectantly for some sign that she was thrilled about this information.

"That sounds like a dream! I can't think about it right now. There is too much left to settle before I get my hopes up." She blew out the breath she was holding.

Frank's smile lost its luster, but he managed to keep it in place. He understood her hesitation.

"There is one last thing...and it involves Gladys."

Here it comes. What has that woman done now!

"I spoke with her after speaking with your father. I explained my feelings, or lack of them, for her. I made sure she knew she was a friend...and nothing more. She was hurt, and I felt bad I was the cause, but, when you saw us talking over there, *she* was apologizing. She said the shock and hurt from the other day kept her from absorbing the information immediately. Now that she's had time to think, she realized she was only pushing herself on me because that's what her ma wanted. It wasn't what Gladys wanted. She didn't tell me who, but she's interested in someone else. Her ma doesn't like it, so, she decided to go with her heart instead of doing everything her ma wants."

Allie's jaw dropped. That didn't sound like Gladys. Maybe she was growing up a bit, too. The sun must be drying up all the wet behind everyone's ears and

277

making them all become full-fledged adults around here. She smiled a relaxed, contented smile and wished she could wrap her arms around this man. Her heart was light. Whatever happens is surely in God's hands and He would not steer her wrong now.

"That is the best news of all, Frank. I can relax a bit, knowing that she isn't going to cause any more problems for either of us."

"Well...Gladys won't. But, we still have to watch out for Mrs. Wimble." He raised his eyebrows to accentuate his point.

Allie stifled a chuckle! "Yes! That's very true. I'll keep that in mind."

"Gladys said she would do what she could to keep her ma out of our business, but she couldn't make any promises."

"I hope that's enough. I can't imagine what life has been like for Gladys. Growing up with the parents she has must have been difficult. I probably should have been a bit nicer to her."

"Don't waste time thinking about what you should or could have done. It's still not too late to start being nice to her. Maybe you'll start up a friendship?"

Frank rested his hand on hers briefly before walking back to the main group. Allie pondered his last comment for a moment. Then she made her way—with much lighter steps—to join her parents in the final cleanup before saying goodbyes.

CHAPTER 36

The fires were relentless, and Eddie's job was monotonous. At least the pay was fantastic! With no experience, twenty-five cents an hour was more than he thought he would make. That was slightly more than he'd made working for the railroad.

The government sure pays well. Too bad I'm stuck in the middle of nowhere and can't spend it on some fun.

He put his head down and continued to slice through the underbrush. The firemen were in a line all doing the same job. The days were long, much longer than he usually worked. Ten-hour days were the average for the railroad, but out here you worked until you physically couldn't keep going or couldn't see any more due to nightfall and thick smoke. Eighteen hours seemed to be the average work day, but he didn't have a way to accurately tell time.

He had to rely on the government to keep track for him. No one talked much. The smoke was thick and just breathing took too much concentration. Lots of stories went around back at camp, though, because the smoke was thinner there.

Eddie's work party was made up of a strange group of men. It seemed no one really had any experience. All walks of life came together on this line. Based on the stories, Eddie decided he might be better than some. He'd made some mistakes and there had been run-ins with the law a few times over the years, but compared to some of these men, he was almost angelic.

The government made a sweep of some prisons to get enough hands to fight this inferno. Keeping his nose clean and staying on the right side of this group was essential, if he valued his life. The boss man was in charge of several groups and wasn't always standing by to be sure order was maintained. They had a party leader that stayed with them, but Eddie knew he was useless. If the men in his group got riled up, he figured no one would be able to stop their wrath.

The work was the same every day. His shovel and axe were quickly becoming his best friends. The calluses were so thick from the repeated digging that his hands no longer hurt.

Their efforts weren't futile. What they were doing was helping. The fire was staying on its side of the line and away from towns. That was some reward for putting in the long days. When sleep finally came, it was fitful.

Dinner and breakfast were served at camp...and

neither were wonderful. The camp cook was a man no one wanted to cross. He kept watch over his supplies and fed the men just enough, so they wouldn't wither away. Potatoes seemed to be in abundance. They were served every day, twice a day. If he never saw a potato again, he would not be upset.

Sleeping was done on the hard ground—surrounded by those he couldn't trust. His whiskey was gone. He realized early on that if he didn't finish it, someone would find it and finish it for him. Now his head ached daily, and he thirsted for the quench only liquor could provide. He used to stumble into towns without any money for alcohol. Now, he had ample funds, but wasn't allowed to leave camp.

The situation was maddening. He'd been here before and knew as his body would work through the dry spell, the ache would lessen. He didn't like it, but he had no choice in the matter. He needed to make money. He needed Allie. And, he would keep his eye on the prize and push forward.

He closed his eyes trying to do the math in his swirling head. Twenty-five cents an hour for roughly an eighteen-hour day...he should be ready in just a few weeks. If he worked for a month or so, provided the fires held out that long, he could go just about anywhere he wanted with her. He knew with her family, the farther away the better.

The government supplied his tools, but he was told he needed to pay for them. The cost would be deducted from his first week of pay. When he was paid it seemed low to him, but he figured that was why. He should have much more the end of this week. He did have another problem...the same he'd had with his whiskey. He feared his pay would be taken by someone. He had to keep it on his person at all times. Sleep would be done with one eye open. This adventure would be short on the calendar, but long on his body.

There was a commotion! Men were yelling up ahead in the line. Eddie stopped to make sense of what was going on. He wasn't sure if he wanted to know. If a fight broke out, he would rather run the other way and wait for it to settle than to charge into the crowd.

Reluctantly, he made his way closer to try to figure out what was happening. The smoke was as thick as pea soup. He could only see a couple men ahead. Then the yells carried back to him in the wind. The fire was stirred up. He got closer and realized there wasn't a fight. It was a rescue. They were calling for help and he hurried forward. He reached the front of the line and could see a man lying on the ground and a group around. The man was awake, but unable to get up.

Eddie stayed back. He didn't know what to do. So, he watched the other men lift and carry the injured man to camp. With those men gone, the rest needed to pick up the pace to keep the progress going. He'd have to find out later that night what had happened. He made his way back to the line to continue his work of digging and scraping. This left the land barren.

He had his own problems to think through. This wasn't a good time to think about others. If they were only one man short, it would increase the demand on the rest of them. Given that, he hoped this man recovered from whatever had overtaken him. He could hear the party leader yelling for everyone to get back to work.

Some of the men were so shaken up, they were just standing around. He knew better. Working on the railroad laying track...he had seen some things. Just because one man had fallen didn't mean the work day was over. Regardless of how bad the injury might be, the deadline was more important.

The fire didn't give a defined deadline, unless it was yesterday. They all wanted the fires out as quickly as could be managed. He knew his place and what was expected of him. He couldn't dwell on the fate of the injured man. The line re-formed without much discussion. The repetitive sounds of metal hitting rocks and plants getting slashed resumed.

The end of the day finally came. Eddie was grateful. His shoulder wasn't cooperating. His stomach was ready for food...until he thought of potatoes. Maybe skipping tonight's meal and eating a big breakfast in the morning would help with his disgust for the tuberous food. He'd get a break from eating them and be more ravenous in the morning. That might be exactly what he needed.

It was a hike to make it back to camp. They were set up near the northern river that fed Lake Pend

Oreille. It was a giant lake and many of the closest towns flanked its shores. There was small comfort knowing the fire would have nowhere else to go after it destroyed the towns. Nothing could jump that lake, unless, of course, it turned and advanced to either side and then down.

One day at a time. That was all he could focus on right now. The absence of liquor prevented his head from thinking further into the future. Making his way into camp, he could smell the dreaded spuds. His stomach wanted to revolt. Most of the men were gathered close to the cook. Eddie wanted to know what had happened, so he ventured closer—even though the cooking smells grew stronger with each step.

The voices became more distinct as Eddie approached, and he knew they were talking about the earlier incident. He decided to hang back to get the news. He didn't want to appear chummy with his coworkers. The loner status could save him from any trouble that might make its way through this group.

He didn't find out much. The man had trouble breathing and collapsed. They took him back to camp and dunked him in water and that seemed to help. He'd rested after that. Eddie didn't see the man around, but figured he was off sleeping somewhere nearby. That's exactly what he intended to do.

As quickly as his tired feet would take him, he moved away from the group towards the area designated for sleeping. Sleep would most likely prove fitful yet again, but tossing and turning was much better than trying to choke down one more bland and mushy overcooked spud. Tomorrow would come soon enough, and he would work at forcing them down his throat then.

Tonight, he would work on trying to get some sleep—and not get robbed...or worse. A group of men without any lady friends could turn ugly faster than a camp cook could turn a whole camp against potatoes. With that revolting thought, he rolled over onto his back and attempted to turn off both his nose and his mind.

CHAPTER 37

Allie was settling into her new schedule at the paper. After only a couple of weeks, her savings were caught up to where they would have been if she hadn't lost her job. Allie didn't know how Frank was able to get her the wage meant for a man, but she was very thankful and wasn't about to question it.

She was sitting in the church pew with many other women and a few men on a Saturday morning. She had signed up to help plan the festival when she wasn't working. Now that she had her job back, her days were cramped, but since she'd already volunteered, it didn't feel right to back out.

Allie hoped she'd be given a simple task. Maybe she could organize the baked goods. The older women loved to bake for the town. She would only need to coordinate with the bakers and make sure there weren't too many of the same item. Most of those women were sitting here with her. If she was lucky, she could get most of the work done for that job today.

The men were sitting behind the women. They

looked relaxed and talked to each other while waiting for the meeting to start. The women were divided into smaller groups. Each group was chatting about something different.

Allie just tried to focus. She was tired and loved that her life was busy again, but it didn't allow much time to be alone with her thoughts. She ran through her mental list of what still needed to be finished today. Watering and more watering! It seemed like the only job she helped out with around the farm now that she was back at the paper.

When Allie did the watering, Ma was free to get other chores done. Days spent at the paper meant Ma was working overtime. The crops were failing, so since Drew had some free time, Pa gave him some of Allie's chores. They were all working together.

Allie continued to give Pa a portion of her money each week. She couldn't match what Pa would have earned with good crop weather, but it was something, and that was better than it would have been. She was starting to feel a little guilty about not giving them all her pay. They were working so hard this year—for so much less reward. They were in good company, though. The paper was reporting that folks throughout the West were suffering from the drought. Things needed to turn around soon, or it would be disastrous.

Mrs. Wimble took her place at the front of the church and Allie pushed those thoughts aside, so she could focus on this meeting. She needed to stay alert and grab a job that she could balance with her other obligations. If she didn't pay attention, she could be left with one of the jobs no one wanted.

"Good afternoon!" Mrs. Wimble stood in front of the group to begin the meeting and all conversations ceased. "It seems this time of year has found us once again. I am happy to announce that I am your festival chair head this year." Chair heads were appointed, and everyone took turns, but she clearly wanted to believe that this made her more important than anyone else. "I would like to start this meeting today by reminding you that our festival last year was bigger than ever. Some people from neighboring towns came to visit, and I would like to increase that number this year. We all know crops are failing. The festival can provide more booths this year. That will allow more families to sell their items and earn a little something to help get through this tough year. I would like to start the discussion with what worked last year...and what we want to continue. Then we'll move to new ideas. And, finally, we will delegate committees to pull off this great event. So...to start us off...I want each committee head from last year to come forward and report on what went well and what didn't. Mr. Wixel, would you please come up and give us a report on the barns?"

Mr. Wixel was a short, rotund man. He owned one of the establishments for men at the far side of town. He always ran the barns and headed the races. That put him in charge of all the betting. Allie didn't know him very well, but her experiences in Idaho gave her some insight into Mr. Wixel's character. Fortunately, Deer

Lodge didn't have too many of those people around. *There were always a few that could be found in any town.*

All the committee reports were given. Water was an issue that ran through them all, including Mrs. Wimble's. She always had a magnificent rose garden that she was very particular with. She liked to choose the best roses in each color and display them every year. Those would need to be kept in water to stay fresh as long as possible. Conserving water, where possible, was a priority. A few questioned even holding the festival this year, given the water and time shortage of all involved. But, the majority agreed it was needed to keep up morale. A little fun goes a long way in hard times. It kept people pushing through. This year would have its challenges...some of which they hadn't seen before, but they would all overcome them together.

The meeting was then open to new ideas. Allie didn't have any to offer, but she was curious about what others might suggest. She had prioritized each committee by ease to plan and carry out. New ideas could add options she hadn't considered.

The baking committee still seemed to be the front runner. Sewing wouldn't be awful, either. Basically, anything that was mostly filled with items from the older female generation ran itself. They had been participating for years and had it down. Many had begun their sewing or planning right after last year.

Allie knew she didn't want animals. They required

care during the entire event—unlike the non-living items. Setting that up and monitoring it would require too much from her. She didn't want any interaction with Mr. Wixel, and she definitely didn't want anything to do with animals.

Various ideas were coming in: a fashion show, music highlighting other countries, a collection of automobiles and farm equipment. Nothing sounded right for her, but she kept listening and considering. Everyone agreed that a fashion show sounded lovely and the current store owners would head that and use their inventory.

The music idea was interesting, but no one was aware of anyone local who had the skills and knowledge required to pull that off. They settled on the church choir taking part and gathering the small group of local musicians to perform at least once.

As for the machinery, Mr. Wixel said he could speak with some of his acquaintances from Missoula and Helena. He hoped they might be willing to help. Shipping them here would be a challenge they might not be able to overcome, but he could ask.

Mrs. Wimble took control of the meeting again. She announced that it was time to decide who would be running each committee.

"To start off the committee head appointments, I would like to nominate Allie and Frank to co-chair the children's activities."

Allie was stunned! *Surely, I didn't hear that right!* Running the children's activities would not work for her. That took too much time. Mrs. Wimble raised her hand and rose. Her mother stood and seconded. The rest of those gathered said, "Aye!" Allie was left standing with a dropped jaw.

"Yes? Allie? Do you have something to say?" Mrs. Wimble stood with a smug look on her face. Allie closed her mouth and quickly sat. *What just happened?!* "That's settled! Let's move on to the preserves. Do I have anyone who would like to volunteer themselves?" Mrs. Wimble scanned the room...and Allie sulked.

I could have done preserves! Why did I get put on kids? She sat there—not listening to the rest of the meeting for the conversation she was having in her head with herself.

Mrs. Wimble was so quick...too quick! And, my own mother! She stood up so fast, I didn't realize what was happening. That was planned! There was no other possible way for that to have occurred without being planned. And, Frank! He sat quiet the whole time. Was he in on it, too? Well!

Before Allie knew it, the meeting was over. She didn't know who had been assigned to the rest of the committees, but it really didn't matter. She was working with Frank on the children's activities. Allie stood to leave. Her eyes locked with Frank's like a magnet to metal. She was trying to bore a hole into his brain. He was returning the same smug look she had seen on

Mrs. Wimble.

It was planned by all three of them! Of all the nerve! I'm supposed to be letting God do His work on His time, but they can just do whatever they want whenever they like? She let out a huff and stomped out the room.

Frank refrained from chuckling out loud at Allie's display as he followed her out.

"Allie! Wait up!" He had to pick up his pace to catch her. She was clearly angry and moving quickly. Allie didn't stop when Frank called to her, forcing him to match her pace. "Allie, listen! I can see you're upset."

"UPSET! OH, why would I ever be upset, Frank?" She stopped abruptly, turned, and glared at him, crossing her arms over her chest.

Frank held his hands up in surrender. "I had nothing to do with that back there, really. Allie, you have to believe me. It was a shock to me, too. I happen to think it's perfect, though," he said, relaxing his stance.

Allie stared at him quietly for a moment. She was looking for the truth in his eyes. "I guess I have to believe you, but why would they do that? Well, my ma makes sense, but Mrs. Wimble? She's been pushing Gladys on you. I don't understand. That's not why I'm upset, though. I don't mind working with you. Actually, I'll enjoy that. I was hoping to have an easier committee to head. With all my work at the paper and helping around the farm, I don't have much time for anything else."

"Maybe that's why. They know I'm basically twiddling my thumbs right now. Sure, I help Doc out, but that's when I want. I'm not scheduled there, and Ma and Pa don't need much help. They just like my company."

Allie pondered that. It could be true, however, she knew Mrs. Wimble, and everything that woman did had a reason. She loved to meddle. She was up to something, but what? She wasn't going to share with Frank, yet. She would keep it in the back of her mind and try to sort it out as the festival drew closer. "All right! Since you have time, maybe you can be the committee head and I'll just help."

"Fair enough! That sounds like a good plan." He turned and motioned for her to join him as he stepped away from the building. "I'll work on some ideas over the next week and you do the same. Then on Sunday...week from tomorrow...after church...we can meet up and share our ideas. Sound okay?"

"That sounds great."

Sundays were a day of rest, but she figured this wasn't really work. A festival was fun. Sunday was the only day of the week she didn't have some kind of chore besides what needed doing every day...like watering. Sunday was the best day.

"I'll see you Sunday, then." Allie didn't wait for him to respond. She saw Ma coming and knew it was time to head home. There was so much to do and this meeting already had them behind schedule at home.

Allie would keep her suspicions about being paired together to herself. Ma wouldn't admit to any of it anyway. She didn't want to let Ma know what she was thinking. There'd be a better chance at figuring this all out if she kept quiet...for now. Once she had some concrete evidence, she'd decide what to do.

Her new plan was to keep her mind busy. She was doing what she was supposed to...waiting for Him...even if others weren't. She fell into step with Ma and shouted out the last few goodbyes as they started the walk home.

CHAPTER 38

Eddie had been fighting fires for several weeks or maybe it was closer to a month. He couldn't tell for sure. The days all blended together. Pay was inconsistent. That also contributed to losing track of time. He couldn't rely on counting the weeks by payday anymore. They were all told accounts were being kept up and they would get their money.

Fires were popping up everywhere and travel wasn't as safe. The out-of-reach places where the fighting men stayed made it even more challenging to get the money to them. He had to rely on trust from men he didn't know.

Trust was not something that came to him easily. He learned at a young age that men, at least those closest to him, couldn't be counted on. His pa did what he wanted with his ma for a while and eventually left. He hadn't seen him since he was around five. For now, he didn't have a choice. He needed that money, and, if he had it, he could probably leave. But, he didn't have it...so he was stuck here lighting backfires.

In some ways, he was glad to be off the line. He was still breathing smoke like a chimney, but he didn't have the dust to battle. The days were hot and the fires hotter. He was working closer to the fire now. He could feel heat like he'd never known. His body felt as though it would burst into flames for the sheer hell of it...much like the trees appeared to do.

The fire would be yards away and a tree would explode into flames as if it just gave up. It all needed rain, but the sky was raining embers. They could tell their distance from the main fire by the wind. The inferno created its own weather. The larger the blaze became, the windier it was and that allowed the fire to grow.

Fire consumed everything in its path. They were told they had the power to stop this. Eddie wasn't so sure. The forest fire was a wild animal released from its cage. The destruction it left in its wake was a contrast to the confinement it had maintained the last several years.

The natives told stories of deliberately setting fires every year to control the burn. The big companies, railroads, logging, and miners, wouldn't have that. They wanted everything to themselves. It was as if the land had had enough. It was shaking its raging fist back at the selfishness of the settlers.

Eddie wasn't going to question it. He had a job to do and needed the money. Regardless of what happened with this fire, he would eventually be paid.

He would be moving from this area anyway and wouldn't need to worry about the politics here.

There would be politics to fight wherever he went. That was a given. But, for now, he could stay out of them and just do his job. He'd heard rumors that troops were starting to train. Eddie had never heard of the military fighting fires, but they did need bodies. That was certainly a way to bring more.

It was only rumors at this point, though. He hadn't seen any new souls since the start. Something needed doing...whatever their plan. This was grueling work and men were starting to drop. Some were not cut out for this type of work. Eddie could keep going. Working was helping with his head at least. Lack of alcohol was always difficult for him, but this physically demanding and repetitive work helped. He took comfort in knowing what tomorrow would bring. There was no guessing involved in this work.

They were told that the fires were receding, but he couldn't see it. He wasn't sure if they were trying to boost morale or if it was honest information. For him, the fire stared him down every day. There were reports passed from fighter to fighter. There were thousands of small fires—three thousand was the number thrown out—and up to ninety large fires.

Eddie was fighting one of the large fires. Ten thousand men were fighting this one. Reports said some of the fires were controlled, but the fact that President Taft was calling in the army spoke volumes to him.

They could talk all they wanted and try to encourage him to keep going, but he wasn't fooled. If the threat was dwindling, the number of men fighting would be shrinking—not growing. Another question he wouldn't ask. There was no sense in it. If the men he was forced to work with thought they would lose their jobs soon, chaos might break out. He would keep his nose down and keep pushing forward towards the fire. The more he could burn up in its path, the less likely it would reach him.

Fighting fire with fire seemed an odd approach before he saw how it worked. He was starting the fires on the back side of the previously scalped earth. The fire would only have one way to advance—towards the existing fire, burning up all potential fuel. The large fire would need to look elsewhere for something to consume. This was big country and they had thousands fighting the fires. There just wasn't enough man power to work all angles of each fire, but they had to protect the towns.

Their focus was to direct the fires into the vast, open wilderness and hope that the weather would eventually work in their favor. So far, the weather had only helped the fires. It had chosen a side and wasn't going to waiver.

Rain had to come at some point. It always came, eventually, in these parts. August was brutal regardless of the year. This one would be no different. The only hope anyone had was that fall would come early. Spring did, so fall could, too.

Winters were harsh, and snow was deep. It was ironic that folks were wishing and praying for winter now. Normally, people dreaded the winter and prayed for summer. This was the first year living in the Wild West that he had seen the flip.

The natives lived with nature. They worked around it. The settlers approach was to confront it. Building a town took a stand against nature. This wasn't any different. Time would eventually declare which approach worked best. Maybe they would win this battle and suppress all these fires. He would keep doing what he was doing to fight them. That was his only choice, right now.

CHAPTER 39

It was already Sunday and almost time for the meeting with Frank. Allie had used any available time to brainstorm ideas, but it wasn't much. Many of her ideas required water and they needed to conserve, but she would still share them with Frank. She hoped he had more ideas and could do most of the work to pull something together.

She stood to join the choir in their final song. Afterwards, church would let out and the luncheon would begin. She hadn't paid much attention today. Her thoughts kept returning to the upcoming festival and the work it involved. They were supposed to work together so neither had the full load. She hoped Frank understood what he was getting into when he agreed to take on most of the work. Allie was already stretched too thin. Her busy schedule was stressful, and it took a lot of effort and energy to keep all the events of the last year from consuming her.

She stared at the words in the well-worn bible. She was singing, but today she didn't feel the lyrics. She felt pulled in many ways and didn't know how to make it all work. She loved that she had a job. She needed to save money and help her parents. There was so much extra work to be done at home right now with the drought. She felt awful when she couldn't be there to help.

On top of all that, she had to help plan and participate in the entertainment for the children. Her focus was no longer on Eddie and that situation. That did free up some time to think. She was busy with other things that diverted her thoughts to the here and now and not the future. She wondered how that would all end, but patience came easier with each day. She felt stronger in her faith and she hadn't seen or heard from Eddie. That helped to increase her strength.

All these thoughts were spinning around in her head as the final notes were sung and people began to fill the aisles to make their way out. Allie followed her ma through the crowd and made her way to a table. Thankful this wasn't a Sunday her family had signed up to help, she sat and waited for the food to be set up before making her way to join the already forming line. She would take every break she could get right now.

She quickly dished her plate and went back to the table. They were sitting with Ma's usual group of ladies. Her pa would sit down at the end of the table and Allie chose to sit closer to him. She didn't want to sit near the other ladies and be expected to join the conversation. Pa and Drew would focus on their food and let Allie do the same. The men usually ate first and made small talk while waiting for the women to eat. She knew Frank would find her soon and this was her chance to be able to eat something before moving on to her next task.

Allie sat across from Drew and he smiled at her. She smiled back and began to eat. Drew kept very busy with Pa. This time of year, she hardly saw him and she missed him. Everyone was busy. When her family came together after dinner, all anyone wanted was sleep. This was a good opportunity to catch up with him. She swallowed her bite of fried chicken.

"Hello, Drew. I haven't seen you much lately. How are you?"

Drew's smile grew. "Good, good. Busy...so busy."

"Thank you for helping to water Ma's garden. I know that's normally my chore, but I'm not home as much right now." She scooped up some potato salad with her fork.

"You're not home anymore. You're working too hard." He stared her down challenging her to argue it.

She closed her eyes and exhaled. "You're right. You're always right. It will calm down a bit in a while though. As soon as the rains come...things will start to settle down again."

"Pa says we need rain or we won't have much for Ma to can this year." He kept eating as though this was not upsetting news.

Not wanting to worry him, Allie just nodded and

ate in silence. She hadn't thought about that. She knew the crops they normally sold every year had already failed, but the garden looked okay to her at this point. All efforts were diverted to keeping their food watered so they wouldn't starve through the winter.

She began to wonder again if she should give her parents all her income to help the family get by. Frank joined them and took a seat next to Drew. She saw him go through the line earlier, but he didn't have a plate now. That meant he had finished. He folded his hands and rested them on the table, waiting for her to finish. He struck up a conversation with Drew. She loved what she was seeing.

Frank was always relaxed around Drew. He treated him like nothing had ever happened. Not many people did that. Even those who were his closest friends avoided him now. His accident had changed him, and he angered easily, but he was still in there.

Allie could draw him out on occasion, but that wasn't often these days. She had very little time for herself. The conversation that she had just had with him was good and now Frank was easily talking with him.

Drew just didn't always understand things. He didn't connect that no canning meant no food for winter. His brain was like a child frozen in time. Some days she wished she could visit that childlike brain. Not worrying about tomorrow would be nice.

But Drew couldn't take care of himself, and that

wasn't something she wanted. He needed to be supervised always...much like a child. Allie knew her parents were tired, but they kept pushing. They refused to send him away and she couldn't blame them for that. She loved that she could still have her brother around.

Someday, her parents wouldn't be around anymore, and she wondered what would happen to Drew. If her life didn't get turned around, she couldn't help. The problems seemed to continue to increase. She felt like she had bricks on her shoulders weighing her down. Frank was eyeing her as he continued to converse with Drew and then Pa. She stood and carried her dishes back—ready for the meeting with Frank.

"Well, I'm ready now," Allie stated. She sat back down across from the men and waited for Frank to finish his conversation.

He looked at the other end of the table and motioned for her to scoot down. The ladies had cleared their places and were out mingling. Allie scooted down a bit.

"You okay? You seemed lost in thought a moment ago."

Allie gave a tired smile. "Yes, I just have a lot on my plate right now. I'm worn out."

"You didn't ask to be a co-chair for this. Do you want to?" Frank's brows were already furrowed in concern as he pursed his lips.

"I'm fine. Life will settle down soon enough. Winter will come, and I'll be twiddling my thumbs. Keeping busy keeps my mind from wandering."

"Except for a few moments ago." He reached into his pocket and pulled out a paper and a short pencil. "I wrote down a few ideas. Did you think of any?"

Allie's cheeks reddened, and she used her hand to smooth her hair. She couldn't hide much from him...and didn't want to try anymore.

"I was thinking about bobbing for apples...maybe some crafts to do...maybe a relay race." That was about it for her ideas. They weren't much, but they were solid ideas.

"Those are good. I had already thought about relay, but crafts are new. What kind were you thinking?" He wrote down the new ideas.

"Oh...I don't know. Maybe we could combine them with some of the other exhibits? A sewing craft in the sewing booth, water color drawing in the arts booth, that type of thing." She was really flying by the seat of her pants with these ideas.

"Those are great! We could spread activities for the children all over the grounds—instead of just one area like previous years. They can mingle with their parents this way. When the parents are in one exhibit, the kids can be corralled in a corner or somewhere close—staying busy, but still near them." He was writing frantically.

Her sad smile returned at the compliment and she looked down at her hands that were in her lap.

"Allie! You're good at this! You're going to make a great mother someday."

She winced, and he realized his mistake. *She doesn't know that I know. I need to tell her.*

"Perhaps," was all she said. She forced herself not to think about it. The wound was still raw. Someday she'd be tougher.

"Allie, there's something you need to know." He looked around to be sure his voice wouldn't carry, and they had a little privacy. "Doc's wife keeps meticulous records. When I covered for him a while back, your pa came in to make a payment. I wasn't snooping around, I promise. I pulled the file out to make a note in it. The record of the procedure was in there." He cleared his throat. "I know about the baby."

She let one tear slip out and quickly brushed it off. "Yes...well...what's done is done."

"Oh, Allie. You don't have to be strong for me. It's okay." He wanted to gather her in his arms but knew this was not the right place.

No more secrets. "You know how Eddie was...is. He was upset that he didn't have a child yet. Little did he know...I didn't even know! At least I'm not saddled to him with a child." She was trying to put on a brave front.

"You don't mean that. You would have cherished that child, I know." He reached across offering her his hand, but she didn't take it.

Her eyes were somewhere else. They were looking at him, but they were hollow. "I'm not sure if I will ever have the chance again. Doc doesn't know. There was a lot of damage." She stood and began walking away from the group.

Frank followed but remained silent.

Allie walked and walked until she had traveled clear to her part of the creek. She noticed that Frank kept a step behind her, letting her have her freedom. He was there if she needed him, though... her rock to lean on. If she did, her heart might fall completely for him. That thought terrified her. She couldn't until she was free to do so. She sat with her back propped against the old familiar tree and Frank sat, too. Her tears flowed freely sitting in silence. Her shoulders bobbed as she sobbed soundlessly. Frank remained at her side—not expecting her to talk but offering himself if she needed it. They sat that way for a long time until she was finally able to control her tears. Frank remained quiet and waited for her.

"I'm fine now. You can go if you like." She used the hanky that was in her pocket to dry her face.

Frank pulled his knees up and folded his arms across them. "I'm not going anywhere. I have all day just to sit here with you. Allie, I can't take this pain away, but what can I do to help?"

She starred into the very shallow, almost stagnant water. She felt like this creek, all dried up and nothing left to give. "I'm tired. I don't know how much help I can give you for the festival. I found out our garden that provides food for the winter might fail us before harvest, I've been patiently waiting for answers, but so far the only answers have been to keep waiting."

Frank lifted his hand and gently moved her chin until she was looking at him. His face was inches away from hers. "You are the strongest woman...person...I know. Don't worry about the festival, I can do it. Maybe I can even come out here a bit more and help with some chores."

She sighed and closed her eyes at the thought of having him take some burdens off her. When she opened them, his lips were brushing hers and she succumbed to his advances. She needed to be replenished somehow. Maybe this would help keep her going. Something she could focus on. It felt good...right...as she relaxed more into the kiss and parted her lips. He plunged with curiosity...searching her. He wrapped his arms around her and the kiss deepened. She startled, and her eyes flew open when she heard a wagon approaching. Her parents were home. Frank immediately stopped and stood offering her his hand to help her up. They made their way to greet her family both silent and calming down.

"Well, there you are, Allie. We looked for you for a

while. A few people mentioned they saw you and Frank walk off this way."

"Sorry" Allie spoke first. "I needed a walk. I've been so busy. The gentle walk home, admiring all of God's creation, was just what I needed today. I should have told you first, though."

Frank chimed in. "I joined her. We had to discuss our festival plans and it was a great time to figure some things out."

Some of those things were clear...but whether they would be able to follow through on them was yet to be decided. He didn't care if she was still legally married. At this point, he was ready to run away with her to somewhere where no one knew them. They could start a new life together, but he had to wait for her to want the same thing.

"I'll leave you for now. I think we came up with enough for me to start in on some details." He winked at Allie and she blushed. "Good to see you all again!" He turned and headed back towards town. He needed to cool down and slow his heart. He knew that would never happen with Allie in arm's reach.

"Bye, Frank! I'll probably see you in town this week." Allie took Ma's arm and they walked together into the house.

By His Hand

CHAPTER 40

Because of the monotony, Eddie had lost track of how long he had been there. There was still no weekly payday to help him keep track. He thought it was somewhere in the middle of August and he was ready to be moving on. Unfortunately, he was stuck here. Here in the middle of nowhere...attempting to save another tree that looked just like the last one he dug by. He was back to working on digging the fire line. They rotated through the two positions. He had a couple more days before he switched back to the backfire group. If the government got their act together and paid him, he could leave as soon as they handed it over. If he left before then, he might never get paid.

There were many men who had left. The number of fires were shrinking and those that still burned were dying out. Not as many men were needed. He was glad to see some of the men leave. It made for a safer camp. He could sleep better with them gone.

The troops that moved in were still a bit rough around the edges, but a much better group to work with. He didn't need to fear being stabbed to death or

311

beaten upside the head by his own shovel. There was a rumor that some of the men who were let go were starting more fires. That didn't surprise him one bit.

With those men, they were lucky that was all they were doing. He could understand why they wanted to do that. For many, this was a second chance at a stable life. Then they were sent packing because the fires were shrinking. The clear answer to them was to start more fires. Then they would be needed again. It could all be blamed on the government. They're the ones who hired the inmates in the first place...and then fired them only a short time later. *Did they really not see that one coming*? He pulled his grubby handkerchief out of his back pocket and wiped his forehead. He smeared the soot and dirt and sweat as he wiped. Each breath felt like he was eating soot, smoke, and dirt. His lungs were tired, and he had a nasty, hacking cough from breathing it all in.

His shovel kept separating from the handle. That made the work even harder. Eddie had tried unsuccessfully to fix it. The stores were clean out. The supplies that could be used for firefighting had been sold out of every store within several miles weeks ago. Nothing had been restocked. That made his broken shovel a treasure to have.

Men were using anything they could. Some were on their hands and knees using what was left of their shovel like a scoop. Eddie was still standing. He wasn't sure for how long. His handle wasn't broken. It just came apart. He kept pushing it back on. He even used nails in an attempt to hold it in place. The nails would hold for a while before they loosened and fell out, and he would start over again. It made for slow going, but at least it looked like they were getting the upper hand with the fire...and weren't being pushed so hard.

When the reports of success came in, some men were released of their duties. The attitude and treatment at camp changed. They were put on twelve-hour rotations instead of their eighteen- hour days. Potatoes were still served at every meal, but with less mouths to feed, there was more food to go around. Some men didn't want to sleep for the full twelve hours so they did some hunting. The meat provided much needed protein. Venison could do wonders for the standard potato when they were cooked together. The juices gave the spud a richer flavor. That made them slide down the hatch much easier. They'd had meat before, but not near as often as now. Eddie was very thankful for that. The improvement was nice. Now, if he could just get his pay and be on his way he would be happy.

Meanwhile, he continued digging. *No sense in wishful thinking. No point in thinking about how many weeks they owe me...or adding up how much I'm owed.* He needed to focus on the here and now. The small changes were such a welcome. Those kept him going each day. He needed something to keep him going since there was no whiskey. Keeping track of how long he'd been sober was impossible. He knew one thing was certain, he'd been sober longer than he'd been in a long while...since before Allie entered his world.

Thinking of Allie also kept him moving from one day to the next. She was a small portion of his past and his future. He needed her—wanted her. She was a feral cat that refused to be tamed, but he was up for that challenge.

Part of Eddie was attracted to her free-thinking spirit. He wanted to wrap that up and direct it for his own benefit. She could do so much for him, if he could only find the way to get her focused. He had a lot of time on his hands to think about Allie. He decided he had allowed her too much freedom. That must have been why she felt she could just up and leave him. There was no other explanation that came to him. He thought that if he gave her some small freedoms— decorating the little house with her handmade curtains and such or deciding what to cook each day—she would be satisfied. She would be busy with the little inconsequential decisions and he could go about his business and not have her in the way. And...he'd still have the best part of her when he wanted it.

Punishing her when she tried to overstep her place was working until she up and left. He wasn't sure how to remedy that. Whiskey would probably help clear the fog and give him some ideas. He knew she needed a baby. He couldn't care less. *Babies just cause a ruckus and disrupt a man's life!* But she needed one to help keep her tied to him and she hadn't done her part.

Eddie thought she might be broken in that department. For a while, he thought she was doing something to prevent it, but he watched her before and after to make sure she had no time for any of that nonsense. He'd have to come out and ask her point blank if she was infertile. Maybe taking in a little orphan child would be enough to cinch the knot. He'd heard those kids were grateful for homes. *Maybe the little bastards would work harder than my own offspring.* He began to fantasize about the rest of his life. The picture was perfect. He just needed to figure out the best way to make it all happen.

CHAPTER 41

It was August 19, 1910. Eddie went to sleep feeling hopeful for his future. He was peaceful. His plan was cast in cement. The fires were under control and he would be out of work soon. Some pay had come, but not all he was owed. Collecting it was his first priority. He wouldn't leave before he was paid in full. While he waited, he had some cash to keep himself occupied. There were tables and fresh meat in the nearby towns.

The night was pleasant. The temperature seemed cooler, but he was so exhausted that he wasn't sure. August was almost over. *I'll finish the month out before I walk away.* There probably wouldn't be any work left after that. Fall should be coming soon, and the fires were tamped down. He'd already worked longer than he thought he would. Two more weeks would be nothing. They might pack him up and send him out sooner. Once he was all paid up, he wouldn't need to hang out in town to pester anyone about it.

Eddie kept that in mind the next day as he faced another plate full of potatoes. He'd need to make sure Allie never cooked any for him...ever! He'd had his lifetime supply over the last weeks. Eating them was just for survival now. He needed something in his belly to keep laboring for the next twelve hours.

He'd been switched to the backfire crew again. He liked this better. The work wasn't as strenuous. Danger was higher, but it gave his body some rest. Cutting the fire line was hard work. The day was cooler—a much needed relief for everyone. Now...if the rain could just come to finish putting out the fires.

That would make everyone happy. Just because they had the upper hand didn't mean they would keep it. The tops of the trees were blowing around, but the wind was calmer down on the forest floor. A few branches had blown out as the day continued. Everyone was paying more attention to their surroundings than usual. The wind provided some relief from the heat, it pushed the smoke out. Moods were much improved. He had buddied up with one of the other guys today. Conversation with him made the day pass much faster. The group had a few decent singing voices. Their songs kept everyone's spirit up.

After working for a few hours, a tremendous sound overpowered the angelic voices. It sounded like a train barreling through the forest. That was the only noise in Eddie's experience that sounded similar. The problem was—there wasn't a single track nearby. There was zero possibility it could be a train.

The winds had been increasing all morning. The combined sounds were deafening. All the men stopped working. They were all confused over what was happening. Eddie was scanning the area, trying to figure out the direction of the new noise. He saw many of the men yelling, but he couldn't hear what they were saying. The roar was overpowering and getting louder.

One group of men started running toward the group digging the fire line. He saw the panic, but he didn't understand why. Then a tree exploded into flames in front of him. That sent him running as well. He still wasn't sure what was happening. Everything was in total chaos. The winds were howling and knocking trees down like toothpicks. Those that remained standing were bursting into flame all around him. Eddie was dodging falling branches...and trees. Flames were reaching out as he ran down the hill. That was the direction of the only water source he knew of. It was down by camp.

Somehow, he made it all the way down. He wasn't sure how. He was running for his life and a slight trip over some briars or a stump would have been the end of him. The fire had been racing right behind him. The pace of the fire hadn't slowed. It was gaining speed.

Camp was just as chaotic. Everyone was screaming. Many seemed to be running in circles. Some were in the water. He could hear them yelling, "Dive in!" Unfortunately, the drought had considerably lowered the water level. Diving in would likely kill you. The river was so shallow, it wasn't even covering anyone completely. He grabbed the blanket off his cot and ran quickly to the water's edge. It was more swamp than river, now. Eddie found a spot to lay down. He was next to another man who was silently crying. Eddie rolled around. He wanted to soak all his clothing and the blanket. Then he spread the blanket out so it covered him and his companion. The fellow had just joined their party a few weeks back. He started out as green as Eddie had been.

Laying under the blanket helped to filter out the smoke. It made breathing a bit easier and his chest didn't feel as heavy. Eddie knew all they could do was wait it out. They hadn't been trained in what to do if the fire attacked them...only how to be the attacker.

Those in charge had given a little instruction about fires in the beginning...the basics, really. No one had enough experience to know what to do with this inferno. Not even those in charge knew what to do in this situation. There was nothing left to do but wait...and overthink.

He tried playing out different scenarios, but in his limited experience he couldn't think of a   better solution. The water was heating up and he could hear men screaming. Trees were falling into the water and he prayed one wouldn't fall on him. He wasn't much of a praying man, but right now it seemed like a smart idea.

Talking to God was the only thing he really could do. So, he prayed. He prayed for his life to be saved, for the fire to turn direction, for the slimy blobs he felt against him to move on. He lifted his head to let some light in under the blanket. The only light source was from the fire. The sun was blacked out by the smoke. The small amount of light let him identify the blobs as fish. And they looked dead. The water was like bathwater and he figured it must have cooked them.

A tree slammed down right in front of them, the fir bows slapping their backs and sending them jumping and running. Eddie wasn't sure where they were heading. The poor soul next to him was terrified beyond belief.

The two of them took off. Eddie was vaguely aware of screams fading in the distance. Their chests were heaving and gasping to find air. The fire was raging in their lungs. It seemed like there was no oxygen in the air. They needed to find shelter. The wet blanket flung over their shoulders like a cape was used to ward off the embers that were raining down on them. Some still found skin and sent searing pain through his body.

They ran into the black—not knowing where else to go. That appeared to be the only way they could go. A wall that seemed like one solid flame was rapidly growing behind them. The fire was behind them and smoke circled around. The blue sky and sunshine from just an hour before were completely gone.

Night had come hours early—and would stay for two long days. Eddie didn't know if others were dealing with the same situation. Three million acres had—or were about to be—raging. Whole towns were running for their lives. He prayed the sun would brighten his dark reality. The sun wasn't coming for Eddie, though. His whole world in all directions turned black as he hit the ground hard.

CHAPTER 42

The papers told a bleak story: millions of acres were destroyed, many lives had been lost, and countless others were still missing. Property was devastated. Allie was working in the office straightening out some files when more information arrived. The stories were too much for one person to digest: Fires burning so hot nothing remained, trains carrying passengers barely escaping as the engines were pushed to their limits.

The people of Deer Lodge were fortunate they had survived to hear the stories—not learn of them first hand. They were south of the disaster areas. Allie put down the papers and decided to take a walk. Her boss didn't even look up. He was too consumed with what was being sent over the telegraph.

Allie paused on the front steps. She wished the sun could wash her face of the helplessness she felt. Deer Lodge hadn't had to deal with any of the burning rage, but they did have smoke and haze hanging low in the air.

According to the telegrams, the fire bypassed them at some distance. Over the weekend and into the start of the week, the sun had turned a pretty shade of pink and the bright blue sky looked cloudy from smoke. Those who ventured into the streets were using handkerchiefs to cover their noses. They hoped it would filter out some of the bad air. Not many were out on this normally busy day of work. Those that did brave the air were huddled in a group—most likely talking about the fires. It would be the only topic of conversation for many days—perhaps weeks—to come.

She started to cough and decided to head back inside. She would need to bear the stories that were beating a rhythm on the telegraph machine. It didn't matter where she was—in or out. It just provided a different perspective to the same information. Everyone was afraid and had refused to speak about it for months. Now, it all roared to life. The amount of devastation was yet to be seen. Some reports were saying hundreds lost, others didn't want to put a figure on it...yet. Everything was in total chaos.

Mr. Ashton walked out of his office with his hand on his face. "I need a drink!" He made his way over to the corner where he had some spirits and poured himself a good portion. "Would you like one, Allie?"

Normally, Allie would have said no. Life with Eddie made her despise liquor. But, today, she could use something to calm her nerves. She nodded her reply.

He handed her the amber liquid. "Whole towns are

gone: De Borgia, Haugan, Henderson, Taft, and Tuscor—all in Montana.

Good riddance to Taft! That town was as evil as they come. She took a swallow and let the burn scorch her throat.

"Falcon and Grand Forks in Idaho—completely destroyed!" Her mind went fuzzy. She missed part of what Mr. Ashton was saying. "Wallace is partially destroyed." He finished his drink in one swallow and headed back to his office.

Allie remained standing there trying to process what he'd just said. She was friends with some of those people. *What had happened to them? Was Eddie still living there? What does this mean for me?* The questions swirled around her brain so rapidly, she couldn't process them. She took another swig and coughed as it went down.

It was already starting to do its job! She walked to the window to sit on the stool placed under it. The stories would keep coming for the next several days. She couldn't listen to them any longer for today. She left without speaking to Mr. Ashton. He wouldn't even notice she was gone for hours. Today would stand still as information was collected. No one knew what to do or how to help. Hopelessness settled onto this small town.

She walked in no particular direction, letting the alcohol take its affect. The smoke settled in her lungs and weighed down her chest. She didn't care. The towns were gone. Her friends...those that helped her escape...who knew what they had experienced. Were they still alive? She didn't know. She found herself entering one of the restaurants and took a seat at the corner table. It wasn't until after she sat down that she realized it was the same table, in the same restaurant, where she'd first met Eddie.

It seemed so long ago. She ordered coffee and waited for her cup to be placed on the table. As she took her first sip, Frank took the seat across from her. He didn't say anything...just sat with her. Everyone was silent now that she thought about it. They stayed that way while she finished her coffee. She placed her nickel by her cup and headed to the door. He followed. She spoke first. "You're a doctor, Frank. Maybe you're needed?

"I already thought of that, but the tracks are badly burned. Trains can't get there. Fires are still raging. That makes horse travel very dangerous. They are isolated right now. They'll have to use the resources they have and fend for themselves for the time being. Wallace has a good hospital if it hasn't burned and people can get there."

Isolated! That single word brought Allie to her knees in the middle of the street. Even in her darkest times, she'd had glimmers of hope from those she had considered friends. They were her small beacons of light. She had never been isolated. She couldn't even imagine what that would feel like.

Frank sat with her. He didn't speak. He wanted to be a rock for her to lean on.

"The towns are gone...where I lived...I don't know what's happened. The people...my friends...Eddie..." She stared blankly ahead as the tears came quickly, pouring streams down both cheeks.

Frank picked her up and carried her off the street. She sank into his arms and buried her head on his shoulder. Instead of setting her down, Frank continued to walk straight out of town. She didn't know where they were going—but she didn't care. She'd been in his arms for a long time when he set her on the ground. She immediately realized where she was and that made her cry more. Frank had carried her all the way to her tree and creek. Her safe spot. *Frank doesn't realize he's replacing my safe spot.* She leaned into him until her soft repetitive sobs drifted into sleep.

When she woke, she had no idea how long they had been there. Frank was asleep with his back against the tree and Allie's head was in his lap. She felt safe for the first time in a long time, but she didn't really know why. The fires were still raging, but the worst seemed to be over for now.

So many questions remained. She didn't know if she would ever have the answers. Everything that she knew had been upturned...like Eddie had once done to the kitchen table when he was drunk and angry. She would have to right what she could and move on from what had been shattered.

With the table, she could see what was lost and what was salvageable. With this...she had no idea. Frank was stirring, and Allie said good morning. She didn't really know what time of day it was, but she thought that was the most appropriate comment. Frank just yawned and gave a sad smile back. He would stay or leave—whatever she wanted. She knew this.

"Let's go back to the paper. I don't *want* to know what the reports are...but I *need* to know."

He nodded and stood. He held his hand out for her and she accepted. They made their way back to town— slowly and quietly. She wasn't sure what more she would learn. She knew she could handle it with Frank there...whatever the news.

As they approached the paper, they could see many townsfolk had the same idea. The building was crowded. Frank and Allie weaved through to the main area. Mr. Ashton had his door propped open and was reading aloud as he wrote down the messages coming over the telegraph.

The previous reports were laid out on the counter for anyone to read. Young Mr. Ashton was not to be seen. He must have been in the back room working frantically to prepare an early edition of the paper.

Despite the sizable crowd and more trying to enter, the only voice was Mr. Ashton's. He was currently giving missing reports. No names, yet. Only numbers were reported so far. The figures blurred together. Allie couldn't add it all up fast enough.

The latest report was a missing train...a whole train of people! Any train available loaded up with as many as they could hold and made its way to either Spokane or Missoula. One train didn't make it in and no one knew where it was.

Whole parties of firefighters were missing, and people were being sent out to the last known areas to search. Allie dropped to her knees and begin to pray out loud. Others joined in slowly. Soon, they all became one voice repeating Allie's short prayer over and over.

"Lord, all mighty and powerful, please help those who are lost and injured and give direction to those who are seeking." It was a simple request for them to make. They could only hope it would be granted...for the sake of those on the receiving end. Allie sent her prayer up after repeating it a few times and another took a turn leading. It continued that way for a long time before people started to make their way back home. Their minds were filled with too much information and their bodies were overcome with emotion and grief. Allie stayed until Frank pulled her up and led her out. He would see her home and she would give in to exhaustion well before dark.

CHAPTER 43

Allie kept busy doing chores at home as Tuesday came and went. She tried to keep her mind off what she knew would be the only topic in town for the next several weeks. That was impossible. She wanted to know what had happened to those she cared about. Keeping her body busy was not enough to shut her brain off.

Today she would get more information. She hoped what she found out would be answers instead of more questions. She was on her way back to the paper. At least she slept well last night. Rain had come sometime during the dark hours. She wasn't sure of the exact time, but the pitter-patter that fell on the roof lulled her to sleep. She hoped it was enough to help quench at least some of the raging monster that lay to the north.

The ground underfoot still showed some evidence it had rained. The heat of today would surely evaporate all of that before the plants could get enough to drink...if they were able to get any. The ground was so hard and cracked that the water had a difficult time penetrating deep enough. She learned that the hard way. She had spilled some of her buckets while carrying the water to the garden. That soil was still soft and manageable, but it had its drink twice a day, every day. The water that fell on the other ground seemed to pool up just long enough for the sun to take it all for itself.

Entering town today was different from Monday. Monday started off as a normal day. Streets were empty while most tended their farms. That only left those living in town milling about. That changed quickly when everyone came to town seeking as much information as possible. Today, it seemed everyone was just trying to process what they had learned on Monday.

She walked through the front doors of the paper and made her way to the broom closet. She was putting her apron on when Mr. Ashton placed a stack of papers on the counter. "Morning, Allie! Got a little rain last night. Seems to have helped decrease the actual size of the fires and lift the spirits of those living with it."

That was a great way to start the day. Good news was all she wanted to hear. "That's wonderful." That was all she could say. She hoped if she didn't add more, he wouldn't add more. She didn't want anything to take away from the good. She walked over to see what he had placed on the counter. One look was all it took. The good feeling changed back into a knot that settled in her stomach...and refused to dislodge. The papers had names—mostly those of the missing. A few had been listed as dead already. She couldn't look and turned away to clean the window on the front door.

Looking out the window gave her a view of the almost deserted town. Someone was exiting the dress shop with a brown paper package. She was too far away to identify. A small group of men stood outside of the restaurant. They probably just finished breakfast. She saw Doc and Mr. Jonson. He seemed to be walking better. His foot must have healed by now. Mr. Ashton usually joined them, but the constant clicking in the other room was taking all his attention. The sheriff was also there. She could see him when he turned. Frank would be there, too. He was probably the other set of feet she could see, but the upper body and face was blocked by the other men. She knew that he joined Doc for breakfast most days. So, it had to be him. The group didn't stay in front of the restaurant long. They began to make their way toward her. Maybe not to her directly...but to the paper.

Allie just wanted to do her job and go home. Dealing with people would take more energy than she had. She stepped aside as they pulled the door open and filed in.

"Morning, Allie!" They all said...almost in unison. She nodded in acknowledgement. "Is Mr. Ashton busy? Didn't see him this morning. Understand why, though," Doc spoke for the group.

Allie just pointed, and Frank made the oddest face. Allie thought it was sort of cute, but turned away. She hoped he would get the hint that she wanted to be alone. He didn't. Frank lagged behind as the rest of the group crowded into Mr. Ashton's office.

At least he waited. She made her way over to the table with the liquor. Depending on Frank, she may need it to give her some strength. She didn't want to turn to liquid courage and be like Eddie, but her life was in shambles. Tragedies continued to unfold in the aftermath of the fire. And she didn't know what else to do. She couldn't cope anymore. It was all so overwhelming.

"You okay?"

Two little words! She didn't know how to answer. Yes, she was—and would be. Somehow, she knew that, but she felt so helpless. She couldn't fix her own life or help those who worked so hard all those months ago to help her. All she could do was pray. She had and would continue to do so. *Was that enough?* She was tired of waiting. Her patience was wearing very thin. Frank must have read her thoughts because he wrapped her in a hug and held her tight. They stayed that way until the group of men came out of the office to pour over the stack of papers on the counter.

"What's the latest?" Frank reluctantly walked closer to see what they were examining.

Sheriff Paul was the only one to speak. "Names."

Realization was written all over Frank's face. Allie couldn't stand to look. She turned away and grabbed the broom to give herself something to do. She felt like running...and would have if she wasn't obligated to stay. She swept harder than necessary. She hoped the continuous strokes over the worn wood floor would drown out the sound of the shuffling papers. Frank watched her but kept his ear toward the group. The men straightened the papers and thanked Mr. Ashton before heading out to start their day.

Doc paused when he passed Frank. "You stopping by the office today?"

"Not sure yet," Frank replied, keeping his eyes fixed on Allie. Doc followed his gaze.

"Good to see you, Allie. You take care." He left before she could respond.

"Have you looked?"

She knew what Frank was talking about. She played dumb anyway. "At what?"

"The list, Allie! Have you checked for names of people you know?" He paused...then continued when she ignored him. "At least tell me you checked for Eddie?"

At the sound of his name she looked up and froze, uncertainty in her eyes. "No, I haven't, and I don't want to."

"You don't want to? You need to know. Maybe this will be your answer."

"I don't want him dead, Frank. I never wanted anyone to die."

"I know that, but we don't know God's way. Maybe this is God's answer...and it was just his time."

"What a horrifying way to die."

"You don't even know. Let's not jump to conclusions. You need to know if his name is listed. Maybe he left the area after you left. He could be long gone."

She knew that wasn't the case. He'd want her back. She just didn't know how he would try to get her. Maybe he found work elsewhere...and is just biding his time. As much as she wanted him gone from her life, she didn't want him dead. She could never wish anyone dead. There was a possibility all the people she knew were dead. That kept her from searching the names.

"I'll look, it would be Edward Coghill? Correct?" He raised his brows hoping for an answer.

She continued sweeping where she already had. "Yes."

Frank stepped over to the counter and began to shuffle through the papers. There were too many names. First, he looked through the list of the dead. She didn't want him on that list...but Frank did. It would certainly make his life easier and be final for her. Frank wanted Eddie punished for what he did to Allie. *No man should be allowed to live after what he did!*

"He isn't listed as one of the dead." He continued to look through the missing. This was a longer list. He suspected that many of these names would eventually move to the other list, but there was hope that some would be found alive. The list was random. There seemed to be no order to it. It made the search take longer, but he eventually found it. Edward Coghill was listed as missing with no other information given. *Well at least I know his last whereabouts give or take a few million acres.* "He's missing." That's all he could say. *What else could he say?*

She paused...then quickly picked up the pace of her sweeping. Frank stepped into Mr. Ashton's office and closed the door. This left Allie alone with her thoughts. *Couldn't he have done that in the first place?* She sighed and eyed the decanter before changing direction. She began to sweep an area she hadn't swept for the third time, yet.

"Can we find anything more about someone listed as missing?" Frank sat facing Mr. Ashton.

"So...you saw? I realized when I was writing it...but didn't have the nerve to tell her. I don't know everything that happened, but she is still Mrs. Coghill."

"She's not dealing with it well. Your floor is going to be cleaner than it's ever been." He attempted a joke, but it failed to lighten the mood.

"I'll see what I can find out. But...we may never know. Some are reporting bodies burned beyond identification."

Frank let out a breath he didn't know he was holding. "All we can do is try. Thanks." He stood, ready to leave and added. "Let me know first...if you hear anything...please. I don't want her to find out without me." He stepped back out where Allie was still frantically sweeping. "Let's go."

She froze. "Go! I'm at work. I can't just leave."

"Yes, you can. Mr. Ashton will understand. Come on." He held out his hand and waited for her to take it.

Allie looked confused, but put the broom and apron away anyway. Then she headed to the door without taking his hand. He was glad she'd listened to reason. He didn't know where they were headed, but knew he wanted to get her away from the information source. Frank didn't think they would hear back soon. He would get her away now and make sure she stayed away for the rest of the day. That would buy him time until she came back on Friday.

So, they walked. He wanted to put as much distance between her and the paper as possible.

"Why don't we go check in on Blinne? I haven't seen them for a while. Little Lena is probably ready for a checkup, anyway."

Doc had just been out not that long ago, but he didn't care. It gave them something to do and Blinne could help take her mind off everything. Allie nodded and remained silent for the entire walk.

Frank hoped that Blinne had some kind of magic that would help. He was fresh out of ideas. The walk didn't take as long as Frank thought it would. Since there was no conversation, they walked a bit faster than usual. Blinne saw them before they saw her. She was outside. Lena was in a blanket contraption that left Blinne's hands free. Frank had seen this before, but it was usually a native trick. Quite genius. She met them at the porch.

"Hi, there. What are you two doing out together?' She thought they were going to keep a safe distance to discourage gossip.

Allie kept her gaze down...so Frank answered for them. "Out for a walk. Need to clear the mind."

Blinne cocked her head toward Allie before opening the door for them. "Everything alright? I haven't been to town in a great while. I don't want Lena around anyone just yet. My mother tells me I'm paranoid, but after our last illness I'm not ready to deal with that again any time soon."

"That's understandable, but she's going on what, four months now?"

"Three and a half, actually." Blinne shifted a bit and removed the contraption. Then placed Lena in her cradle. "Please...come...sit. I'm getting a bit lonely out here. George doesn't bring any news home. He's afraid I'll get too worked up, I guess." All three took seats with Blinne on one side of the table and Frank and Allie across from her.

"There is no easy way to tell it, so here goes. As I'm sure you have been aware there are many fires burning around right now. Seems they converged a few days ago causing a fire storm." Frank paused to let her absorb that information before continuing. "Now, of course, we are all fine down here, but..."

Allie interjected. "Eddie is missing."

"What?" Blinne stood, shocked by the news.

"We don't know any details. It seems he was in the area and now he's missing. His name is on the list."

"What list?" She directed her question to Allie, but she knew Frank would answer.

"The paper has been receiving information at a steady pace. There is a dead and a missing list."

Blinne kept her focus on Allie, as she pointed to the door. "Frank, please leave. I'll handle it from here."

Frank was shocked. He was being dismissed. "I'd like to stay and walk Allie home when she's ready."

"No, sorry. I need you to go. You're only adding to the problem. I'll make sure she makes it home from here." She walked to the door and held it open for him.

He reluctantly stood and scratched his head as he walked out. When he passed Blinne she whispered to him. "Find out whatever you can—as quickly as you can." He nodded and left. He was still confused. *How did sweet Blinne just take control* like that?

She closed the door and took the recently vacated seat next to Allie. Allie fell into her open arms but remained silent. She didn't know what to do. Cry, laugh, or shout? She wanted to do all three. Blinne understood this in a way Frank never could, but she didn't blame Frank for that. Allie opened up more to Blinne. She knew the whole story. Being with her was comfort enough—even if they didn't speak. Yet she felt the need to let it pour out now. "I don't want him dead."

Blinne was petting her hair. "Of course not, honey! I know that."

"Why? Why would God do that?"

"Oh, Allie. God wouldn't do that. Eddie made his own choices. We don't know any details of what happened. Whatever they are...it wasn't God's doing. It was Eddie's. I know Eddie hurt you and probably others, too. God isn't punishing him for that. Bad things happen to good people, too. Just look at all those people who are affected by this inferno. Not all of them were like Eddie. God helps us through those times if we let Him. He never promises a perfect life, but he does promise to be there to walk through it with us. All we can do is pray. We pray for everyone affected. We pray for the dead and injured. We pray for those who can and are helping. And, we pray for the government and land owners and managers to have the knowledge and wisdom to know how to move forward so this won't happen again.

Allie let her tears flow. She would have to wait for the story—if one ever came. She may never know what happened. They stayed that way for a while until Allie felt like she could head home.

Blinne started wrapping the blanket again to carry Lena, but Allie scooped her up first and headed out the door. Blinne didn't mind. She knew her little girl could give the love that Allie needed right now. Nothing like the love from an innocent baby who could laugh in the midst of the storm to cheer you up. Lena would work her magic on Allie...all the way home.

CHAPTER 44

News was slow now that the main event was over. The stories that came in over the next several days were mixed with heartache and triumph. They were stories of lives lost in unimaginable painful ways, most burned beyond recognition. The fire overtook anything and everything in its path. Fighting it was impossible. People stood by and watched their livelihood destroyed in seconds. Everything that they had worked so hard to accomplish vanished as if it was never there.

There were stories of people running for their lives and wandering back into civilization without their eyesight or with feet burned so badly the flesh was gone. And stories of those surviving the raging fire just to succumb later from wounds suffered. It was gut wrenching to read through them all.

Some of the stories, however, were amazing acts of survival. The missing train was found in a tunnel with the tracks burned and destroyed on both sides. The survivors on board were mostly women and children. The lawmen had forced the cowardly men off at gun point to allow more women and children to board.

People, including a young boy by himself, turned up in Missoula after wandering through the forest for days to escape the raging vegetation. Some braved the flames to push through. Others hunkered down in areas already burned. Some were licked by the fire...but not killed.

All of this was too much for Allie to process. She took some time off from her job at the paper, so she wasn't around it all the time. It was depressing, and it raised too many questions in her mind.

The number of those missing shrank. Many were moved to the dead list. The number of dead grew significantly. Eddie's name was one of those that moved. Mr. Ashton did his best to learn the story. They knew he had joined the firefighters early on and was stationed in Northern Idaho. Those who had survived from his party said he worked both lines: backfires and cutting fire lines.

Allie was told Eddie was a great worker. That didn't really surprise her. He did fine at his work. It was his personal life that was lacking. Those that were there the day the fire overtook them said Eddie was in the river one minute and gone the next. Only two ran from their party and only two partial human remains were found a few days later. One of them had to be Eddie. He was buried where he lay—no marker left.

Allie felt nothing after this news. She had been so raw over the last several days with all the stories that she had nothing left to give. Her body was empty and numb. Her problems were solved. God didn't do it though, as He wasn't allowed. Eddie took care of it for Him.

The prospects for her future should have made her ecstatic, but she couldn't feel anything. She had felt so much for so long. She was ready to put it all behind her and start fresh. This time with more knowledge than she ever knew she would or could possess. Every decision would be patiently considered and prayed about. She knew her body would feel many emotions as it slowly let her process everything in the days ahead, but that didn't scare or worry her. She would have God there to help her through it. And, most likely, Frank. He hardly left her during this whole time.

They were together now. The festival committee decided to bump it up a few weeks earlier this year. Everyone needed cheering up and they were hopeful this would be just the ticket to do the job.

Allie was going through the motions...and Frank knew that. He had taken sole responsibility for their committee and didn't ask her for anything. He had even taken bits of paper and strung them together to make decorations that matched. They would be hung to mark the kid section in each booth. No one would wonder where to find them.

Moving the date up didn't allow for time to plan and prepare. The fire created big transportation obstacles for the out-of-area exhibits. It would be the same run-of-the-mill festival they always had, but this year the people would make it special. The hunger for something good to focus on was more than enough to make this year the most memorable festival ever.

Frank was stringing more and more paper and rattling on and on with mindless conversation to help comfort Allie.

She knew she was looking at her future. She had known that for a while, but now she was free to take what was hers—when she was ready. She needed time to process and heal first. She wanted to be whole and healed for Frank. What their lives together would look like was still a mystery. She enjoyed imagining it. She didn't know if they would be blessed with children. Time would tell if she could carry a child. If it turned out to be only the two of them, that would be enough.

Allie knew they would move away from here. Frank was a doctor and he needed to be where he could run his own office. This town was a good size, but not more than Doc could handle. She didn't care where she ended up. Just knowing she would be with someone who loved her and would cherish and protect her was more than enough.

Allie knew that was all that mattered to Frank, too. She could tell by his eyes when he looked at her. Life would have its ups and downs, but she would have a wonderful man beside her to hold her hand, and an amazing Father above to guide her future. That is—and was—all she ever needed.

By His Hand

Continue reading Allie's story in book two of the Carried Through Chaos series, In His Time.

A NOTE FROM THE AUTHOR

Thank you so much for choosing to read my first novel. Writing was something I thought about doing off and on for a long time before I finally decided to take the plunge. I had read about the Big Blowup by chance and the story idea just came to me. I'm not really sure where in my brain these characters crawled out of, but I feel that they have somehow always resided with me just waiting for the right time to show themselves. This was a work of love that I fit into my spare time for a couple of years. I did it just to see if I could and after my first editor and a few beta readers gave it praise I decided to follow through with publishing. I hope you enjoy reading it as much as I enjoyed writing it. You can leave a message or ask a question on my website stefaniebridges-mikota.wixsite.com, email at stefaniemikota@gmail.com, or Facebook Stefanie Bridges-Mikota. If you could take a moment and leave an Amazon review I would greatly appreciate that. I love to hear from my readers. I have begun working on additional works and hope to incorporate interests of my readers.

By His Hand

ABOUT THE AUTHOR

Stefanie Bridges-Mikota grew up in a small town in SW Washington halfway between the beautiful Pacific Ocean and Majestic Cascade Mountains. She was raised by two hard working people who instilled old time values in a modern world. She married her high school sweetheart and together they have two children. The small town they call home is not far from Stefanie's childhood roots and an easy place to be a writer without all of the business found in the cities to the north and south.

Stefanie is one of those people who, despite quickly approaching middle age, is still trying to decide what to do when she grows up. She has worked in a variety of fields which has given her some great knowledge to work into future books. Now she is trying her hand at writing which she finds quite fulfilling. Stefanie has other works started and anxious to introduce to the world in the near future. To follow Stefanie like her Facebook page... or send her an email at stefaniemikota@gmail.com. You can also visit her website at stefaniebridges-mikota.wixsite.com. She loves hearing from her readers.

By His Hand

Made in the USA
San Bernardino, CA
22 March 2020

65949581R00219